Holidays in the Heartland
Ohio Christmas Tales

Holidays in the Heartland

Ohio Christmas Tales

Wayne Novelist Guild

Prickle Forrest Books LLC
Published in Wooster, Ohio USA

COPYRIGHT

First edition November 2025

Book Cover design by Getcovers
Editing by Prickle Forrest Books
Formatting and layout by Firesmyth Press

Library of Congress Control Number: 2025908922

ISBN: Paperback 978-1-965780-04-6
ISBN: Hard Back 978-1-965780-06-0
ISBN: Ebook 978-1-965780-05-3

www.prickleforrestbooks.com

ACKNOWLEDGMENTS

To the ten brilliant, slightly bonkers authors who braved deadlines, plot twists, caffeine crashes, and holiday-induced chaos to craft the delicious stories inside this festive bundle of joy — I see you, I adore you, and I owe you cookies... Or maybe some carrot cake.

Thank you for pouring your creative hearts into the first-ever Christmas anthology for Prickle Forrest Books (cue the jingle bells and confetti cannons!).

Whether you wrote by the glow of a Menorah, blinking Christmas lights, or under the glare of your laptop at 3 a.m., your stories made magic. The North Pole has nothing on c souls. You survived wild brainstorming sessions, frantic cries of "Does this title even make sense?" and the emotional rollercoaster of final edits. You gave up your holiday movie nights and tolerated spontaneous readings of dialogue aloud. You deserve medals. Or wine. Probably both.

From the sparkly title debates to choosing a cover that didn't involve Santa in questionable poses (you know who you are), to formatting woes that nearly turned us into Christmas gremlins — we made it! We proofed, we tweaked, we might have cried into our eggnog a few times, but in the end, we created something beautiful, festive, and full of heart.

This anthology is a love letter to the holidays and the messy, magical act of storytelling. So thank you, dear Chrissy, Cary, Cyndi, Linda, Ruth, John, Patricia, Judy, and Ryan for gifting the world your words — and for trusting Prickle Forrest Books with your holiday spirit. May your next cup of cocoa be extra sweet, your inbox empty, and your readers merry and bright.

With mistletoe madness and editorial love,
Christina H. Benchoff

Editor-in-Chief, Santa's Favorite Word-Wrangler,
Number One Reindeer Cuddler

Contents

Mistletoe Kisses 1
Chrissy Hartmann
Home for Christmas 59
Cary Harter
Stranger than Christmas in July 83
Cyndi Brec
Tinsel Touched 115
Linda Morgan
Christmas Village.. 159
Ruth Reifsnyder
The Light of Cleveland 185
John Newton
Christmas Giving 207
Max Willi Fisher
A Timeless Christmas 235
Patricia Miller
The Abandoned Cottage 269
Judy Cicero
Sleigh Watch 293
R. W. Shultz
Notable Ohio Holiday Celebrations 337
About Ohio...345
About The Wayne Novelist Guild 354
About Prickle Forrest Books 356

Mistletoe Kisses

A Whiskey Salvation Christmas Short Story

by

Chrissy Hartmann

Kash Tyler's determined to win back the woman who's still got his heart tied up tighter than a steer at a rodeo. Between dilapidated gingerbread houses, frosting fights, and some strategic mistletoe placement with help from his dog, he's ready to prove that loving Rose Shanklin isn't a burden — it's the best kind of trouble.

Get ready for a holiday tale located in Wooster, Ohio that's full of sass, second chances, and enough sugar to give a bull diabetes.

Chapter 1

Kash Tyler gripped the steering wheel, knuckles tight, as the GPS blared its latest lie.

Recalculating ...

A muscle jumped in his jaw. "*Yeah*? Try recalculating your life choices."

Hank let out a low huff from the passenger seat, his chocolate brown head resting against the dash. The old lab had been watching the road like he had a personal stake in Kash getting to Wooster without losing what little patience he had left.

Didn't help that Columbus had more highways than a rattlesnake had scales. One wrong turn and suddenly he'd been spinning through city streets like a cowboy in a ballroom brawl—no rhythm, no grace, and definitely no idea where he'd land.

Finally, after an hour and a half of driving a sign. Wooster 5 Miles.

Relief cooled his temper just enough to keep him from punching the glitching GPS.

Two years. Two damn years tracking Rose Shanklin across half the country. And now here she sat, tucked away in a town so Christmas-obsessed even the squirrels probably wore Santa hats.

Hank shifted, ears twitching. His milky eyes followed the movement of Kash's hands as he reached for the coffee in the cupholder. The dog didn't see much these days, but he sensed everything.

"Almost there, bud." Kash scratched behind Hank's ear, feeling the thick warmth of his fur beneath his fingers. "Don't get too excited. Not like she's been waiting by the door for us."

Hank licked his chops and settled deeper into his seat. Either he didn't care, or he already knew Kash was full of it.

Wooster appeared like something straight out of one of those holiday movies Rose used to make him suffer through. Storefronts dripped in twinkling lights. Christmas banners hung from every garland wrapped streetlamp. A plump Santa statue waved like it had an agenda. The kind of place that smelled like cinnamon and friendly neighbors.

Too bad Kash wasn't feeling either of those things.

The truck crawled down Liberty Street, tires crunching over a thin layer of snow. Christmas stores sprawled along the sidewalks, packed with people carrying red DORA cups of spiced cider and shopping bags bursting with holiday cheer.

Rose had left Texas without a word. No note, no phone call—just an empty house and an engagement ring sitting on the kitchen table. And for what? Some so-called "eye trouble"?

Rumors swirled worse than a dust storm back home. Some claimed she'd gone to Ohio for a fresh start. Others said she was sick. One old-timer had insisted she'd run off to become a nun, which Kash really hoped was just small-town gossip and not the truth.

He barely made it past the city square before his truck got caught behind a parade of miniature horses wearing elf hats going down Liberty Street heading to the fairgrounds. Tiny hooves clopped against the road as their handlers tossed candy canes to onlookers.

His fingers drummed the door's armrest. He hit one control. The driver's window inched down with one tap to allow for the chill to seep in.

A soft whimper intermingled with his mumbles as he scanned the GPS on his phone.

He grumbled low in his throat. "I hear ya, boy. Everyone's got eye trouble in some way or another. Right?

And so what. Think I care if she has to wear glasses. Well that's just plum crazy."

Kash released one hand on the steering wheel and patted the dog's head. "But I gotta feeling..."

Not paying any attention to anything else, but the houses just up ahead, he rolled past a makeshift Christmas tree bodega in a small parking lot. The air smelled like cinnamon, pine, and the kind of cheer that could suffocate a

Man.

At the next red light, he scowled at his useless phone. The screen sat frozen on a spinning wheel of death. "Sure, yeah, take your time. Not like I'm trying to find a house in the middle of a snow globe," he muttered, tossing it onto the dash. The truck's heater wheezed, barely keeping up against the Ohio cold, and the wipers scraped across the windshield, smearing more than clearing.

Hank let out a deep sigh, fogging up the passenger window. "Don't start with me, buddy. You ain't the one squinting at house numbers in this here flurry of snow like a fool."

The truck continued down the street, passing a set of glowing snowmen and an inflatable Santa that had given up on life, half-deflated in a heap on a lawn. About two seconds from calling it quits, movement caught his eye.

The truck eased to a stop at the red light.

His pulse did something stupid. Like a colt trying to gallop on ice.

Two figures stepped out of a porch up ahead bundled up like they were fixing to climb Mt. Everest. And wouldn't you know it — the barely visible house number on the post matched the one he hunted. His GPS spoke up. "Your destination is in two-hundred feet on the right ."

Kash rolled his eyes. "Thanks, you idiot. Glad you decided to finally show up." He stepped on the gas and mumbled. "Where were you an hour and a half ago when I got lost in Columbus?"

Hank leaned into Kash and licked him.

Kash grimaced as he used his red and green flannel plaid to wipe off the slobber. "Hey buddy. Not now, I'm driving."

But Hank paid him no mind as he squeezed under Kash's arms.

"Come on, buddy. I think we've found our destination."

As they crossed through the intersection of Liberty Street and Columbus Avenue, Kash spotted her.

Rose Shanklin, the woman who had slipped away like a wisp of morning fog left nothing but a cold bed and an emptier chest. She wore a dark green coat cinched at her waist, auburn hair tumbling from beneath a knit hat. She stepped out of the door and onto the porch with a man at her side.

A man?

Something in Kash's gut coiled tight, hotter than a branding iron pressed to raw hide.

Kash idled the truck in the side alley running between the chamber of commerce and the house. With a stab to the window control it lowered further. The frigid air provided no relief to the tightness that gripped his neck. His breath caught in his throat. A flurry of happy voices danced between the falling snow. Kash's heart kicked as if to bust loose of some ice. He examined her closely. Well in all honesty, as much as he could from his truck's rear-view mirror.

She tossed back her head laughing.

Kash hadn't heard the happiness of her laughter in a year, and now some townie in a plaid scarf was soaking it in like he'd earned it?

A sharp twinge of pain hit his chest, while bitterness crawled up his throat.

Hell no.

He slammed the truck into park and yanked on the doorhandle.

Two years. He'd spent two years tracking her down, only to find her cozying up to some Ohio farmhand.

Hank sat up, ears perking at the sudden tension in the cab.

"Stay put. This ain't your fight."

Boots hit pavement. He strode toward them with fists clenched at his sides ignoring Hank's bark of protest.

The two figures turned at the sound of the bark. Rose slipped on a pair of pink glasses while the other person cocked their head.

Kash slammed into something soft, yet unyielding.

Time slowed.

The world tipped. A tangle of synthetic fur, oversized hooves, and blinking LED lights engulfed him. He crashed backward taking the monstrous inflatable reindeer with him.

A chorus of shrieks followed. A group of carolers ready to step up to the porch collapsed like dominoes, tangled in garland and flailing scarves. The reindeer, still blinking maniacally wedged itself between them. Rudolph's glowing nose blinked like it mocked him.

Hank whined louder, and somewhere in the distance, a kid yelled, "The cowboy killed Rudolph!"

And of course, the two on the porch, well they stood there — All warm and smug, like two barn cats watching a mouse struggle in the snow.

A faint, tinny murmur, almost like someone left a tiny radio on low volume broke the cold crispness of the air.

Silence.

Then, laughter — rich, unmistakable — Rose's.

Rage BOLTED up Kash's spine. He shoved the tangled mess off him, surging to his feet. He squared his shoulders and growled.

The carolers scattered.

Rose's mittened hand covered her mouth, but those green eyes sparkled with wicked amusement.

With three quick strides, Kash hit the top of the porch. Puffs of air pressed past his lips. His hands opened and closed into tight fists.

A peppermint-scented mitten collided with his chest.

"You planning on ruining the entire Christmas display, cowboy?"

He caught her wrist, holding tight. Her breath hitched, the barest tremor running through her. Kash stepped closer.

He leaned into her. "You run off," his voice rougher than he intended, "and now you're cozying up with some other man?"

Rose stiffened. "What?"

He jerked his chin toward Plaid Scarf, who, to his credit, had the sense to take a step back.

Rose's nose scrunched in confusion — then her lips curved. Dangerous. Like a match held too close to kindling. "Kash, that's Talia ."

Talia?

Kash scowled, searching the man's face. Then glancing at Rose with his voice lowered. "You're laughing?"

Rose yanked her hand free with an arched eyebrow. "I could be crying. Hard to say."

More snow danced around them. But the flurry of flakes melted before they could pile up on his vest.

"You disappear," his voice edged with something unreadable, "and now you're shacked up with some guy?"

Rose blinked. "Excuse me?"

Kash tilted his chin toward Talia.

A slow, cheshire grin formed on Rose's lips. "Oh," she purred.

Kash's brow furrowed, recalling that tone, his neck hairs stood. He shot a warning. "Rose."

Rose shifted toward her friend. "Talia, honey, this here cowboy thinks we're lovers."

Talia spun on her heel. Eyes wide. She clasped her hands over her heart. "Oh, bless your heart!"

Kash went still. He watched as the next moment played in slow motion.

Rose clasped her mittened hands together. "You came all this way because you were jealous? That's adorable. Do cowboys always get this dramatic, or is it just the ones with commitment issues?"

His jaw flexed.

Talia stepped out of the shadows of the porch and draped an arm around Rose's shoulders. "You should have seen our last dinner date." She sighed theatrically. "Candlelight. Slow dancing. Rose fed me tiramisu off her spoon — "

Recognition slammed into him like a rogue bull.

Rose's old college roommate. Not a man. But her best friend. The same snarky Talia who he had once gotten a black eye for rescuing her.

Should have let her fend for herself. She's definitely got the mouth to do it.

With a low growl, Kash held up a hand. His jaw tight. "I get it."

He watched Rose bite her lip.

She's laughing at me.

"You sure?" She fluttered her lashes. "Because I could—
"

Not ready to give up, he closed the space between them faster than she could crack an egg. He loomed over her. His breath puffed small clouds of air between them. Heat stirred within him. The crisp winter air suddenly not cold enough.

"I didn't come here for games, Rose."

The tension flamed as if someone threw another log onto it. Something dangerous. His heart kicked. A quirk of a smile uptick from the corner of his mouth appeared.

Rose licked her lips.

Okay, Darlin' what's your game. Temptation? A dare??

And this wouldn't be the first time she did something like that to him. No. Not at all. In fact, their senior prom appeared in front of him. She wore a black formal with three-inch heels. She'd told him she'd go with friends. You know, a girl group. But what would that say to everyone? What would it tell her if he didn't provide the escort? After all, he'd been the one to ask her long before anyone had discussed the dance. Better yet, what would she think? So, not wanting to disappoint, he spent the whole night on his feet without complaint. He bit the bullet and escorted her to their prom. Heck he even danced the night away. Sure, he wanted to make the love of his life happy, but standing there for four hours straight on the gym floor, in a monkey suit, and with one foot booted in a walking cast, might not have ever been the smartest thing he'd ever done for her. And yes, today, he still had a slight limp. But it's only noticeable now when it got real cold. But what else could he have done. Right?

He had only one person to blame. Himself. So now, would he give in again?

Could she be tempting him? Could she be daring him?

Talia cleared her throat. "Hey buddy. Look at you."

Hank reached the top of the steps and huffed. He let out a soft whimper and nudged Kash's leg.

Talia bent down and held out a hand.

Hank stretched his neck forward and sniffed.

"Come on, buddy."

The dog didn't move.

"Hmm?" Talia stood.

Kash nodded.

Talia straightened her coat. "There's good things happening these days with cataracts. You should check into it."

Silence.

Talia squeezed Rose's arm. "Should I go?"

Kash snapped out of his thoughts.

Breathe slow. *Think rationally.*

Rose reached into her coat. A white metal tube appeared. "I got this."

Talia grinned and squeezed Rose's arm. "Now don't hurt him. Be gentle with the poor boy." She laughed.

Rose chuckled. "Yes, ma'am... I'll try."

Talia shook her head. "Oh girl. You got this."

"I do. Remember, tomorrow. Seven pm were taping the Christmas special."

Rose nodded.

Talia pulled on the collar of her coat and vanished down the steps.

Kash's gaze returned to Rose.

Rose lifted her chin. "You done causing problems, cowboy?"

Kash blew out his breath between his fingers covering his face. Tinsel clung to his flannel sleeve. "Not even close."

Rose extended the white metallic rod with a button. Tapped the floor and moved back a few feet. She dug out her keys and unlocked the door.

Kash watched in curiosity.

14

She pointed with the stick. "If you're done making a fool of yourself, get inside before you destroy any more innocent reindeer."

Pride warred with relief, but Kash had learned one thing about Rose Shanklin — when she gave an order, you either followed it or got bucked faster than eight seconds flat.

"Fine." He grumbled. He'd go inside. But this wasn't over. Not even close.

He patted the side of his thigh. "Come on, Hank, you heard the lady. Inside, now."

Chapter 2

Kash entered the house.

Rose followed. She barely made it two steps inside before Hank barreled past her, tail whipping against furniture like a caffeinated tornado.

She toed off her boots with the kind of determination usually reserved for battling a rogue stand mixer.

Thump. Crash. Something clattered to the floor.

Rose cringed.

Kash blew out his breath. "Hank, settle down."

She pivoted in her socks and felt for the edge of the doorframe.

The lights clicked on.

Rose removed her coat, hanging it and the stick on a hook next to the door.

Hank whined.

She turned.

In front of her, Kash lingered. Silence stretched between them, heavier than a cast-iron skillet to the shin.

His presence pressed against the room.

Boots scraped against the wooden floor. "You gonna talk, Rose, or just let me hang here?"

Oh, so now he wanted to talk. Convenient.

She scoffed. "Yeah sure. And give you an excuse to stay longer."

His chuckle rumbled low sliding beneath her ribs in a way that shouldn't still matter. "Darlin', I don't need an excuse."

He stood in her living room like he belonged there. Like she hadn't run halfway across the country to make sure he never had to see her like this.

Hank launched himself onto the couch. Well, almost. A yelp, a scramble, a tangle of limbs — then a very undignified thud as he flopped halfway off, rear legs dangling, tail wagging like optimism could fix bad decisions.

Kash huffed. "That dog's got more enthusiasm than coordination."

Rose leaned back against the door, arms crossed. "Ever wonder if he's your emotional support chaos."

The cowboy moved closer. His footsteps steady, unhurried, like a man measuring the distance between what he wanted and what he feared losing. "Still waiting on an answer, Rose."

The air shifted. The way it always did when he got serious. She sucked in a slow breath. "You want to know why I left."

Kash's vest rustled as he folded his arms. "I deserve that much."

He did.

Rose tapped her fingers against the door, letting the rhythm fill the space where words should be.

Hank wriggled himself fully onto the couch, let out a long-suffering groan, then began the loudest licking session imaginable.

Rose's lip curled. "Is That normal?"

Kash covered his eyes shaking his head. "Oh, yeah. That's the sound of my last shred of dignity."

Rose snorted.

A pause.

Then, softer. "Why, Rose?"

No more jokes. No more stalling.

She dug her nails into the door... The smooth wood, the faint scratch where Talia had banged a sweeper handle against it last week — familiar things. Safe things. Unlike this conversation.

"Two years ago," her voice barely cleared a whisper, "I got diagnosed with Stickler's Syndrome."

Kash stayed quiet. No quick reply. No boots shifting. Just that solid, steady presence.

Rose exhaled. "Doctors told me I'd already lost too much vision. My retinas? Like duct tape that's been pulled one too many times. Detached. They tried to fix them, but..." A shrug. "Too late."

Kash's mouth fell open. He raked a hand through his hair.

Hank whimpered.

His gaze shot to his dog, then back to Rose.

Something flickered in the space between them. Not pity — she would've smelled that from a mile away. Something else.

Kash's voice dipped low. "So, you up and left?"

Her chest tightened. "I didn't want you stuck with this."

"This?"

Hands clenched at her sides. "Me."

Kash muttered something under his breath that sounded suspiciously like a curse word too impolite for church.

Boots moved closer. "Rose Shanklin, if you honestly think I — "

"Kash ." Her voice cracked, but she powered through. "You didn't sign up for this. You wanted a wife, not — "

"Not what?" his voice heated. "Not a woman who still bakes circles around the rest of this town? Not the same

19

stubborn, infuriating, incredible woman I wanted to marry?"

Something stung behind her ribs.

Hank flopped onto his back, letting out a dramatic groan that, honestly, felt personally timed to ruin the moment.

Kash sighed, rubbing his temples.

Rose forced out a laugh. "Hank's right. This conversation is exhausting."

"Rose."

She turned, slow and careful. "You still don't understand."

"Then make me understand."

Deep breath. Fine.

She reached toward the door, finding her coat. Her fingertips brushed cool plastic. Glasses. Not just any glasses — her Meta glasses. She pushed them onto her nose and tapped the right arm of the frame, activating the tiny AI voice nestled inside. "Hey Meta, describe my surroundings."

A crisp, robotic voice replied, "One person in the living room. Male, standing by the couch. Chocolate Labrador, upside down, paws in the air."

Kash's brows lifted. "Well, damn."

Rose huffed. "Yeah. Welcome to my new reality."

He reached out, not touching her, just hovering close. "Rose, why didn't you tell me?"

Words stuck, thick as molasses. "Because I wanted you to remember me before. Before I needed tech to tell me where my own things were. Before I —" She swallowed hard. "Before you saw me like this."

Kash moved then, fingers grazing her jaw, tilting her face up. A gentle, careful touch that burned.

"I see you," he murmured. "And I still love you, Rose."

Her chest ached.

Hank chose that exact moment to roll off the couch, crash into Kash's legs, and send all three of them toppling into a heap of limbs, fur, and questionable life choices.

Rose let out a strangled laugh. "Oh my Gosh."

Kash groaned beneath her. "Hank you're becoming a menace."

Hank licked Kash's face in response. Sloppy. Enthusiastic. Probably with extra slobber just for fun.

Rose tried — and failed — to stop laughing.

Kash grunted. "You enjoying this?"

"Immensely."

A beat of silence.

Then Kash, deadpan: "You still in love with me, or do I gotta wrestle the dog for your attention?"

Rose's breath hitched.

His hand, warm against her back. His voice, steady as ever.

The answer sat right there, waiting.

She let it hang between them, caught in the space where fear and hope tangled.

Hank sneezed directly in Kash's face.

Rose lost it.

Maybe — just maybe — love wasn't off the table after all.

Rose wiped tears of laughter from her eyes, still half-sprawled across Kash and the ridiculous dog that had just body-checked them. But as the giggles faded, something heavier settled between her ribs — the weight of what came next.

She pressed her palms against Kash's chest and pushed herself upright. "Alright, cowboy," she said, tilting her chin. "You say you still love me. You say none of this changes how you see me." Her fingers found the edges of her Meta glasses, the sleek frame cool beneath her touch. "But can you handle my world?"

Kash sat up, rubbing a hand over his face. "Rose, I — "

She held up a finger. "No. No pretty words. Actions, Kash." A challenge sparked in her voice, something daring, something that dared her as much as him. "You want me back? Fine. Then show up at my class tomorrow night. Christmas baking at the art center." A slow, deliberate smile curved her lips. "I'll be the one wielding the rolling pin."

Silence.

Rose arched a brow. "Problem?"

His jaw tightened, just a little. "Not one."

She stood. "Good. Because before I give you my heart again, I need to know you're ready for all of me. Blindness, chaos, and whatever else comes with loving me."

Kash rose to his feet, towering over her, solid and sure. "Darling," he drawled, a slow smirk creeping in, "if a little baking is all that's standing between me and you, then I'll see you in that kitchen."

Rose smirked back. Oh, he had no idea what he was in for... And to be honest, neither did she.

Chapter 3

Kash had handled wild stallions, raging rivers, and more than one ornery ranch hand in his lifetime. None of that had prepared him for a Christmas baking class.

The scent of peppermint filled the air, warm and inviting — like Rose herself. If she'd wanted to torture him, she'd found the perfect way to do it.

She stood at the front of the Wayne County Art Center's kitchen, apron dusted in flour, her hair pinned up except for one unruly strand that kept slipping free.

Kash curled his fingers around the edge of the counter. That damn strand had no business being that distracting. She adjusted the Santa-shaped timer on the counter, its plastic red hat crooked like it had just staggered home from an eggnog bender. And in all reality, somewhat like he felt standing so close to her.

Could either of them forgive and forget. Maybe move on together?

"Alright, folks," Rose said, running her hand over the items of flour, sugar, eggs, cream cheese, and a pile of candy canes on the counter in front of her to orient herself. Her confidence stirred something deep in his chest, a mix of admiration and something more dangerous. "Today, we're making candy cane cookies. And let's not forget, Talia will be video taping it all for my Substack channel. So smile pretty."

Perfect. Simple. Straightforward. How hard could it be?

He cracked his knuckles, ready for battle.

The class hummed with movement, a steady mix of laughter, clanging bowls, and the occasional panicked yelp when someone overestimated their whisking skills.

Talia moved stealthily from station to station filming the class.

Kash stood in the middle of it all. He looked about as comfortable as a cowboy at a ballet recital. But not ready to lose this battle. And especially the woman he loved, he unleashed his inner bull and let loose.

Twenty minutes later, it looked like a blizzard had hit the kitchen.

Talia cupped her hands around her mouth. "Cleanup on counter five, please."

The class laughed.

Kash growled.

Rose Unfolded her cane and edged closer. Her cane tapped gently against the tiled floor. "Kash, how's your cookie dough coming?"

Silence.

Then, an exasperated sigh. "Looks like a gunfight."

Across the counter, Rose's lips twitched. "Kash."

He lifted his hands in surrender, white powder coating every inch of his skin. "Before you say anything, this is not my fault."

She tilted her head straightening the pink Meta glasses on her nose, unimpressed. And with one tap of her finger a slight click and a blink of light emanated from the arm of the charcoal grey frames. The tinny AI voice described the scene. Not wanting to laugh out loud, Rose slipped a hand over her lips once the description finished. She mumbled through her fingers. "You mistook powdered sugar for flour?"

"Honest mistake."

"What did you do? Throw the bag in the air?"

He gestured toward the offending bag, currently slumped over like a spent gunslinger. "Listen, it got away from me."

"And Hank? What's he doing?" Her shoulders shook, barely contained laughter bubbling beneath the surface. "So, what's his excuse?" She nodded toward the mess behind him.

One of Kash's eyebrow's rose in an arch.

The clip of nails and clatter of a tin container rattled as if someone scooted it across the floor.

Rose tapped her Meta glasses. The light from the corner of the frames where the camera sat blinked again.

Her face fell. "Oh Hank. I thought you were going to be good?"

Damn. Those glasses are amazing.

He turned slowly dreading what he'd find.

Hank sat in the middle of the floor, nose buried in an empty tin, tail wagging in triumph.

Rose sighed. "Those pecan clusters were for the Christmas charity drive."

Kash rubbed a hand over his jaw, smearing sugar across his face. "I'll make more."

"You don't even know how."

"Then you'll teach me." He leaned in, close enough to catch the faint hint of vanilla clinging to her skin. "Unless you're scared, I'll out-bake you."

Rose snorted. "The only thing you'll be baking is your pride."

She turned to grab something off the high shelf behind her. Kash, ever the gentleman, reached for it first. The rolling pin and handful of candy canes slipped from his grip. They bounced off the counter, careened into a stack of Christmas platters, and sent them tumbling down like a festive avalanche.

Silence.

Rose pressed her lips together.

Kash exhaled. "Just go ahead and laugh."

She did. Loud, full, and completely unrestrained.

The sound wrapped around him like a warm blanket, tightening the noose he'd been trying to ignore since he first set foot in Wooster. He'd come here ready to fight for her. Now? Now, he was just trying to keep up.

Chapter 4

Rose grabbed a stack of gingerbread cookies and a fresh bowl of frosting. "Let's start over. But this time, we'll make a gingerbread house instead."

He sighed, shoulders dropping. "Fine."

The minute she handed him the supplies, a new disaster began.

An hour later, Kash stared at his gingerbread house like it had personally offended him.

Rose edged her way back over to Kash. Her fingers tiptoed across the counter and found the edge of the platter Kash's masterpiece sat on. She squatted to get eyelevel with it. "Hey, Meta describe this gingerbread house."

"You're looking at what was supposed to be a gingerbread house, but currently resembles a gingerbread disaster zone. One wall has completely given up, the roof is sliding like it's trying to escape, and the icing — meant to be glue — is more like a sad, sugary landslide. A few gumdrops cling for dear life, while others have abandoned ship and now lie scattered in the debris field. There might be a faint smell of charcoal with the burnt edges, suggesting things went south before construction even began. Despite the structural failure, it still has 'homemade charm'... if you squint. And hey, at least it's still edible — probably."

Rose stood bracing herself against the counter. "Sounds like a tornado hit it."

"I'd like to see you build a house using only icing and betrayal."

Her grin slowly widened as she leaned toward him.

Uh-oh.

"What are you — "

Rose smacked a dollop of frosting straight onto his cheek.

The war began.

Ginger Cookies, icing, and candy buttons flew.

Hank, sensing an opportunity, lunged for a gumdrop, knocking the table — and Kash — straight into the half-finished gingerbread house.

Sticky. Everywhere.

The others shrieked and dove for cover.

Rose gasped, hands covering her mouth. "Oh my God."

He glared at her, chest heaving. "Help me."

She bit her lip, struggling. Failing. "You're stuck."

"No kidding."

"Ms. Rose," one of the students spoke up from peaking around the station behind her. "Here's a towel."

She reached for the towel. "Hang on."

The towel did nothing.

The gingerbread held fast.

Kash gritted his teeth. "You're enjoying this."

Rose didn't deny it.

A few students laughed.

"Did you put glue in that frosting?"

Rose tried to contain the laughter, eventually, she grabbed a bottle of grapeseed oil and drizzled it over the disaster.

He shivered. "You could at least buy me dinner first."

She rolled her eyes but couldn't quite hide her blush.

Minutes later, freed from the mess, but dripping in oil and more determined than ever to kiss the woman grinning at his misery.

A perfect moment.

But Hank released an unholy sneeze right on both of them.

Rose yelped wiping at her face. "Seriously?"

Kash groaned, defeated. "Merry Christmas."

Talia lost it. "I swear, this is the best Christmas gift I've ever gotten. And your fans? They're going to love it."

Rose exhaled, long and slow. "This isn't how I pictured my Christmas special."

Kash chuckled, low and rough. "This ain't how I pictured my comeback."

A beat of silence.

Rose turned toward his voice. Kash watched her. Something deep in her gaze, something he wasn't ready to name.

Her breath hitched.

He leaned in —

Hank sneezed again, right in their faces.

Rose gagged. "I'm convinced he's allergic to me."

Kash wiped at his cheek, grumbling. "Like I said, Merry Christmas."

Chapter 5

Later that evening, Kash strolled with Rose through the town square. Lights twinkled like fireflies against the night sky. Snow crunched underfoot.

"I gotta admit," he said, glancing at her, "this town does Christmas right."

Rose exhaled, visible mist curling in the frigid air. "It's home."

Something about the way she said it punched him in the gut. He could picture her here, laughing, cooking, thriving. She didn't need him to swoop in and save her. She never had.

They reached the towering Christmas tree, its colorful glow softening the sharp edges of reality with its large candy canes decorating it.

Rose nudged him. "You okay?"

He turned to her, really looking. The set of her shoulders, the way she turned slightly to listen — every little thing that made her Rose.

Yeah. Looked as if trouble had found him.

Behind them, a shepherd's hook lamppost stood wrapped in garland with twinkle lights and clusters of mistletoe.

His pulse kicked. "Rose ."

Out of old habit, she looked around. "What?"

"Mistletoe."

"Oh."

No teasing, no laughter. Just her lips parting, breath catching — Hank chose that moment to shake himself off, sending snow and lingering cookie crumbs flying.

Rose groaned. "Your dog is the worst."

Kash rubbed his temples. "He's lucky I love him."

Rose's laughter softened. "You always love the difficult ones, don't you?"

He tightened his arm around hers.

Always.

Chapter 6

The Wayne Center for the Arts buzzed with holiday cheer, the scent of cinnamon and sugar thick in the air. Christmas music drifted through the space, slightly offbeat from the hum of chatter and the occasional clatter of mixing bowls. Rose stood at the front of the class. Her sleeves were rolled up, apron dusted with flour, and cane tucked neatly against the counter.

Tonight, she belonged here surrounded by warmth and laughter. The steady rhythm of baking familiar beneath her hands. Teaching these classes had become more than a job — it reminded her she still had control, still had something to offer.

She didn't need Kash barging into that. And yet, there he stood, all six feet three inches of stubborn cowboy, arms crossed, eyes fixed on her like she might disappear again.

His boots scuffed against the tiled floor as he stepped closer. "Hope I'm not late." His slow drawl sent a shiver down her spine.

"Not at all," she said lightly, ignoring the way her pulse skipped. "Plenty of time to ruin a perfectly good batch of sugar cookies."

A snort. "I ain't ruining nothing."

Rose smirked. "We'll see." She waved him toward an empty station. "Get settled. Recipe's in front of you. Try not to set anything on fire."

A low chuckle rumbled from his chest, but as Kash moved to his place, a new problem surfaced.

"Hank."

The overgrown menace had wormed his way past the door and now sat beside Kash, tongue lolling, eyes locked on the trays of dough.

"Be a good boy."

Rose sighed. "Who let your partner-in-crime in here?"

Kash scrubbed a hand over his face. "That dogs got a mind of his own."

A mind currently focused on cookie theft.

Rose shook her head, returning her attention to the class. "Alright, folks. First step, grab your rolling pins.

We're aiming for a quarter-inch thickness. Even cuts make for even baking."

The sound of dough being flattened filled the room. Rose worked alongside them, fingers pressing into the soft, cool surface, relying on the muscle memory that had become second nature.

Beside her, Kash's approach seemed less... Graceful.

A thud. A muttered curse.

Rose turned toward him. "Everything okay?"

Silence.

Then, the unmistakable whoosh of flour exploding into the air.

She coughed, waving at the cloud that engulfed them. Someone let out a surprised yelp. Kash muttered something under his breath.

She wiped at her Meta glasses and barely contained a laugh. "Did you just try to open the bag with brute force?"

A pause.

"Might've pulled too hard."

Rose arched a brow. "Like a grizzly tearing into a picnic basket?"

Another pause.

"Bit like that, yeah."

Laughter rippled through the class. Kash, now thoroughly dusted in white like a misplaced snowman, exhaled and shook his head.

Rose bit the inside of her cheek. "Maybe next time, use scissors."

He wiped his hands on his jeans, sending another puff of flour into the air. "Got a little carried away."

"Clearly."

Hank seized the opportunity, lunging forward. His nose disappeared into the flour pile, tail wagging like mad.

"Hank, no!" Kash reached down to grab him, but it only made things worse.

Hank yanked free, sending a mixing bowl clattering to the floor, then charged straight for the nearest table, paws skidding. The table wobbled. Someone gasped.

Rose's stomach lurched. "Hank .!"

Too late.

The entire tray of cookie cutters tumbled down, clanging onto the floor, a Metallic avalanche of stars, trees, and candy canes.

A stunned silence filled the room. Then —

A sniff. A sneeze.

And Kash, bless his ridiculous soul, sneezed so hard he nearly knocked himself backward.

Rose covered her mouth. "You good?"

He sniffed. "Tastes like cinnamon."

That did it. The laughter she'd barely contained spilled over, shaking her shoulders.

Kash looked down at his flour-covered self, sighed, then shot her a lopsided grin. "Admit it. This is the best entertainment your class has ever had."

Rose folded her arms. "I'll give you points for enthusiasm."

As the class slowly regained order, Rose guided them through the next steps. Kash, to his credit, kept up — mostly. His cookies came out lumpy, his icing attempt bordered on abstract art, but he stuck with it, stubborn as ever.

And despite herself, she softened.

Kash Tyler, a cowboy who made me melt with a single touch, the man I'd run from because I refused to let him sacrifice his future for me — he'd come here. He'd stepped into my world. Mess and all.

Maybe — just maybe — he really meant it.

But before that thought could settle, a voice drifted over from the next table.

"...if Rose takes the cookbook deal, she'll probably have to move. Big publishers always want their authors in-house, right?"

Rose's stomach tightened.

Talia's voice came next. "It's just an offer, nothing set in stone. Besides, Rose isn't leaving Wooster."

A beat.

"I mean, unless she wants to."

Silence stretched for half a second too long.

Rose didn't have to see Kash's face to recognize the way his entire body tensed. Nope, not at all especially when the thud of a rolling pin hit the countertop near her.

Her pulse kicked up. "Kash — "

"Don't." His boots scraped the floor as he pushed off the counter.

Rose reached out, but he'd already stepped away.

"Cowboy?"

Boots stomped against the tile. A clipped, "Got what I came for."

And then, he disappeared.

Chapter 7

Wooster's winter air bit at Kash's skin as he threw a duffel bag into the truck bed. The old Chevy groaned under the weight, or maybe it just groaned in solidarity. Leaving never sat right.

Hank circled the truck, snuffling at the tires like they might hold the answers. Smart dog. Kash could use a few answers himself.

The sky stretched above him, an endless quilt of gray and white, thick with the promise of more snow. His breath came out in short, sharp clouds, vanishing into the cold just like Rose had vanished from his life. Twice now.

He yanked open the driver's side door, but a flash of green snagged his attention.

Mistletoe?

Dangling from the rearview mirror, a cocky little sprig tied with a red bow.

Hank sat beneath it, tail sweeping in slow, lazy arcs. He panted, looking far too pleased with himself.

Kash narrowed his eyes. "Where'd that come from?"

The dog gave a full-body wiggle, then lunged forward, licking Kash's chin with enough enthusiasm to count as a Christmas assault.

"Alright, alright!" Kash wiped his face on his sleeve, scowling at the mistletoe. Wooster had it out for him. First, a woman he couldn't stop loving. Now, a dog practically shoving him under holiday tradition like some matchmaking elf.

Hank barked once, then climbed down from the truck and trotted back to the house, nose high like he had unfinished business.

Kash should've just left.

Instead, he followed.

The porch creaked under his boots. Every step dragged, his body moving on pure instinct. Hank had wedged himself between the door and a battered cardboard box left outside.

Kash crouched. The label stared back at him, bold black ink spelling out a truth he hadn't been ready to see.

"Cookbook Drafts — Do Not Toss."

His stomach knotted.

This wasn't a box for a big move. It wasn't sealed for shipping, wasn't stamped with some fancy New York address.

It sat ON THE PORCH like it belonged here.

His fingers twitched. He could open it, flip through the pages, find out if she'd really been planning to leave.

But he didn't.

Because Rose wasn't his to claim.

He straightened, muscles stiff, heart heavier than the snow-laden sky pressing down on him.

Behind him, Hank huffed, then bolted.

"Hank!"

Too late.

The dog shot off the porch, bounding toward the garage like a reindeer on a sugar high. More importantly — Hank had a piece of mistletoe clamped between his teeth.

Kash cursed.

By the time he caught up, the dog had cornered Rose.

She stood near the garage door, bundled up against the cold, her hair a mess of auburn curls peeking from beneath a ridiculous Santa hat.

Hank skidded to a stop, plopping his butt down, mistletoe hanging from his mouth like a trophy.

Rose sighed. "You're relentless."

Kash leaned against the doorframe, arms crossed. "He's got an agenda."

Her head tilted toward him. Snow dusted the tips of her boots, the hem of her coat, the curve of her cheek.

"And what's yours?"

That voice. Soft, but sharp enough to cut.

Kash exhaled, gaze flicking to the dog still holding the sprig of mistletoe in his mouth by the red and green ribbon like he was officiating a Christmas showdown.

"Leaving."

Rose didn't move.

Hank whined, shifting his weight.

The silence stretched.

Then —

"You always run when things get tough?"

Kash stiffened. "Not running."

"No?" Rose stepped forward. Her cane tapped against the frozen ground, steady and sure. "Could've fooled me."

His heart slammed against his ribs.

This woman. *This impossible, beautiful, maddening woman.*

He swallowed hard. "You've got plans."

She crossed her arms. "Do I?"

He nodded toward the porch. "And what about the box near the door?"

Rose blew out a breath. "That's not — "

"Hank," Kash cut in, voice tight. "Drop it."

The dog spat the bunch of mistletoe and its Christmas colored ribbons onto Rose's boot. His tail thumping like he'd just solved world peace.

Rose bent searching for the sprig and its berries — finding it she picked it up. "You gonna let a dog make your decisions for you now?"

His jaw clenched.

He'd spent days — hell, years — trying to be what she needed.

And here she stood, acting like he'd never mattered.

"Doesn't seem like you need me, Rose."

Her breath hitched. Just barely.

But he caught it.

And it wrecked him.

She shook her head. "You idiot cowboy."

That did it.

Kash stepped closer, close enough to catch the faint scent of cinnamon and vanilla clinging to her skin, the warmth of her breath curling in the cold air.

His hands fisted at his sides. "If I'm wrong, tell me."

Rose's lips parted.

Hank yawned.

Then — because the dog had no sense of timing whatsoever — he lunged forward, knocking them both straight into the garage door.

Rose gasped. Kash caught her elbows, steadying her.

His fingers brushed the wool of her coat. Too soft. Too warm. Too damn much.

Rose sucked in a sharp breath. "Are you really leaving?"

He didn't answer.

Because if she asked him to stay —

He might not be able to say no.

Chapter 8

Wooster's air carried the sharp bite of winter, the scent of woodsmoke curling around Rose like an old friend. Snow crunched beneath her boots as she teetered waiting for his answer. Each step a quiet reminder that she hadn't moved from this spot in front of the garage in far too long. Kash stood there, stubborn as ever, arms crossed, jaw clenched like he was bracing for a storm.

Which, given her tendency to speak first and figure out consequences later, he probably should be.

Hank, ever the opportunist, sniffed at the ground between them, uninterested in human dramatics unless they resulted in food. Or belly rubs. Or — based on the way he suddenly trotted off — whatever new disaster he could get into next.

Rose inhaled, fingers tightening around her cane and the sprig of mistletoe. "You ever heard the saying, 'If you can't stand the heat, stay out of the kitchen'?"

Kash's gaze flicked to her, wary. "Might've heard it once or twice."

"Well, cowboy." She tilted her chin, feeling the warmth of determination spread through her limbs. "I live in the kitchen."

One of his brows inched up. "And that's supposed to mean what, exactly?"

"That I don't run when things get hard." She gestured toward him, her hand brushing his coat. "That I know what I want."

That last part came out quieter than she meant. She let the words hang there, balancing on the thin wire between terrifying and true.

Kash didn't move. Didn't speak.

Hank did, however, choose that exact moment to barrel into her legs again with the force of a wrecking ball covered in fur.

She stumbled, catching herself against Kash, who caught her in return, because of course he did.

His grip burned through her coat. Not from the cold. But from the sheer presence of him — solid, steady, impossible.

Hank sat at their feet, tail sweeping the snow. If dogs could smirk, he would have.

Kash groaned. "You'd think someone trained him for these moments."

Rose's lips twitched. A barely-there almost-smile that hit him like a shot of espresso straight to the heart.

Rose braced herself, then grabbed ahold of his coat lapels. The distance only helped. "I want to be with you."

His jaw ticked. "Rose — "

"No, I mean it." Her pulse kicked up, but the words poured out anyway. "Winter here. Summers in Whiskey. Maybe we argue over which town gets Christmas, or maybe we split holidays like a couple of divorced parents with joint custody over our sanity. But I don't care where we live." She inhaled sharply. "I care that we live it together."

Kash leaned his forehead into hers. He wrapped his arms around her. The weight of it pressed into her ribs. The kind of silence that could build a home or tear it down in one breath.

Hank, thoroughly unimpressed with the lack of immediate resolution, trotted off.

Kash exhaled, his breath visible in the cold. "You sure about this?"

Rose pulled the Meta glasses from her coat pocket, slipping them on. "You're a six-foot-three tall cowboy who thinks powdered sugar is flour and once tried to fix a rocking chair with duct tape and prayer."

His mouth opened. Closed.

She crossed her arms. "Yeah, I'm sure."

A chuckle rumbled low in his chest. Like a gravel road before a winter storm.

Hank chose that moment to reappear, a Christmas wreath clamped in his mouth, dragging half a string of tangled lights behind him.

"Oh lordy." Kash shook his head. "You don't want to know what he's got now."

Rose sighed. "Perfect."

Kash smirked. "Fitting."

Hank pranced between them, stopping just long enough to shake snow onto Kash's boots, then Rose's. The wreath bobbed in his mouth like he was officiating some kind of backwoods holiday wedding.

Kash snorted. "You realize we're probably stuck with him forever, right?"

Rose smiled, eyes still locked on him. "I believe I can live with that."

Kash grinned. "Good. 'Cause forever sounds about right."

Hank barked, sending the wreath flying straight onto Kash's boots.

Rose laughed.

Kash swore.

Wooster sighed with the winter wind wrapping around them like an old, familiar quilt. Not perfect. Not easy. But absolutely right.

Rose leaned into Kash. "Let's not waste his efforts."

Kash's brow rose. "Which means?"

Rose held up her hand. "Don't waste this mistletoe, cowboy. Kiss me."

The End

Candy Cane Cookies

Serving Size: 1
Servings: 24
Approximate Calories: 120

Ingredients:
- 1 cup grapeseed oil (or exchange 1 cup unsalted butter, 2 sticks)
- 8 oz cream cheese
- 1-1/4 cup granulated sugar
- 1 large egg
- 1 teaspoon vanilla extract
- 1/2 teaspoon peppermint extract
- 2-1/2 cups all-purpose flour
- 1 teaspoon baking powder
- 1/2 teaspoon baking soda
- 1/4 teaspoon salt
- 1/2 cup crushed candy canes

Topping - Optional
- 1/2 cup white chocolate morsels/chips - melted
- extra crushed candy canes
- Red and green sugar sprinkles

Instructions:
1. Preheat oven to 350°F. Line baking sheets with parchment paper.

2. In large mixing bowl, beat grapeseed oil and cream cheese together until light and fluffy.

3. Gradually mix in the sugar until fully combined. Then, add egg, vanilla extract, and peppermint extract. Continue mixing until smooth.

4. In separate bowl, whisk together flour, baking powder, baking soda, and salt. Gradually add to the wet ingredients, stirring until just combined.

5. Gently fold in crushed candy canes for peppermint crunch.

6. Drop rounded teaspoon balls of dough onto prepared baking sheets. Space about 2 inches apart to allow for spreading. Gently press fork into top of dough to create stripes to fill with sugar sprinkles for candy cane stripe effect.

7. Bake for 10–12 minutes or until the edges are lightly golden and centers are set. Remove from oven and let cookies cool on baking sheet for 5 minutes before transferring to wire rack.

8. Once cookies are slightly cool, if pressed with fork above, sprinkle with green or red sugar sprinkles and extra peppermint or let cookies completely cool, drizzle with melted white chocolate and sprinkle extra crushed candy canes on top for festive finish.

9.

Nutritional Value:

Based on a 2000 calorie diet		
Total Fat:	6	g
Saturated Fat:	3.5	g
Cholesterol:	25	mg
Carbohydrates:	14	g
Sugar:	8	g
Sodium:	80	mg
Fiber:	0.5	g
Protein:	2	g

Grumbles from the Chuckwagon

Ain't nothing worse than a pack of grown men whining like calves over candy cane cookies, but here I am, busting up peppermint sticks with the butt of my revolver like some deranged Christmas elf. Gotta grind 'em down real fine, too — last thing I need is one of these halfwit cowpokes cracking a tooth and crying about it for the next hundred miles. Ain't got time to play nursemaid between driving cattle and keeping these cowpokes from burning themselves on the coffee pot. If they so much as breathe a word about sprinkles, I swear I'll salt their beans for a week.

Merry Christmas!

About Chrissy...

Award-winning blind short story writer and contemporary western romance author, Chrissy Hartmann hopes to one day rope in a Best Sellers list title with her contemporary western romances from the Whiskey Salvation series.

Now following her 5-star Readers Favorite debut novel, "Rescuing Whiskey's Salvation" and her novella, "Cherishing Whiskey's Salvation" is her short story to the Whiskey Salvation series, "Tacking of Hearts," published in the Great Lakes Fiction Writers anthology "Love on the Lakefront: Romantic Tales from the Great Lakes" and her Whiskey Salvation cookbook, "The Grub Wrangler: Heartfelt Grapeseed Oil Recipes with Benefits."

Rolling in like a tumbleweed, but hopefully sooner will be her third book of the series, "Treasuring Whiskey's Salvation" and her anthology of suspense short stories, "Tales from the Prickle Forrest," and her Whiskey Salvation Christmas novella, "Merry Christmas Whiskey," and finally her Whiskey Salvation anthology, "Hearts and Kisses."

Not only does Chrissy two-step words across romances, but she loves creating short stories and blogging for the Prickle Forrest Chronicles... But only when she's not galloping around the countryside with her hubby or son.

For more info, take a gander at

https://ChrissyHartmann.com

And don't forget to hitch your wagon to her newsletter at

https://PrickleForrestChronicles.com/follow-me

Join the herd and follow her on Goodreads, X, Instagram, Facebook, and Substack at USAWriter355.

Now kick off your boots, grab a Whiskey, and settle in for some romance!

Home for Christmas

by

Cary Harter

It was a blue Christmas season for Donna after the death of her husband. Then on Christmas Eve a lost dog showed up in her life. A dog who strangely made her feel like her beloved Alan was with her again and showed her the way home for Christmas.

Donna watched as the lights on the Christmas tree in the center of town became four pointed stars, then multiple pointed ones, until they finally all blurred together the moment before a tear ran down her cheek. She dashed the traitor away with the back of her hand. Before more dissidents could escape, she squashed the rebellion with her fingers and rubbed until there was no evidence of their presence. Emotion was attempting to stage a coup, but she was refusing to be overthrown. Even so, feelings were dangerous and had been for the last ten months.

There was no way she would let herself cry here in the center of town. Not when she had a perfectly good home to cry in and hadn't let more than a single tear fall there. She knew if she started, she could never stop.

In the beginning, she had to maintain tight control to keep working. After ten months, she had become used to keeping it all in. Though, she had to admit, it was getting harder the last couple of months. The initial numbness had morphed into a constant pain in her heart. Now it was Christmas, her first Christmas without Alan. The pain was getting sharper, and so fierce it was almost physical. But she was a strong woman, that's what everyone said, and everyone knew strong women did not cry.

She blinked rapidly a few times, letting the cold air remove any trace of the recalcitrant tears, stiffened her spine and turned to continue her walk back to her car. In her haste, she almost tripped over a large dog that had come up behind her.

"Oh, sorry, fella." She had no doubt that it was a male even though she had seen no physical proof. "It's a cold night. You'd better get home. It's Christmas Eve and your family must be waiting for you."

She pictured the dog in a house full of smiling people. And children. Lots of children. She dashed the picture away before it could embolden those rebellious tears, and brushed past the dog to continue on her way.

She walked briskly, almost reveling in the familiar dull pain that filled her heart when she thought of the children she never had and the husband that was no longer with her. Little puffs of smoke escaped her lips as her breath quickened and fell into rhythm with her steps. Puff...step...puff...step...puff...step. The small bag she carried bumped rhythmically against her thigh and her heart pounded, seeming to follow its tempo. She felt like a human metronome, each breath, each step, each heartbeat clicking away another moment of her life, until she reached her car parked at the end of the block.

She turned to look for oncoming traffic before walking out to the driver's side and noticed that the dog was still following her. In the brighter light of the streetlight, she could see that he was muddy and rather thin. Perhaps he didn't have a home, or couldn't find it. She sighed. She couldn't leave a poor dog on the street in the cold, especially on Christmas. And there was just something about this dog ...

"Are you lost, boy?"

The dog hung his head and looked up at her in that perfect sad, puppy dog look that guaranteed he was going home with her.

"Christmas is a bad time to be lost. Believe me, I know." Her heart seemed to squeeze in her chest as she said this, the pain becoming almost unbearable. She inhaled a shaky breath.

"Tomorrow, I'll take some pictures of you and put them up around town, so you can find your family. In the meantime, I'll take you home with me so that neither of us has to spend the holidays alone."

The dog seemed to understand. He began wagging his tail, walked up to the car and pointed his nose at the door expectantly. Donna smiled. She shook her head, reaching her hand for the handle and then stopped as she realized she had nothing at home for him to eat. She had a little cereal, a couple cans of soup and a frozen turkey dinner she was planning on eating tomorrow for Christmas.

Without Alan, she didn't see a need to keep much food in the house. It didn't make sense to her to cook for one. She didn't seem to want to eat much anyway.

She looked around and spotted a Jimmy John's a couple of doors down.

"We've got to get you some dinner," she said as she started walking toward the deli, the dog following behind.

"You'll have to wait here. Sorry no dogs allowed. I'll be right back."

The dog sat as she opened the door.

He'll probably be gone by the time I come out. Off looking for handouts from someone else.

Donna ordered a Big John, but asked for the tomato and lettuce on the side. The boy making her sandwich gave her a strange look, but she didn't care. If the dog stayed, she doubted he'd like lettuce and tomato, but if he was gone, well, she'd be damned if she'd eat a plain sandwich.

She felt a twinge of regret as she passed over a few more of her precious dollars to the boy, wished him a Merry Christmas, and went out to see if the dog was still there. He was, and he rose from the sitting position he'd been waiting for her in, wagging his tail.

"Alright, I've got your dinner. Let's go home."

Donna wondered if she was making a stupid mistake as she opened the passenger side door for him to get in. Some dogs did not travel well. She had a dog when she was younger who walked back and forth from window to window, not caring who he stepped on, or if they could see where they were driving or not. As she walked to get in her side of the car, she sent up a fleeting thought, almost a prayer, but not quite, because she was still upset with God over taking her Alan, that this dog would not be like that.

Her fears were unfounded, or God heard her. The bag with the sandwich sat between them untouched. The dog sat perfectly still, only his head turning, watching the passing scenery, or as much as he could see of it at six o' clock on an Ohio winter night.

When they got closer to her street, the dog's awareness seemed to increase. His eyes seemed to sharpen, and his ears perked up. As they turned and drew closer to the house, he grew visibly excited. He shifted from paw to paw and let out a whine. When she pulled into the drive, he knew they were home. The excitement emanated from within him, like an aura, filling the space around him.

She pushed the garage door opener and looked over at him. He was looking at her with what she could only call a smile on his face and a look in his eyes that was so warm and familiar it was as if he had been hers forever. Strangely, it reminded her of Alan. She felt a tug at her heart as a few of the bricks from the wall surrounding it crumbled. The toppling of her defenses wasn't a relief. It wasn't a breakthrough that made her see things differently. It just hurt.

She turned facing forward again and pulled into the garage, her hands shaking slightly. *Maybe I am losing it like they said at work.* The thought gave her a burst of anger, just enough to sharpen her thoughts. She turned off the car, closed the garage door, grabbed the bags from the seat between them, opened the car door and slipped out. She walked around and opened the passenger door where the dog was waiting patiently.

He sat there for a moment as if waiting for her to look at him, but she refused, and he finally hopped out of the car and walked to the door leading into the house.

It's just for a night. I will not get close to this dog. He will be gone just like everyone else, and I can't hurt any more. She grabbed the mental mortar to put the fallen bricks back in place.

"Alright, buddy, I'll let you in, but it's straight to the bathroom with you. No eating until I've scrubbed you clean."

She entered the house and wearily set the bags on the table to the right of the door, putting her keys in the bowl sitting there. As she hung her coat on the hook on the wall beside it, she felt exhaustion sweep over her again and wondered how she was going to have the energy to wash the dog. She sighed. *Well, it's no one's fault but mine. I should never have brought him home. Oh, no. Where is he? I hope he hasn't made more of a mess for me to clean.*

She heard the sound of his toenails clacking on the hardwood floor of the hallway and followed. He went into the bathroom, turned back around facing her and sat, looking at her expectantly.

"How did you —?" Donna shook her head as if to clear it, as the dog gave her one of his doggy smiles then turned and jumped into the bathtub.

She took the shower head down before turning on the water and adjusting the temperature. As she sprayed the warm water over the coat of the muddy dog, he seemed to relax into it. She didn't think dogs liked getting a bath, but this one obviously did. He was smiling and clearly enjoying the experience. He let out a sound that had her freeze at first, thinking it was a growl. But as the sound emanated from him again, she realized that it was a moan of pleasure.

She let out a snort. Not exactly a laugh, but the closest she had come to one for what seemed like an eternity.

Alan had enjoyed a good warm shower too. Who was she kidding? It was one of his favorite things in life. She asked him once why he didn't just marry the shower, it's lower maintenance. He had just smiled and said, "I would have, but her kisses are too wet. I like mine just like this," and he had kissed her till she laughed.

The pain ripped through her heart again and she realized she was on her knees spraying the dog with a smile on her face, and tears streaming down her cheeks. A sob broke free from its imprisonment deep inside her. She struggled with its comrades trying to prevent their escape as the dog turned to face her. The doggy smile slipped from his face and the look in his eyes changed to one of compassion. At that look, the prison door was thrown open and emotions were running amuck all over the bathroom. Donna hadn't the strength to corral them back in, and so, knelt in the center of the whirling emotions, eyes closed, the tears continuing to fall.

She was brought back to reality by the feeling of something warm and wet on her cheek, other than her tears. The dog had laid his muzzle against her cheek. She stayed that way for a minute or two, her tears drying, as she reveled in the touch of another living being. It had been so long. She had forgotten how good it felt.

Finally, she took a deep breath and pushed herself back until she sat back on her heels.

"Well, we're not getting things accomplished like this. Come on, let's finish up."

She had to accomplish something, if just to prove to herself that she could. Her coworkers had made no disguise of the fact that they didn't believe she ever would.

She turned around, opened the bottom drawer of the vanity and pulled out Alan's bottle of shampoo she had put there. She hadn't been able to get rid of it yet, and was glad she hadn't. It would come in handy now.

"I didn't think you'd like smelling like a bunch of fruit. We'll give you a more masculine scent."

She squirted some on her hand and as the scent filled the bathroom she was filled with sweet memories and longing at the same time. But she quickly threw off her meandering thoughts. She had a job to do. She began rubbing the shampoo all over the dog. As she worked up a foam, she thought about work.

Her coworkers had been very nice to her the first few weeks after Alan's death. They had brought meals or little gifts of sympathy, but as time wore on and she didn't spring back into her old self, that sympathy faded. They began to complain that she wasn't holding up her end of the load. That she was loafing off. She overheard one woman who she had considered a friend say, "I think she is taking advantage of us. I mean, six months is long enough."

But none of them understood. They all still had husbands. Most had children. They didn't know the feeling of being childless and losing the love of your life after forty years of marriage. Asking her to go back to her normal life was like asking an athlete to run a marathon after losing their leg. Some would run again, but it wouldn't be in six months. It would take years of training and determination, and it would never be the same. Some would never run. Some wouldn't have the support and self-determination to ever do it again.

She was one of the ones who would never run. She had no support now that Alan was gone. It was hard enough moving at all, but it seemed everyone was insisting that she had to get up and run with one leg. It was an impossible situation. Finally, they had complained to management. Now, after thirty years of working for the same company, she was a sixty-four-year-old unemployed woman. She hoped that the social security and Medicaid she filed for would come through or soon she would be a homeless sixty-four-year-old woman.

She finished rinsing the dog, and grabbed a towel as he sat patiently without shaking water all over the bathroom, to be dried. She had to use two towels to dry him, but was grateful she didn't have to wipe down her whole bathroom and told him so. The dog smiled back and leaned into her.

She let out a sigh, her eyes feeling heavy. She had forgotten how much work it was to bathe a dog. It had been years since her old dog, Trixie, died, the same month and year as her mother. She had never gotten another animal since then. She knew well before Alan passed how much death hurt the living. Ah, but she would not do that to anyone. There was no one in her life, so there was no one to hurt.

The dog sat still as she dried his fur with the hair dryer. When she was done, she stood up to put the dryer in the top drawer of the vanity. As she looked up from her task, she caught sight of herself in the mirror. The contrast between the freshly washed dog and herself shocked her. She leaned in closer, and realized she had not even looked at herself in the mirror for weeks. A stranger looked back at her.

Her hair looked thin. The style it had last been cut in had grown out so it was now shapeless, and there was two inches of gray roots before it became a drab brown. It looked like it had not been brushed for days, which if she thought about it, it probably hadn't. The dark circles that had begun the week Alan died had become larger and darker. The number of wrinkles had increased, and her neck looked drapey, something she had always tried to prevent with daily exercises consisting of facial contortions that Alan had laughed at her about.

She looked old. And haggard. And she stank. When was the last time she had taken a shower herself? She gave up trying to remember, deciding it didn't matter. She was taking one now.

She walked into her room, followed by the dog, over to the pile of washed, but unfolded, clothes piled on the chair in the corner. She pulled out a pair of gray sweats and an old baggy t-shirt that said Niagara Falls on it. That marked it as over fifteen years old, because she and Alan had gone there for their twenty fifth anniversary.

She stood for a moment with them in her hands thinking. Then she looked down at the dog beside her.

"I think I'll go all out for you tonight. You're the first guest I've had for months and that's worth a nice outfit, isn't it?"

The dog's tongue lolled out as he grinned and nodded his head.

"I'll take that as a yes."

She smiled faintly back and walked over to her closet. She picked out a pair of black pants that she remembered being comfortable as well as dressy and a soft baby pink sweater that had been one of Alan's favorites.

"Alright, it's my turn now. I'll be done in a jiff."

As the water flowed down over her shoulders, she felt herself release a deep tension she didn't know she carried. She was suddenly overcome with intense exhaustion. Her arms felt like lead weights as she raised them to work the lather through her hair. She definitely felt the workout she got washing the dog, and her carpel tunnel was acting up again. In fact, her whole left arm was hurting.

I sure hope Medicaid will pay for carpel tunnel surgery. I should have gotten it years ago when the doctor recommended it. I guess that's what you get when you put things off.

She closed her eyes and leaned her head back to rinse her hair, sighing as the water ran down over her. She could hear her heartbeat pounding in her ears, *thud, thud, thud,* as if hammering in the fact that she was alive, whether she wanted to be or not.

Suddenly she was almost overcome with dizziness. Her eyes flew open, and she threw her hand out against the shower wall to support herself. *The water must be too hot, you ninny.* She adjusted the water to a cooler temperature, hurriedly washed herself, rinsed and shut off the tap. She grabbed a towel, wrapped it around her quickly and sat shakily down on the toilet. As soon as she felt steady enough, she stood and opened the window about an inch and sat down again. She breathed in the cold air and, after a few minutes, began to feel almost normal again.

When was the last time you ate, you idiot? She rolled her eyes at her stupidity and sighed. She toweled her almost dry body off, dried her hair and dressed. By then she felt much better and decided to go all in. After heating the curling iron and throwing a few curls in, she decided to put on a little makeup. She put on a little blush and was applying some lipstick when she realized she had left the bags on the table by the door, a table that could be easily reached by a large dog.

She sighed as she thought of the mess that she would probably have to clean up.

Well, it's my own fault. I guess I might as well get on with it.

She put away the lipstick and opened the door expecting to find the hallway covered with shredded paper bag. It was clear. She walked down the hall and looked over at the table. Both bags were still sitting exactly where she had placed them. She looked toward the living room and there was the dog sitting, waiting for her, exactly where Alan always sat. His eyes lit up and he smiled at her, straightening as she entered the room.

"Well, thank you for being such a gentleman and waiting for me before eating supper. I see you've made yourself comfortable."

She was about to tell him to get down. She had never let an animal sit on furniture. Her mother had always told her that dogs belonged on the floor and people on the furniture and that idea had always stuck, but her mother wasn't here, and this was a unique situation. She decided to let things be.

She walked over to the table and picked up the bag with the sandwich. She sat down on the other side of the couch, opened the bag, withdrew the sandwich, unwrapped it and set it on the console between them.

The dog looked at her, then at the sandwich, then back at her.

"Go on. Eat your supper."

The dog continued to look at her expectantly.

"What? Do you want to share?"

The dog broke out in one of his smiles and gave a nod.

I must be going crazy. This dog can't talk, and he certainly wouldn't be waiting to share his sandwich with me.

But she said, "Alright, if you insist. I have to get a knife to cut it. I'll be back."

Donna took her time getting the knife. She was positive that when she came back, she would find that the sandwich had vanished, right down the dog's throat, but when she walked in, she was surprised to find it still sitting untouched on the console. She cut off a third of it, retrieved the lettuce and tomato from the bag, put it on her sandwich, and took a bite. It tasted wonderful. It had definitely been too long since she had eaten.

"Mmmm," she said and took another bite. The dog nodded and took a small bite from his part of the sandwich. They ate in companionable silence. Donna marveling at the delicate bites the dog took. She ended up giving him half of her piece. Her stomach must not be used to eating, she felt a little nauseas. It was probably because she was so tired, but she was loathe to go to sleep.

"Well, since it is Christmas Eve, would you like to watch a movie?"

The dog seemed to smile and nod his head.

Donna got up and started looking through the collection of DVDs that she and Alan had collected over the years. Lots of people started streaming instead of buying DVDs, but she and Alan had liked the actual physical copy in their possession. She found one and held it up.

"How about Christmas Vacation?"

The dog's smile seemed to get bigger, and he wiggled a bit in his seat.

"I'll take that as a yes," she said laughing. The sound surprised her. It had been a long time since she had laughed. She became suddenly serious and busied herself with slipping the movie into the player.

As she sat down with him, she said. "I can't watch a movie with you and keep thinking of you as the dog. It may sound funny, but something about you reminds me of my husband. Would you mind if I called you...Alan?"

The dog leaned over and licked her cheek. Donna laughed again, but the sound didn't shake her as badly as last time, and as the movie progressed, laughter became a familiar sound once more.

Sometime during the movie, she fell asleep, dreaming that Alan was petting her hair, but when she awoke it was to find the movie had ended and the dog had its paw on her head.

She shook it off and raised herself up. The sweetness of her dream receded. Alan had not been smoothing down her hair, and he never would again. The pain ripped through her chest once more. She took a deep breath, as deep as she could when her chest felt so constricted by grief and pushed herself up to a standing position.

That turned out to be a mistake. It was obviously too soon after she had awoken. She felt dizzy and reached out her left hand to grab the arm of the couch only to find that she must've been lying on it as she was sleeping. Her arm was all pins and needles and had no strength at all. Alan quickly stepped over the console and leaned against her to steady her.

"Thank you, Alan." The words felt odd falling off her tongue, but strangely right. "Let's go to bed."

She pushed the button on the remote to switch off the T. V. and started down the hall, Alan staying close to her side. She was so tired she could hardly slip into her pajamas and for the first time in forever she didn't brush her teeth before she slipped between the sheets.

Alan was on the floor, lying next to the bed. She lay between the cool sheets as the pain in her chest grew heavier and her arm still wouldn't wake up. She felt enveloped in pain. She was so tired of being alone, she decided to do something she had spent her whole life believing was sacrilege. She patted the bed beside her. "Come on up, Alan."

The dog jumped up on the bed so quickly it was like he was just waiting for her call and snuggled down beside her. Donna felt an almost immediate sense of comfort. With the smell of Alan's shampoo, and the feel of a warm body pressing against her side, she could almost believe it was Alan himself beside her. She felt herself drifting off to a peaceful sleep.

She awoke the next morning in the dimness of predawn. Even though the sun was not quite up, she was wide awake. She felt more awake than she had in what seemed like years. Grief, her constant companion of late, had risen from his perch on her chest and she felt she could breathe easily again. Her arm had its strength back, the pins and needles had vanished. Her body felt clean and fresh and surprisingly painless.

She wanted to lay here just a while longer luxuriating in the feeling, before getting up to make herself a cup of the tea she had bought yesterday at the shop downtown, a little treat for Christmas morning. She smiled to herself. *That dog sure is something. I wonder if it would be wrong not to put up posters to try to find his owners.*

She stretched and turned her head to look over at the dog she had named Alan last night sleeping beside her, but he wasn't there. In fact, where was the bed? Her forehead creased in confusion. She sat up and looked around feeling disoriented. She felt higher up than she should be.

She looked down, and saw the bed below her with the dog curled up against... her! *What in the – Oh no.* Tears filled her eyes as she realized she was dreaming. All this wonderful feeling was going to go away as soon as the sun's rays reached her eyes and she woke up. The funny thing was, it didn't feel like dreaming. It felt more real than anything she had ever known. It was as if life was the dream she was finally waking up from.

A movement from the bed caught her eye. Alan, the dog, was moving. His body wasn't moving exactly, except for the steady up and down movement as he breathed, but there was a sense of movement around him. The movement seemed to gather and rise up. It twisted and rose until a thin, silver cord could be seen. It started from the body of the dog in the bed and ended at a dim blob that slowly formed into ... Alan! It was her Alan! Looking exactly as he had when they'd first married. His auburn curls falling down on his forehead, curls the same color as the dog on the bed below. How had she not noticed that before? His boyish smile that had never dimmed as he aged, spread across his face. His eyes sparkled as he reached for her hand.

She reached for his, and when they touched, she was filled with such love and joy it spilled out like the rays of the sun she had feared would wake her.

"Don't be afraid, Donna" she heard him say without moving his lips, as if she ever could be with him by her side. "I've come to take you home."

She felt herself rising higher. As she did, she felt a slight tugging at her stomach. She turned to look back down at the bed and saw that she too had a silver cord attached from her body below to herself. It was stretched thin, and fear filled her.

What happens if the cord breaks? Does that mean —

"Just let go," Alan's voice said from inside her head.

She turned to look at him and felt herself rising once more. She began to see a brilliant light behind Alan. It seemed brighter than the sun, yet she had no need to shield her eyes from it.

"Come on," Alan said tugging at her hand once more.

She turned and took another look at the bodies snuggling close to each other on the bed and then back at Alan

"They're all waiting for you there. It's a wonderful place. It's home."

Donna looked around the place she had called home for most of her adult life. She felt a wisp of sadness rise up at the thought of never being here again, and then, as quickly as it came, it was gone. Was this place really her home? For months, she had been feeling more and more like a stranger in a strange land. She turned away from the scene below and nodded.

"Yes, let's go home for Christmas."

The light seemed to grow brighter around her as she began to rise once more. Her hand gripped Alan's tighter, as she let out a laugh. She hardly noticed the final tug from the area of her navel, as the cord snapped, and, together, they soared off into the light.

The End

About Cary Harter...

Cary Harter has had an interest in writing since the first grade and has the many illustrated books her mom saved to prove it. When she's not writing or working her full-time job, she likes to sit on the front porch of her northeastOhio home playing guitar with her dog at her feet. Unless, of course, it's winter, which she doesn't want to talk about because if you can't say anything nice you shouldn't say anything at all.

You can find her on Facebook or the website https://www.inkerspen.com/cary-harter.

Stranger than
Christmas in July

by

Cyndi Brec

Christmas in July isn't normal, but neither are secrets, visions, or strange happenings. Someone—or something is causing bizarre things to happen and things to disappear.

The deeper Callie digs for answers, the more she questions her sanity. Is Gramps losing it or is she? Or is something more mysterious happening?

U nder a sweltering Ohio July night, Christmas lights flickered like a warning in the dark. Why the Chamber of Commerce felt they could pull off Christmas in July for one weekend baffled me. However, every year, they succeeded with my precious Nana, their biggest cheerleader. The faint scent of rain clung to the breeze as if trying to fool my senses. The lights strung from the posts along Liberty Street hummed faintly, their colors offbeat and wrong for the season—greens too sharp and reds that carried an omen.

Nothing seemed right—And Christmas in July was as bizarre as Gramps's dark moods. His shifting moods only intensified my frustration. What was wrong with this world? Jings. Nothing made sense. Navigating two worlds without a compass kept me lost, and Gramps's bizarre behavior left me questioning my motives and sanity.

"Do you remember when Nana would bring us down to the square every Saturday we visited in the summer?" I tightened my grip around my hoodie tied to my waist. Even the weather's unpredictability weighed on me. One minute, it was hot, and within ten minutes, the temperature could change.

"Don't remind me, Callie." Ella's forced chuckle sounded brittle. "N-nana never let us sleep in on Saturday mornings. We had to be up, ready to beat all the other customers to the fresh produce."

A distant *Crrooaakk* built in intensity as a flash of purple shifted beneath the streetlights, allowing me to catch fragmented glimpses. A rhythmic whisper hovered in the night.

"I never liked the Farmers Market." I chuckled, scanning the shadows. "It seems like the only day we got to sleep in was our birthday."

"I can't believe you're sixteen."

"You'll always get wrinkles before me." My mind worked in overdrive. I pulled a chocolate bar from my hoodie, peeled the wrapper back, and took a bite. A smooth, creamy blend of sweetness and bitterness filled my mouth. Gramps always said food stabilized one's thoughts.

"I'm two and a half years older." Her lip twitched at the corners. "Anyhow, wrinkles are just the face's way of showing off the memories you've collected."

It broke my heart watching her face dissolve into a pursed pout and hearing her talk about Nana. Ella, my sister, was closest to Nana. They had a connection I never understood. With all my powers, I couldn't fix the past, my sister, or my life. Knowing I was Theran only added more questions to an existing puzzle. My life was a puzzle, missing all the edge pieces. I glanced down the street at the courthouse. Dang it. The courthouse clock tolled 11:30 pm—I hope the church doors weren't locked. I glimpsed Ella, biting her lower lip. I had to keep the conversation going. "Ohh my, do you remember that older dude that hung out here every Saturday and lurked around all the vendors?"

An unsettling *crrooaakkk* sang in the distance like a mournful cry. "What is that noise?"

I shivered, feeling as if the dark had eyes. I untied my hoodie from my waist, put it on, took another bite to sustain my thoughts mentally, and stashed the rest of the chocolate in my pocket. My mind worked in overdrive.

Ella shook her head. "N-no."

"Hmmm …. Maybe that was after …" Mom and Dad were murdered. I swallowed. Don't go there. Get a grip. I swallowed, collected my thoughts, and did a mental one-eighty. "Yeah, the dude dressed as Santa. He swapped his heavy red suit for a vibrant tropical patterned shirt in shades of red, green, and yellow paired with khaki shorts. He wore the ugliest orange flip-flops, but the dang cowboy hat tripped him out. A colorful lei hung around his neck, adding to the festive Christmas-in-July vibe." I glanced overhead at the streetlights. "H-he always seemed out of place but had the nicest smile."

"Who was the guy?"

"Some veteran Gramps befriended. Really cool dude. Sheriff Travis always checked in on him at the Salvation Army."

Ella paused, listening to the chime on the courthouse, but a sudden crash of thunder echoed in the distance. She grabbed my forearm. The pain etched on her features tore a hole through my chest, and the part of me that wished to fix everything yearned to ease her pain. "We've been out for over an hour. Why are you entertaining me with stories? This is the third one tonight. I can't even breathe without you watching my every move. You don't need to babysit me. I'm not gonna leave—I've got nowhere to go."

She released her grip on my forearm. I caught her hand and held it. "I'm not following you—this is all new. New for both of us. I thought you were d-dead."

"I'm not gonna disappear on you, Callie. But I need my space. I need time to separate my feelings and get through the mess my g-guardian, Bio Dad, made. I don't get over things by forcing a smile and making it through the day. I can't."

The storm brought a crisp coolness to the air. I pulled my hoodie over my head as a shiver of dread chilled me.

Her guardian was my worst nightmare. He was why my life was a puzzle of missing pieces—no borders, no boundaries, just scattered fragments I couldn't put together, no matter how hard I tried. The best thing out of the entire mess is Ella was alive—he never killed her. I clenched my fist, knowing I almost died at his orders. What good were my powers of strength and visions if I couldn't keep people safe? OMJings. Was I always gonna be a freak?

Thunder rumbled like the low growl of an approaching beast.

"Is that why you're constantly looking over your shoulder?" she hissed. "You're so tense. And Gramps just adds to the mess with him constantly asking questions. Something is wrong with him."

"What? What did you say about Gramps?" I arched my brow, wiping the sweat. Had she noticed, too?

"Callie, I know it's been a long time since we've seen each other, but I can tell something's wrong. What's going on?"

"Nothing." I shook my head and released her arm. I stepped off the curb. "Let's go."

The glow of headlights cut through the night, painting golden streaks on the asphalt from the previous rainfall. The screech of tires ripped through the air as the car barreled toward us. Another set of headlights streamed from the opposite end of Liberty Street.

My heart slammed against my ribs, every nerve screaming to move, but time seemed to slow. The rush of wind from the car's momentum hit me—its red front bumper was a mere inch from my toes. Without thought, I shoved the car into the oncoming lane, and into the other vehicle, it raced.

One guy crawled out the window. "What do you think you're doin'?"

Another guy leaned halfway out the car window, their voices cutting through the sirens like jagged edges. Shouts of drunken laughter and nonsense echoed in the air.

"You could've killed us."

The energy was wild and chaotic, as if the night dared the world to pay attention.

"What did you do to my car?" The redhead stalked toward us. His curly Einstein added a menacing vibe.

My breath froze, and my legs trembled as reality caught up. I caught Ella by the wrist and yanked her. "Get behind me."

"Me?" Her brow arched.

Redhead's face contorted as his scowl became pinched lips. "How? I should've hit you, but ... my car is ..." He shook his head. "How did you do it?"

Jings! I scanned the streets, keeping him in view. How do I get us out of this?

"Answer me. How did you do that?"

"Look." I pointed to the cameras at the intersection, keeping my face concealed within the hoodie. "I did nothing wrong. But you keep standing here. Your face is gonna be plastered on every Facebook scanner's page across Ohio."

"You." He lunged—

"Callie, be careful." Ella's words died on the wet pavement.

I blocked his hand, did a squat spin, and swept his legs out from under him. The ground came up and smacked him with an *oomph*.

"You can't do that." He gripped the back of his head.

"Get away from her, Peter." A guy yelled from the other car.

The sound of sirens rose and fell like a haunting wave.

"Move. Move. The cops."

"Let's get out of here." Frantic words from another's voice carried on a kaleidoscope of flashing blue and red lights that clashed with the Christmas colors. The cops snaked up the side streets.

"Watch your back. This ain't over, girl." The red-haired boy jumped back into the driver's seat and drove off without looking back.

"Ella, run up the road and hide from the cops."

"But—"

"Just go, Ella. I don't want them to see you."

"Okay—" I hated damaging public property, but I wasn't about to leave evidence that could incriminate me. Crimson light exploded into view, and a solid wall within my shield changed it to orange—at its darkest, right before me. I narrowed my eyes, and the color amplified, glowing like a fireball about the size of a quarter. I narrowed my eyes. The orange light stayed within the shield's wall, always in eyesight and responding to the direction of my stare as I took out all four digital cameras at the intersection.

The camera's plastic melted like butter around the post and dripped onto the traffic lights.

"One problem solved. And my secrets safe." I turned and headed toward Ella and found her in a door alcove.

Ella backed away from me like an abused pup. "You don't think the guys will follow us, do you?"

"I'm not waiting around to find out." I lowered my shield and grabbed Ella's arm.

She flinched. "Where are you taking me?"

"You don't wanna know."

"I don't like it when you talk like that, Callie."

"We've got another few miles to go."

"Why can't we drive there?"

"Because Gramps stalks his phone, watching my every move—those dang tracking apps. And don't think you'll get off easily. I borrowed Trystan's phone and left mine with him. If my plan works out, Gramps will think we met up with Erica in town, and I left my Jeep in the parking lot."

A solitary car drove by its headlights, cutting through the silence, just the quiet hum of the night that felt like something waiting, watching.

Forty-five minutes later, soaked to the bone, we finally reached the church's back door. I slipped down the cellar steps and pulled out a key when pressure built up in my pocket like a squirrel burrowing. "What's that?"

"What?" Ella asked.

"I don't know ... something is—" I pressed my palm against my drenched hoodie and reached into my pocket. Jings. It was at that moment the candy bar wrapper fell from the sky, and a distant *crroooaaakk* invaded the night.

An explosion of panic lurched me forward. I jammed the key into the keyhole and felt the tension from my shoulders once I heard the click of the door unlock. "Why'd it steal my candy bar?" I shook my head. "I'm hearing things."

"What are you mumbling?"

"Nothing. Let's go." I nudged Ella on the shoulder and stared behind her.

"Why are we breaking into the church?"

"We aren't. I borrowed the key from Trystan."

"This place gives me the creeps. What are we doing here?"

"This is the best place to find answers."

We finally entered the underground library, a mausoleum of ancient dusty books. A faint hint of aged paper lingered in the air, mingling with the scent of leather.

"What do you hope to find?" Ella's words slice through my anxiety.

"Shh ..." I flicked the flashlight on Trystan's phone, grabbed my sister's hand, and moved deeper into the Historic Hall. His cell shined a ray on the far wall, illuminating a row of forty or more switches. I flicked them all on. A succession of lights came to life, echoing in space. The lights lit up a wall that stretched into a long hallway, where fifty or more pictures hung from floor to ceiling. Ashworth Library lit up like a Christmas event.

As the lights illuminated the underground library, the shadow in the far-off corner didn't retreat—it moved. An eerie sensation shuddered through my body. Not even July's weather could warm me mentally. I turned off Trystan's flashlight. "Jings. Get a mental grip."

"What'd you say?"

"Nothing, Ella."

We rounded a corner, and Ella gasped.

She pointed at the Greek Coliseum—the underground amphitheater's dimensions expanded to the size of a football field, and several tiered platforms descended into the earth. Wooden benches covered each raised area. Large stone columns stretched to the ceiling and disappeared behind the lower lights.

"This is beautiful. In all my travels, I've never seen anything so cool. Wow." Ella cleared her throat.

"Come on. I want to look at the books."

"Use the flashlight on your phone to see better. Some of these aisles are dark."

"Disturbingly dark?"

We moved through the amphitheater and deeper into the aisles and bookshelves full of books. I scanned the words on the endcaps of the bookshelves.

"It's cold in here. What are you looking for?"

"Creatures." The words fell from my mouth as a stack of books smacked the floor louder than the thunder *probably* cracked outside.

Ella's hands clutched my arm like a vice, pressing so hard I swore she'd leave marks. Her fingers dug in with a trembling urgency. It wasn't just a grip, but a plea, a silent scream for stability.

I faced Ella and placed both my hands on her shoulders. "Relax. No one else is down here." Not a human or Theran, just … *maybe* a creature. I needed to figure out what the creature wanted. Was my mind conjuring up images? Why couldn't I get the image of the feathered wraith-like creature out of my head? Nothing made sense, and I didn't have the guts to tell Gramps or Trystan.

Ella shivered. "Okay, w-we're here. Let's find it and get out."

"Great." I swallowed and looked over my shoulder. Something knew we were looking for it. But I wasn't scared of it.

"This way." She pulled me down a passage where the scent of paper hung heavy. "Creatura is Latin for creature. Maybe you can find your mythical creature here?"

"How'd you know that?"

"The benefits of boarding school—I speak three languages. Now, hurry up. I don't like being here."

I squatted and dug into several old leather books.

"Try this book." Ella placed it on the narrow, rickety table. "Maybe there's something in this big tome."

I scanned through the thick pages, feeling anxious. Picture after picture of hand-drawn fictional-looking creatures filled the pages. The images of creatures chilled me. "Do you think one person drew all these images?"

Ella crowded my personal space. "No."

"That's what I thought, too. Look, Ella. These pages have different thicknesses, and the images are drawn in charcoal."

"And others look like a kindergartener drew it."

"That looks like a woolly mammoth, doesn't it?" I pointed to the illustrations on the page. Some parts of me still believed my mind worked in overdrive.

"Sorta, Callie." Ella leaned over the tome. "But the hair on its back looks like porcupine quills."

"Nothing's making sense." I pressed a palm to my forehead when Ella closed the book on my other hand.

"Ouch!" I jerked my hand from between the pages. "Why'd you do that?"

"Because I'm tired, hungry, and … Callie, I just want to go home."

Jings. I wasn't gonna argue with her. She was also trying to make sense of the missing puzzle pieces around the edges of her life's story.

Over an hour later, I couldn't find a picture of the legendary feathered creature in a sanctuary full of knowledge. In the past, I loved libraries. They were a place to visit and lose myself in stories and research until my heart was content, a simple, peaceful retreat from the chaos of the outside world. Now, they're nothing but a prison of uncertainty—especially Ashworth Library.

***

The door slammed behind me through the house like an angry clap, sending the candy cane ornaments swaying. For a split second, I wondered if the entire season might just come crashing down with the next bang of the kitchen door. "Jings. The wind is horrific out there."

"Sure is, dear. It's July with a little extra attitude." He moved into the kitchen archway.

"Gramps. You aren't still mad, are you?"

"I told you to hang them lights on the left side, not the right. There's some short in that outlet, but you don't listen."

The ornaments swayed over the door, half in sympathy, half in fear of the next-door thump. "I'm sorry, Gramps. I want to put the Christmas lights up like Nana always did. She loved Christmas in July."

"We need to be starten' some new traditions, especially with Ella back home." He gave me a weak smile and shifted on the balls of his feet. "And you need to be clearing up all them boxes. Those ornaments are ending up in weird places."

I reached the sink and rubbed my hands together, sending flour flies up like smoke and coating the granite kitchen counter. Jings. I looked like a ghostly version of myself. All the work at the mill left me in powdery mayhem. "I like the old traditions, Gramps. Plus, with you building that new water wheel, I bet it's nice coming home to a house full of color. At least it's not the same color as brown day in and day out."

Gramps mumbled as bad as a starved man's tummy grumbled. "... Life is a collection of questionable choices, dear."

"Gramps, you've got to get into a better spirit. Ella needs us. I can't believe you don't want to carry on Nana's traditions. It's not like we're putting up a Christmas tree."

"Thank goodness." Gramps opened an envelope. "It's July, dear. No one else's gotta house with Christmas lights. With your Nana gone this," he gestured with his hand over his head, "'Tis the *wrong* season' for glittery lights."

"I'm just trying to distract Ella from her misery. But she's hibernating, and I feel chased out of my own bedroom. She keeps the curtains closed and won't let any light in." Anger rose in my heart. Why'd her Bio Dad do this?

"Ella's life is not normal, girl." Gramps' voice shattered on the last word. "You are tryin' too hard to make things right. You had nothin' to do with her life breaking. This is another season in the life of decisions, some small, some questionable, but all leadin' to the same conclusion—"

"I know. I know—you've gotta have the strength to persevere in life. That starts with finding out who you are." I wiped my hands on the towel. "You either had too much eggnog, or something is bothering you. And since it's the wrong season for eggnog, you've got to be mad about something." My lips rolled in over my teeth.

Gramps fisted the paper in his hand and lowered his eyes to the floor. "Ahh ... you girls are eatin' me out of house and home."

"Gramps, you know that ain't true. Ella's never down here, and I'm always working."

"Food is vanishing. Disappearing. I can't make sense of it."

The silence stretched and my chest tightened.

"Okay, Gramps. I get it. I'm trying too hard to make things right in a bad world. But please, what's wrong with you? Ella commented about it. And you can't be so mad over how I decorated the house. Or your messed up chocolate latte order this morning. What's up?"

"I'm feelin' a little touchy today, dear."

I cocked my head. "Now, I know something is wrong. Touchy isn't a word you use. What's really wrong?"

"Overdue library fines." Gramps forced a chuckle, the smile never sparking his eyes. He placed the wrinkled piece of paper on the secretary. "You got another library, fine. You know, I'm not gonna be paying those fines. You really should get that Kindle All-You-Can-Read Buffett and save your money."

"What?" I blinked. "Dang, Gramps. You are confusing me. And you are avoiding the question."

"Callie, you need that Kindle Binge-a-thon device. Don't look at me with them funny blue eyes. I got me modern ways of understanding things. Anyhow, Max calls it his Kindle Gluttony Pass."

"Yeah, but that's because Max's reading appetite can go totally unchecked and he uses his phone." I leaned over and placed the towel on the island. "And what, have some people tracking every book I read?"

Gramps swiped his finger over the stack of historical books on the table. "Hey, if you're gonna get buried under a mound of books, it might as well be readin' something good instead of off these pictures of monsters." He picked up one of the books from the library in Wooster. "Uhh ... since when are you interested in all these pictures of animals and legends? Looks kinda boring."

"My TBR isn't that bad." I chuckled, knowing Gramps dodged every question to spill his guts. He sucked at avoiding questions. Gramps wore his heart in his eyes. Troubled eyes. Was he bothered by Ella living with us? I did a mental shake. No.

"TBR. Did you hear a word I said, Callie?" Gramps shook his head. "Don't be using that language around me."

"Language?" I crossed the room and grabbed Gramps' hands. TBR means 'to be read.' Gramps, what's going on? You won't keep eye contact with me, and you dodge questions. And only I can do that."

"Since your Nana has passed away ...." He released my hand and raked his fingers through his hair. "I'm losing it ... Nana's accident then ... almost losing you."

I wrapped my arms around Gramps and held him tight as his shoulder shook. My heart hurt for a new reason. I couldn't spill my thoughts about the creature, but I couldn't let Gramps think something was wrong either.

He lowered his arms, stepped back, and wiped a tear that fell into his white beard. "Ever since Ella came home, you are tryin' to be strong and hide" – he gestured at the Christmas lights – "your own emotions and distract yourself. And I know you're grindin' your teeth at night, too."

"Okay, maybe I'm stressed out—we both are."

"Yeah." He scratched his head. "But you ain't the one forgettin' where you done put something. That dang elf keeps movin' from shelf to shelf. And I found it in the refrigerator yesterday. Last night, I found it in Tesla's bed. I know Telsa' ain't sleepin' with a doll. Now, you ain't moving things around on me. Are you?" Moisture softened his eyes.

"No, Gramps. I'm not moving things around, and Ella's never downstairs unless I drag her out of my room. I'm not sure what's going on, but nothing's wrong with you. Neither of us is moving it."

He made eye contact with me. "I ain't so sure."

"Gramps, you're under stress with the waterwheel construction. What's going on with Ella and now me? Maybe it'd help if you talked to Doc?"

"Travis said the same thing—"

"Without a doubt, you are fine." I bit my lip, wanting to say more, but then he'd think I was the one losing it if he knew I'd been looking up information on different creatures last night.

I gave Gramps another big hug and headed into my bedroom. Curtains closed off the outside world, shrouding my bedroom in an oppressive darkness that seemed to swallow sound. Ella draped a blanket over the curtain rod, and the faintest ray of sunlight stretched through a crack in the drape.

A breeze brushed my cheek. I spun around, feeling like every squeak on the floor seemed unnaturally loud, as if the room was alive and watching.

***

I gripped the steering wheel, thumb tapping to the beat of the classical music. How long does it take him? Thick traffic covered the streets. Monday night, and everyone tried to get out of work and home. Wooster bustled with excitement. I glanced at the glass door with its sign 'Friendsville Family Physicians.' I wiped the sweat from my face and continued to pass the time away, listening.

The tempo changed with unpredictability. The pulse of the drums quickened, each beat closing in like hurried footsteps. I tapped the steering wheel. Whenever a smooth measure came in, my heart paused, and then the piano hammered out a sharp, staccato note. The bass, once a reassuring thrum, pounded. Jings. Maybe something was wrong with Gramps? It'd been over an hour and a half since I dropped him off at the doctor's office. What took so long?

Then, the clawing sound of the violin swelled, layering on itself until the tension was unbearable. I pushed the radio button and turned the volume down. Then—silence.

The world stopped for a moment, and I took a calming breath.

Until the sound crashed back, faster, louder, relentless. "Are ya ever gonna let me in?"

I did a mental shake. And glanced at the passenger window.

"Let me in. It's hot out here."

"Oh, my, I'm sorry, Gramps." I swallowed and pressed the button. *Click.*

Gramps slid into the seat. "It's a furnace in here. Why don't you have the air conditioner on?"

"I was listening to music and just forgot."

Gramps cocked his head to the side. "You ain't listen' to music. You've been out here worrying, haven't you?"

I nodded. I wasn't gonna lie. "What'd the doctor say?"

Gramps's lip twitched at the side as he pulled a paper from his t-shirt pocket. "He done say, I have a lot of cortisol."

I arched a brow.

"Cortisol is the stress hormone." He handed me the paper. "Stress affects my brain. Doc says I'm on sensory overload. He says the headaches will go away, and I won't see the visual flashes of color zigzagging if I change a few things."

I opened up the page.

Go to bed at a decent time.

Deep breathing techniques.

Prioritize rest.

Cut out processed foods.

Drink water.

Exercise.

Eliminate caffeine and sugar.

I glanced over at Gramps and smiled. "So, what? We can't celebrate the good news with chocolate lattes and a double shot of espresso and Coccia House?"

"Nope. On our way home, let's grab a salad from The Barn Restaurant and a few things from the auto store in New Cumberlin Falls."

Relief anchored me for a moment until he mentioned The Barn Restaurant. The restaurant was great, but I'd give anything for a Coccia House pizza. "Ahh ... if you are watching what you're eating, don't expect me to miss out on pizza."

"As doc told me, everything in moderation."

I chuckled, pulled into the traffic flow, and headed toward Smithville. Dinner was excellent—the salad at The Barn was out of this world. Not to mention all the soups.

***

The old Auto store squatted between two buildings in the center of town. Its once-bright sign faded to a dull, streaked memory. A neon "OPEN" flickered in the window, buzzing like it was just as tired as the place itself.

Gramps pushed open the door, and the bell chimed with a frenzy. "Hey, Doug. Are you tryin' to compete with Wooster?" Gramps' blue eyes sparkled as he pointed to the

Christmas lights. "Wooster took them down last night. Callie took ours down, too. What's your excuse to havin' them up still?"

"No. Us old timers have enough problems." Doug, the store owner, shifted and unplugged the string of Christmas lights. "I leave my lights up all year round. Never have to worry about putting them up or taking them down. Anyhow, I don't care about competing with Wooster. There's too much going on up there. I heard on the scanner there was a police chase the other night. Did you hear about it?"

"No, I reckon the police caught the buggers."

"I don't think they did. I'm glad I keep my grandson home with me—he's a good boy. Always helping me out here at the store in the summer. Taking in a kid is not easy, but it helps me through the summer when I have no one else to help."

"Yeah, Doug. I like having my Callie around." I could hear the hesitation in Gramps's voice. "Callie and I opened our doors to Ella, an exchange student. She's stayin' with us."

Now, the rumors would fly through New Cumberlin Falls like a train out of control. Doug shared gossip like Steve's uncle. They always stayed ahead of the gossip curve, so people knew who to call for the town's social news.

"That's good of you to open your home."

Gramps placed his hand on my shoulder. "We like having Ella around. You'd like her, Doug."

Doug rested his hip against the counter. "Keep the girls close to home. There's a lot of crazy things happening in Wooster ..."

I let my right shoulder drop, easing myself out of Gramps's grasp, and headed past the rows of dented oil cans and dusty-covered spark plugs. The air held a mix of motor oil, rubber, and time—thick and unshakable.

An orange cat with a big caboose sat near a relic of a cash register. A peg board covered one wall, crowded with wrenches and belts that hadn't moved in years, except when an occasional breeze moved the cobwebs. I moved back near the tires. The floor, once checkered black and white, had faded into a patchwork of stains and scuff marks. Near the back of the store was the coolest pop machine. Glass-bottled pop was always better than pop from a plastic container.

I reached into my back pocket and fished for a couple of quarters as the orange tabby circled my legs. The coin slot was so scratched up it looked like someone tried to pick a fight with it and lost. I pressed the button, and it stuck, requiring me to push against the old machine. It wheezed like a tired old man. The pop dropped and landed with a *thunk* so loud you'd think it was trying to escape.

"Here, beautiful." A husky voice invaded my space as his hand entered my peripheral view. "I'll get that for you." The stranger leaned in and grabbed my pop.

The familiar voice chilled my heart. I glanced sideways, long enough for him to hand me the glass bottle.

"You. It's you," The redheaded boy said. "You're that girl from the other night. You damaged my car."

"You're lucky you aren't dead." I fisted my hand around the glass.

He growled.

I took a deep breath. "I'm surprised the cops don't have you behind bars for leading them on a chase throughout Wooster. You almost hit us—"

"You pushed my car into the other lane. What are you?"

"My granddaughter." Gramps's words stole the air from my lungs.

"So, Peter, you were the one speeding." Doug's voice registered an octave. "Here I am telling Al Croskney how good having my grandson help me is. And what? You're the menace that's kept the town on high alert." Doug crossed his arms over his chest. "Did you also damage the street cameras?"

"No, Papa. I didn't destroy the cameras."

I cleared my throat. "Sir, he's telling the truth. He didn't have time because he was on the run from the cops."

Doug reached through our circle and grabbed Peter by the ear. "Don't think you're getting off easy, boy? You're going to talk to the Chief of Police. Move it." Doug looked over his shoulder at me. "Nothing good happens after midnight."

"I know, sir. But it wasn't midnight." I sweetened my voice to a low, silky ooze. "Ella and I went to church."

It wasn't a lie, and giving Ella's name only added to my alibi.

"Doug, there's no reason to mention this." Gramps pointed at Peter. "Talk to the police and make things right, but there's no needin' for anyone to know around the neighborhood."

"You're a good man, Al. Thanks." Doug dragged Peter toward the back office.

Peter cried like a piglet stuck in a fence. Their voices slowly disappeared into the silence.

Gramps's eyes locked on me—unblinking, unyielding, and a little too intense. His blue eyes glared at me like he tried to read the fine print of my soul. "Stay out of the church, and don't be goin' near the underground library. Do I make myself clear?"

Gramps didn't ask about the street cameras. I don't think he wanted confirmation that I destroyed them to avoid incriminating myself. I was so thankful for my black hoodie.

I crossed my fingers – I would've crossed my toes, too. I nodded.

He paced the floor in utter silence and shook his head. He spun around and made eye contact with me.

I drew back and stared into his eyes.

Gramps broke contact with me, his eyes lowered to my trembling fingers, and then he glanced back at me.

His eyes weren't a natural warm blue, but a deep jean blue like the growing worry before the storm. He licked his lips and shuffled from the auto store with the weight of a sack of cornmeal on either shoulder.

My hand shook as I uncrossed my fingers. My choices could damage us all.

An ancient ancestral library, Ashworth, held the answers to legends, myths, and, more than likely, lies. Jings, I hope it had the answers to the creature that slithered between the shadows.

***

I covered my mouth, yawned, and entered the kitchen. The morning sun spilled through the sliver of open curtains, painting the world in hues of peach and amber and casting shadows throughout the room. I opened the refrigerator and blinked. Double blinked. "What the—"

An elf sat on the shelf of the refrigerator.

I snatched the elf and stepped back. The floor was cool beneath my feet. Shadows stretched and shifted across the floor as if they had a life of their own.

Tesla trotted over to me. "What's in your mouth?"

He dropped the ball at my feet.

I rubbed my eyes and stared at the disfigured ball. Glitter covered his snout. "Dang it. I put all the Christmas stuff away in the attic. How'd you get that?"

Tesla ran into the living room.

"Get back here," I murmured. "Give me a few minutes to wake up. I'll toss the tennis ball for you."

I squeezed the elf's belly. Since Ella and I visited Ashworth Library, she hadn't come out of my room but to eat. She wasn't responsible for messing up my mind. Who could've done this?

I heard the faintest, briefest hiss of air as if Tesla had sucked his breath in through his teeth. I spun and stared into the morning shadows that hugged the walls.

Tesla ran from the living room, passed me, and stopped. I jumped when I heard the *thudding roll* of another Christmas bulb smacking the floor.

Tesla scooped up another bulb, his lips barely brushing it before he let it tumble from his mouth with a wet plop onto the floor. The bulb rolled across the span of the floorboards, swallowed by the deep pool of the corner's shadow.

I swallowed a mouthful of anxiety. "I'm o-over here, Tesla—"

Tesla's tail swayed as he danced in circles.

Two beats of silence stretched tightening my nerves.

Tesla stopped and cocked his head, staring into the abyss, whining. He lowered himself to the floor, stretching his paws outward, when the Christmas bulb returned to him. He caught it in his mouth and wiggled with enthusiasm.

My heart plummeted, and a surprised cry left my lips. "D-did that ball ... bulb just—"

A wraith-like sharp talon stretched from the blackness, shoving at a red bulb. The bulb scraped along the hardwood floor, leaving glitter flecks and hitting my feet.

I blinked over and over, not understanding what happened. Visions haunted me, each carved deep—like a scarred vision I couldn't escape.

I dropped the elf and rubbed my eyes.

"Okay, I did not just see that?" I'm seeing things ... right? I inched away from the island and grasped the countertop, stabilizing myself. "G-get over here, Tesla!"

Nothing's there. Nothing's there. Nothing's there. I recited the words as I inched through the kitchen until I found the light switch and flipped it. The room illuminated, removing all the shadows and leaving over fifteen Christmas bulbs of varying shapes and sizes, some broken like cracked eggs, scattered across the floor. Tesla playfully shuffled from front foot to front foot. He whined in frustration not able to reach the tennis ball sitting within the broken shards of ornaments.

My throat thickened, and pressure built up in my lungs as my breathing became shallow. Was I seeing things? Or did it want to play ... *play ball?* Or with my - mind?

The shadows revealed and concealed, hinting at a presence without form, and sometimes, they held more mystery than the objects they left behind. What was this creature?

The biggest thing, Gramps wasn't losing it ... but this was challenging my sanity.

The End

About Cyndi Brec...

A three-time five-star Readers' Favorite recipient, YA fantasy romance novelist, Cyndi Brec writes her heroine into dangerous webs of deception while she sips French vanilla iced coffee.

She and her husband have traveled across the U.S. and abroad. However, Ohio is her home, where she and her husband raised two great kids and several energetic dogs.

She owned a 200-year-old historic watermill with her husband for over 20 years, which fostered an appreciation of historical knowledge and cultivation of The Therans Series.

Cyndi is currently working on an anthology and co-authoring a historical nonfiction book. She also speaks on Time Management Strategies for Authors to inspire fellow authors to live their dreams.

She is a co-host of the P English Literature podcast interviewing authors and serving book banter.

latest update

www.cyndibrec.com

Sign up for Legends, Myths & Lies Newsletter: https://cyndibrecauthor.wordpress.com/follow-me

Tinsel Touched

by

Linda Morgan

When Sarah Richards returns to her hometown to help with the Christmas Festival, she never expects to collide with Ryker Jameson—the boy she loved and the man she left behind. Old sparks re-ignite, but so do past regrets. As the town's matchmakers weave their holiday magic, Sarah must decide if love is worth the risk.

Can a tinsel-touched Christmas bring them the second chance they never saw coming?

Back to Where the Tinsel Shines

Sarah Richard's cell phone buzzed on her desk. The screen flashed "Mom." Uh-oh. That could only mean one thing—trouble, or travel plans. Maybe both. "Hey, Mom. How's the vacation going?"

"Great, honey, but … we need a favor." Her mother's voice sounded determined.

Yep, that's her mom. Get right to the point.

"You see," her mother continued. "Your father and I hopped a plane to Hawaii. Isn't that crazy? And here's the problem? We won't make it back to organize the Christmas festival."

Hawaii? She loved and adored her parents, but since her dad's retirement, he had embraced the role of world traveler like a penguin discovering it could fly.

Sarah scrunched her nose. If this conversation had a GPS, she'd hit "reroute." "Mom." Sarah sighed. "I thought you guys were on a cruise."

"We were, but things happen, and well, your dad couldn't pass up the pre-Christmas promotion our travel agent offered."

"But, I ... I don't know if I can get away right now. This is our busiest season, and I'm swamped." Sarah looked at her watch. She had a finalization meeting for a Christmas event in ten minutes and a client meeting in two hours for vendor coordination for the Columbus New Year Extravaganza, and she didn't even want to think about the event coming up in Cincinnati.

"I know this is a lot to ask, but the festival means so much to the town. Plus, it won't be the same without a Richards at the helm, and I already let everyone know you'd love to take charge. Plus, you haven't been home for Christmas in years. And everyone always asks about you. Sarah, they'll be so happy to see you."

Sarah closed her eyes and let the vision of Main Street unfurl—glittering lights strung like stars, wreaths twinkling in shop windows, and the majestic Christmas spruce standing tall in Snowberry Hill's town square, draped in festive decorations.

The annual festival had always been Sarah's most favorite event growing up, but that was a lifetime ago ... and a Ryker-Jameson-memory ago.

Since that time, she'd built a new life, one far removed from the small-town charm. Still, she couldn't shake the tug of obligation. Her parents had never asked anything of her, until now. How could she disappoint them? Or the town? And, and the children? She couldn't let the children down. It was Christmas, for goodness' sake.

"Let me see what I can do." She heard herself say. "I'll call you back soon."

She hung up and scanned her overflowing inbox and the stack of event proposals sitting on her desk for her approval. She dropped her head into her hands. The busy city thrummed outside her snowy window, the pulse of her day-to-day life.

She couldn't walk away from her job right now, and she really didn't want to face her past—the very thing she'd spent years avoiding. But her parents needed her. And that changed everything.

After four hours and thirty-two minutes of fine-tuning her agenda, Sarah headed home to her condo, packed her suitcase, and loaded it into her SUV. Her stomach fluttered. She was doing this. It took a gut-check to convince her boss she'd be back in a week at the most and return in time for the events already scheduled on her calendar. Thankfully Breanna, her secretary, happily, if not eagerly, intervened to help fill in for Sarah.

***

As she merged onto the highway, the skyline of Columbus shrank in her rearview mirror. The car phone flashed on the dashboard's screen, and Sarah hit the speaker button on her steering wheel. "Hey, Nic. I'm headed your way and can't wait to see you." Nicole was more than a friend; she was the sister Sarah never had.

"Look at you, our own little Snowberry Hill hero!" Nicole's warm laugh filled the SUV. "I bet the mayor is rolling out the red carpet as we speak."

Sarah snorted. "Hardly. I'm just there to make sure the festival doesn't implode."

"Uh-huh. And I'm sure you'll be in and out before anyone notices you're gone, right? No shared hot chocolate, no cozy fireside chats, no *Ryker* to distract you? You know he's still single."

Sarah rolled her eyes at the same time her stomach fluttered at the mention of his name. "Stop. Ryker has his own life, and I have mine. That road closed ten years ago."

"Mm-hmmm." Nicole giggled. "Just remember, a Snowberry Christmas has a way of bringing the unexpected. Sometimes the best tinsel-touched surprises are the ones we never see coming." Nicole's voice sparkled with a hint of holiday cheer dipped in mischief.

Sarah's grip tightened on the wheel. "I'm serious, Nic. I've got a job to do, and I intend to do it. I haven't seen Ryker in ten years, not even when his sister passed last year. I was out of town and couldn't make it back. I sent him a sympathy card. But still, I feel horrible for him."

"You know, he hasn't been the same. He'll be happy to see you. So, don't avoid him. Got it?"

Sarah could practically see Nicole's eyebrow arch through the phone. "Got it. For the record, I'm not avoiding anything, and I don't need any tinsel-touched surprises—whatever that means. It's just ... oh, for the love of reindeer giggles, sometimes I really despise that you know me so well."

"Hey, don't get all Grinchy with me."

"There is no Grinchiness here. I adore Christmas. You know that, but right now, I don't need surprises—of any kind. I need focus."

"Mm-hmm."

Sarah rolled her eyes. "Bye, Nicole. I'll see you—"

"—when I see you." Nicole finished their age-old goodbye.

Then in unison: "Love ya."

Tinsel-Touched Trouble

Two hours later, Sarah drove through the heart of Snowberry Hill, the town's quaint charm wrapped around her like a familiar hug. Twinkling lights lit up the street, wreaths adorned every lamp post, and sweet Christmas melodies filled the air through the town's outdoor speaker system. Snowberry Hill, if anything, was a replica of a Hallmark Christmas card.

Sarah parked her SUV, stepped out, and simply stood in awe. This. This was Snowberry Hill—family, tradition, togetherness, iconic town square. The age-old town's charm tugged at her heart—its familiarity both a comfort and a cage.

Sarah pulled her coat tighter, flung her wool scarf around her neck, and inhaled the crisp pine-scented breeze.

She watched a team of workers preparing to hoist and erect the symbolic Christmas tree in the town square. Their movements precise and well-practiced, each gripping a rope in their hands to stabilize and guide the tree to an upright position. Snowberry Hill did not use a crane or tractor. Tradition all the way: ropes, pulleys, and calloused hands.

As she hurried forward, she turned and looked at her SUV. *Nah, it'll be okay.* When she stepped into the snow, her scarf slipped off her shoulder and fell, tangling around her leather boots. Sarah stumbled and did a couple of bunny hops to regain some semblance of balance.

But no matter how hard she tried to stay upright, Sarah tumbled backward and rolled. "Ohhhh, for the love of jingle belllllllsss." She landed with a thud, sprawled among the life-sized nativity figures. A shiver ran down her spine as she met the unwavering gazes of Mary and Joseph, their stoic eyes locked with hers.

Scrambling to her knees, she found baby Jesus staring up at her from the comfort of his manger. Just then, a thin strand of tinsel floated down from above, settling beside the infant like a whispered blessing.

Sarah's mind parroted Nicole's words: *"Sometimes the best tinsel-touched surprises are the ones we never see coming."*

As Sarah looked around at the nativity mannequins, she pointed at the tinsel and mumbled, "Not funny God, not at all. That random tinsel means nothing."

Sarah brushed the snow from her hands, took a deep breath, and stood. With a quick nonchalant glance at the workers, she thanked God they were laser-focused on keeping the tree upright, not on her impromptu nativity audition. A few people waved, but no one paid her any attention.

No one, that is, except Ryker ... Ryker Jameson.

Sarah's traitor heart skipped a beat. She'd recognize that face anywhere. He strode toward her with those magnetic blue eyes and a stupid to-die-for grin. Her cheeks so hot a snowflake could've burst into flames. Holy heck, out of all 1182 people who populated Snowberry Hill, it had to be Ryker walking her way.

As he drew closer, his amused expression gave way to concern. "Are you okay?"

Pride's a little bruised, but other than that ... "I'm fine." Sarah bent, readjusted the baby Jesus, gave the infant a discreet double thumbs up, picked up the lone tinsel, and set it free in the breeze.

Then, with all the dignity she could muster, stepped out from under the makeshift stable and walked toward Ryker.

Might as well address the awkwardness and get that out of the way. Her heart thudded against her chest.

"Well, Sarah, you always knew how to make an entrance." Ryker grinned.

Sarah lifted her eyebrows. "Ummm, thank you?" She planted her hands on her hips. "I wanted a closer look at the tree, but my scarf had other plans, and, well... the rest was a free holiday comedy special." She dipped into an exaggerated bow.

"Welcome back." Ryker chuckled, and when she stood, he pulled her in for a quick hug. "You look great."

"Aww, thanks. You're looking good too." She smiled. "Ah-hah, there's my scarf."

She and Ryker bent to pick it up at the same time. Their hands met, and a spark of old chemistry ignited in the frigid air. Sarah jerked her hand away, stood up, and stepped to the side. In her haste, she bumped into a rope worker struggling to hoist and stabilize the majestic tree. The worker lost his balance, and the tree teetered precariously.

"Oh. No!" Sarah reached out to steady the worker but missed him. "I'm so sorry."

By that time, all the tree workers scrambled one way, then another. Their shouts of alarm echoing across the square. The massive evergreen rocked one way, then another, its branches swaying like an unsteady skater at the Snowberry Ice Rink, wobbling before losing control.

Sarah covered her face and peeked through her fingers. The pine toppled, and with a sickening crunch, the majestic top half of the tree crashed down onto the hood of Sarah's SUV. The sound reverberated through the square, a jarring contrast to the "Have a Holly Jolly Christmas" song playing throughout the town.

With mouth agape, hands on her cheeks, she stared at the surreal scene. One car space over, just one, and her SUV wouldn't be hissing and billowing steam from the radiator.

"This cannot be happening."

Ryker put his arm around her shoulder. "Well, it is, and it has." He grinned, picked a piece of tinsel from her scarf, and released it to dance away on the breeze.

"You are soooo enjoying this, aren't you?"

Ryker shook his head. "You bet. Nobody's ever taken out the town's Christmas tree, especially with—what is that, a brand-new Lexus Hybrid?" His eyes sparkled with mischief, and he let out a long, slow whistle.

Okay, she deserved his snark. After all, she'd hurt him big time when she left years ago without a second glance. But, to be fair, he never fought for her to stay. In fact, he watched her drive off.

A quick "bweep" of a siren shattered the moment. The town's one and only police cruiser moseyed onto the scene, its lights flashing.

As the officer stepped out of the car, Ryker shot her a wink and squeezed her hand in a gesture of reassurance.

"I'm thinking you might want to have your insurance card and driver's license handy," he whispered in her ear, before turning and walking to greet the sheriff.

His whisper caused a shiver, and she mentally cursed him to Hades and back.

After a brief exchange with the police officer, a tow truck arrived for her SUV, and Ryker loaded her suitcases into his truck. "I assume you're staying at your parents' place. I'll give you a lift, but first, I think we both could use something to warm us up."

"I'm game," Sarah said with a dramatic sigh. She frowned as the tow-truck driver winched her vehicle onto the trailer. Glad she had her parent's car to use as backup. She glanced over at Ryker. "So, you thinking ... Margie's Sweet Treats?"

"You know it."

The mention of Margie's croissants sent a wave of nostalgia washing over her—afternoons spent huddled over steaming mugs, pastries disappearing between stolen glances and laughter. The memories hit her with a bittersweet ache of missed opportunities and paths left unexplored. Sarah feigned a smile, almost as bright as the early moon peeking through the clouds.

Carved in Time

The bell jingled as Ryker opened the door to Margie's Sweet Treats, and Sarah stepped inside. The rush of warmth and the scent of peppermint and chocolate hit him like a memory-laden punch to the chest. Cozy. Comforting. A place where life slowed down—unless you were his Aunt Margie, who ran on sugar-fueled adrenaline.

"Oh my." Sarah inhaled, scrunching her nose in delight. "The smell ... it's like heaven in my nose right now."

Ryker glanced at Sarah. Man, he'd missed her. Her emerald eyes. Her comments—unrehearsed, unforced. He even missed the way she crinkled her nose.

Before they even made it to the counter, Margie bustled out from behind with arms wide open. She wrapped Sarah in a doughy hug like they were long-lost kin.

"You made it! I'm so glad to see you." Margie beamed, her cheeks as pink as a peppermint swirl. "Knew you wouldn't let the town down. You're such a beautiful soul."

"Aww, Margie, bless your heart." Sarah's grin so big it practically outshone the twinkle lights framing the windows. "And I'm delirious for one of your chocolate-peppermint croissants."

"They're fresh out of the oven, honey." Margie winked. "I'll have Bethany bring you a tray. There's a table over there in that cozy little corner—perfect for catching up." Margie winked at the two.

Ryker raised an eyebrow and glanced at Sarah. Her face froze mid-smile. He narrowed his eyes at his aunt, but she only grinned and bustled away. What is she up to?

Ryker shook his head, ushering Sarah through the chaos of hugs, handshakes, and warm smiles from half the town. Compliments and gratitude for her help with the Christmas Festival flooded the space around her.

"Sheesh, I'd forgotten how fast word travels in a small town." She said as they reached their table.

Sarah looked flushed—not from embarrassment but from something deeper. Like she was missing a piece of home or the basic hometown connection. Maybe she actually missed Snowberry? Ryker took a deep breath and helped Sarah with her coat, hanging it on the empty chair at their table.

She murmured her thanks, but the stiffness in her movements told him she was still mulling over Margie's matchmaking comment. He wasn't about to bring it up, though. Some conversations didn't need kindling.

Bethany arrived with a tray, setting down croissants and steaming drinks. Sarah's hot cocoa came in a festive mug, while his black coffee sat in its usual no-nonsense cup.

She studied the two mugs, her gaze lingering a second too long. Ryker didn't mind. Classic Sarah—always analyzing.

"You know ... this place hasn't changed a bit." She curled her hands around the mug. "And by your cup, neither have you." She laughed.

Ryker shrugged. He should have never suggested coming here. The memory of his sister lingered in every corner. He faked a smile and took a sip of his coffee.

Sarah followed the strings of lights hanging from the ceiling to the twinkling windows. "My goodness, it's like being inside a snow globe."

"It is, isn't it." His chest warmed, despite the memories choking him. He swallowed hard. "My aunt loves Christmas as much as she loves raising half the town on sugar cookies. She's the glue around here."

Sarah nodded and sipped her cocoa, a quiet smile tugging at the corner of her lips. "I've seen your name everywhere, Ryker. The Winter Carnival, the charity auction, the Christmas Festival. You're like Snowberry Hill's unsung hero. It's impressive."

He shook his head, shifting in his seat. "It's nothing, really. Just keeping the spirit alive. Staying busy." His voice wavered. He hated that. Hated that no matter how busy he kept himself or how tightly he wrapped his grief, it always leaked through the cracks. "Since Samantha..."

He couldn't finish. Didn't have to.

Her hand slid across the table and settled over his—warm, steady. "Ryker, I'm so sorry. I've been praying for peace and calm for you and your family."

He nodded, clearing his throat, and sitting up straighter. "It's been a year, Sarah, but it still feels like yesterday. Especially now—with the holidays."

Her touch stayed, solid and sure. Somehow, it helped, and a surge of admiration coursed through his veins for her.

He squeezed her hand. "What about you, Sar? Big-city girl now, right? I hear you're making waves." He took a sip of his coffee, glad for the shift in conversation.

"Not really, but it's going well." She brushed off the praise.

Typical Sarah—humble to a fault, except the day she left for college and never came back.

Sarah closed her eyes and quickly placed her hand in front of her mouth. "Mmmmm, this is so good. Just the right amount of creamy chocolate mixed with peppermint.

Oh. My. Word. It's like the North Pole whipped up a truffle, and I'm the taste tester."

***

As they left the bakery, the cold hit them like a wall. Sarah fumbled with her scarf and almost dropped her cocoa-to-go cup. "Yikes."

"Hold up." Ryker handed her his to-go coffee, stepped closer, and wrapped the scarf around her neck. The scent of peppermint and cocoa mingled with her vanilla-sugar perfume. For a moment, he forgot what he was doing. He blinked and stepped back. "There. Can't have you tumbling in the snow again. We normally hold the gymnastics events at the high school."

She gave him a wise-guy squint. Ryker held back a smile and waited for her to fire back, but she didn't. He took his steaming cup of coffee from her hands.

They walked in silence, snow crunching beneath their boots. The glow of the town's Christmas lights lit the streets like something out of a postcard. He stopped by the old oak tree. It stood just off the sidewalk, its branches heavy with snow.

Sarah smiled. "Hey, I remember this tree."

"I figured you would." He laughed.

Ryker followed Sarah as she ran to the side of the tree. She pointed to the S + R carved into the bark like a fossilized memory.

"Oh, my goodness, we were such rebels." Sarah reached out and traced the lettered grooves with her leather-gloved fingers.

"We used to think our biggest worry was getting caught by old man Henderson, especially when we scarred this oak tree." The corner of Ryker's mouth formed into a half-smile. "What did he call us? Oh yeah, something like: Defiant Rebels, but you let him know we were the Invincible Rebels."

Her laugh was soft, barely a whisper in the cold. Their eyes met, and the past hit him with a sharp, bittersweet jolt straight to the chest. Her gaze held him captive, and the twilight's gentle shadows enhanced the nostalgic irresistible pull of yesteryear.

"How about surviving your sister's relentless teasing?" She smiled, then gasped. "Oh, Ryker, I'm sorry. Sammie just popped into my head. She was such a big part of our life."

The weight of his sister's loss settled over him, sharp as falling icicles. He shook his head and quickly masked his hurt. "It's okay." His jaw tightened against the pull of the past. Keep talking, keep it light. He forced a smile. "Now that I think about it—how many times did she sing the "K-I-S-S-I-N-G" song to us?"

"Too many."

"That's for sure."

They both laughed.

As they started walking, Ryker's heart skipped a beat, and he opened up to Sarah, the girl he used to tell everything to. "You know ... I swerved to avoid a head-on collision, spun out on the ice, and crashed into a tree. Sammie ... was killed instantly."

Sarah's breath caught in her throat. "Oh, Ryker, I'm so sorry. I never knew the full story. No one ever told me."

"We were heading home after a long day of running the toboggan chute and keeping track of the four-wheelers and snowmobiles. The storm hit quick, and she wanted to drive the snowmobile home, but I told her it was too dangerous. So, I drove." Ryker shook his head. "I shoulda let her take the snowmobile, she might still be alive."

"Ryker, we don't know why God allows things to happen. But He always has a plan. I know that can sound lame, but it's the truth."

He nodded. How many times had he heard that? "What I can't get out of my mind is: we argued in the truck about me being an overprotective big brother, and how she wasn't a baby anymore. She wanted to live her own life. In all that is holy, Sarah, she died angry, mad, ticked off at me and the world."

"You were protecting her. Because you loved her. She was your baby sister, and she loved you. That argument? It doesn't define your relationship, and it sure as heck isn't the reason she's gone."

Ryker nodded and kept walking.

"Sammie knew you loved her. Even if she was mad in that moment, love doesn't disappear because of one fight. And if the roles were reversed, would you want her carrying this guilt around for the rest of her life?

Ryker exhaled, tipped his head back for a second, and stared at the stars. "No, not at all." His eyes locked with Sarah's. "If the roles were reversed, I'd tell her she was crazy for blaming herself." He let out a bitter laugh, barely more than a breath. "Wow, I guess that makes me a hypocrite."

"No, just a big brother who loved his little sister more than he loved himself."

Ryker swallowed hard. The air hung heavy with unspoken words, and the night cocooned them like an old secret only they shared. Then Sarah stepped closer.

Before he could process what was happening, Sarah's arms wrapped around him. His whole body locked up, his breath caught somewhere between his chest and throat. He didn't deserve this—not her kindness, not her warmth. But she held on, solid and steady, like she wasn't going anywhere.

His jaw tightened. He should pull away. He should say something—anything. Instead, a shuddering breath slipped out of him, and before he could stop himself, he sank into the hug. His fingers curled into the back of her coat like it was the only thing keeping him upright. Her warmth and caring, her analytical rationalization of all his

135

whys was the quiet understanding he needed. His Sarah ... she was home, and he couldn't be more grateful.

After a moment, he pulled back, rubbing a hand over his face. "Thanks, Sarah, it's really good to have you back home."

"It's good to be home ... I apologize for not being here for the funeral. I was out of town. I knew about the wreck, but had no idea about anything else."

"That's because I never told anyone that we argued. I ... I couldn't."

She looked at him long and hard. "Oh, Ryker. I am so sorry. I'm here if you need to talk, no matter the time. Always. Got it?"

"Got it." His shoulders dropped with a sigh. "We should probably get moving and get you to your parent's house," he muttered, his voice rougher than before. "You still have to unpack."

"Yeah. Plus, there's a snow watch in the forecast, right?"

"We're looking at seven to ten more inches of heavy, wet snow over the next three days."

Candy Cane for Your Thoughts

The next three days flew by. On the fourth morning, Sarah sat in the breakfast nook of her childhood home sipping coffee and crossing off tasks for the festival. The daily meetings with town leaders proved productive—as well as last night's snowfall, which blanketed the town in its heaviest layer yet.

Ryker's attendance at every meeting offered Sarah a sense of comfort and reassurance, a feeling she didn't fully understand but found herself clinging to. His steady presence eased the weight on her shoulders, and she couldn't deny the warmth it stirred in her chest. It was unsettling yet wonderful, leaving her both grounded and slightly adrift in emotions she hadn't allowed herself to acknowledge before.

During those three days, they had talked, planned, and reminisced. She understood the town's vision, the budget, and the festive theme her mother had carefully crafted. The snow loomed as a potential problem, but for now, everything seemed to be falling into place, especially with Ryker by her side.

What she couldn't understand were the photos on her parent's mantle. She wandered into the great room, coffee mug in hand. She paused by the fireplace and gazed at the framed photos. Pictures of her parent's wedding, family Christmases, her graduation photo and baby photo. But right there in the middle of it all, a picture of Sarah and Ryker at their prom, another picture of the two of them ice skating.

Sarah gently traced her fingers over the glass and stopped below Ryker's smiling face. Their young love captured in a single candid moment—Ryker's lanky limbs and Sarah's flashing grin, her braces gleaming under the light. Oh, how she hated those braces. Why on earth were these pictures on the mantle?

"Oh, Mother, what are you doing?" Sarah sighed.

A tear dropped onto the glass. Ryker's eyes glimmered from within, young and full of promise. That's the guy she could talk to about nothing and everything. And, for the first time in a long while, hope flickered through the fogginess of confusion.

She'd hurt him—crushed his spirit years ago. But she never had a choice. When she tried to explain, Ryker wouldn't listen. He couldn't comprehend why carving out her own life mattered, why she'd left for college and never looked back. Her parents demanded fierce independence— always.

With a big breath, Sarah placed the picture back on the mantle, set her mug in the sink, grabbed her briefcase, and headed for the door.

Focus, Sarah, you've got a festival to run.

As far as she could tell, everything was in order. Her list of tasks included more lights on the town tree. Actually, more lights on all the trees in the Winter Wonderland Forest, decorate the skating rink, check in with the band, and meet or call all the vendors. Some needed a map for their parking spaces.

Sarah's cellphone buzzed. "Hello."

"Sarah, it's Lydia Davis." Panic edged her voice.

"Hi, Mrs. Davis. I'm about five minutes from town. Everything okay?"

"No, it's not okay! The storage roof collapsed overnight—took out all our extra lights and decorations. It's a disaster."

"I'm on my way. We will make this work." Sarah bit the inside of her lip as she waited for more panic from the mayor's wife. Nothing but a quick goodbye.

As Sarah drove through town, the overnight snowfall had left a thick, quilt of snow, rooftops sagged under its weight, tree branches glistened like frosted lace. It was the kind of snow perfect for snowball fights, sledding, and snowmobiling—but not for a Christmas festival in two days.

She parked the car and rushed to untangle a strand of lights that hung like they were plotting their own holiday heist. Wet snow and the icy mess stung her fingers.

"Oh, for the love of Saint Nick's beard. This is bad, s-o-o-o bad." She blew on her cold fingers. The crunch of footsteps made Sarah turn.

Ryker approached, wearing a Carhart vest and knit hat. He pulled out a small candy cane from his pocket and slipped it into her coat pocket. "Candy Cane for your thoughts."

"This is not a candy cane moment, Ryker. The Grinch snuck in last night and left his mark."

"Yep, he did a number, but it's nothing. We just need some extra hands to clean up."

"I doubt if a hundred hands could fix this mess. I have one day—" Her hands swept over the whole town while still holding the tangled mess of lights. "—one day to fix this. And then there's Lydia—who hit the tilt button with both hands."

Ryker gently took the strand of lights from her frozen fingers. "Hey, how about using the pronoun *we*. I'm here.

The town is here. I've already called around, and volunteers are on their way to help and salvage what they can from the storage building." He offered a reassuring smile. "We'll get this town, Snowberry ready. So, don't turn into a Snow Scrooge just yet."

Sarah laughed through teary eyes. Only Ryker could lighten her mood during a catastrophe like this. Side by side, they re-strung the garland. They picked up the broken branches, revived all the trees, bushes, and fences with old and new lights, re-staked the lighted deer, brushed off the nativity, and hung new giant bulbs in places that needed some color, all before noon.

Sarah's heart swelled with warmth as the laughter and cheerful chatter floated through the crisp, sunny winter air. The townspeople had restored the small town into a true yuletide winter wonderland. Lights twinkled to the beat of the *Little Drummer Boy* echoing from the loudspeakers. Nearby, volunteers had temporarily patched the collapsed storage roof as best they could, salvaging what remained while bringing fun and hope along with it.

"Now for the moment of truth." Ryker flipped the switch to illuminate the town Christmas tree.

Nothing happened. Zilch. The magnificent fir remained ominously dark, the ornaments barely visible beneath the thick snow.

Sarah's heart sunk in her chest. "Oh no ... the lights must be too wet. Is the plug wet? Someone check the outlet.

Where is the outlet? Oh, for the love of reindeer giggles, this cannot happen."

Ryker squeezed her shoulder. "Don't worry. It's gotta be something simple. Say a prayer with me."

Following the prayer, Ryker joined a few retired electricians who were using electrical test meters.

"Found it," an older man yelled from the other side of the tree.

Sarah watched as he fiddled with a few wires and plugs. A moment later, the colored lights twinkled to life. The fresh layers of snow made the magnificent spruce glow to perfection.

Sarah let out a breath.

Thank you, Lord.

Her phone dinged, and as she checked the text, her smile faded. "Oh no, we're short on construction mix for the yearly gingerbread contest. You know, the floury stuff they use to build the walls?

Ryker gave Sarah an only-in-Snowberry look and pulled his keys from his pocket. "I'll call around and see what I can do. You have time to ride along with me?"

Within minutes, they were cruising down snowy streets headed for Sweet Tooth Bakery in Wooster, which had extra gingerbread construction mix. Who would have known, right? But Sarah didn't complain, she enjoyed the extra time with Ryker.

"I can't thank you enough, Margie." Sarah spoke into her phone. "We are on our way back now. You saved the day. It also gave Ryker and me a chance to catch our breath after this morning's chaos." She looked at Ryker and smiled.

"Well, sweetie, if you need anything else, I'm just another phone call away. Take care and be safe." Margie said.

Sarah put her phone in her coat pocket and looked at Ryker. "Your aunt is the best, Ryker."

He nodded. "No doubt. Amazing thing is she knows everyone from Snowberry Hill to Wooster to Shreve and any other outlying town you can think of." He laughed.

As they turned onto Snowberry Main, Sarah spotted her old elementary school.

"Look, it's Nicole's class!" Sarah pointed to the school's art room.

The floor-to-ceiling windows framed the children seated at the tables. Nicole walked up and down the rows of tables laughing and handing out paintbrushes.

Ryker pulled over and parked. "I'm thinking they need a couple of elves to help." He grinned and the two hurried inside.

"Sarah! Ryker!" Nicole's face lit up like a Christmas lightbulb.

Sarah rushed to Nicole and gave her a hug.

"Snowberry elves at your service." Ryker said.

Sarah looked around the room and sniffed. "Did the kids make salt dough ornaments?"

"They sure did, and you couldn't have come at a better time. Don't mind the mess. It only means the students are having way too much fun. Right, everyone?" The second graders cheered like another snowstorm was on the way.

Nicole introduced Sarah, but Ryker didn't need an introduction—his presence alone sparked excitement. The kids lit up at the sight of him, their eyes gleaming with recognition and affection. Sarah stood in awe. They waved at Ryker and the words zipline, giant swing, and Jameson Adventures chattered from the mouths of every child in the room.

"Alright, little elves. Listen up. Does everyone have their ornaments and is everyone's workplace ready to bring them to life? Each table should have paint and glitter and candy to use. Are we ready?"

A chorus of eager "Yep!" and "Let's go!" filled the room.

"Alright ... annnnd go," Nicole said to the children. She looked from Sarah to Ryker. "Feel free to mix and mingle with the kids. I'm sure help is needed." Nicole giggled.

Sarah and Ryker jumped right in.

Sarah knelt beside shy Millie and helped her glue peppermint stick legs onto her reindeer ornament. They used brown pipe cleaners for the antlers. Across the table, Ryker steadied Jimmy's eager hand as the boy glued red M&Ms onto an already painted green wreath.

As the classroom transformed into colorful, glitter-filled chaos, Sarah glanced up and caught Ryker grinning at her from across the room. He held up a purple snowman that bore a striking resemblance to a purple gorilla. Ryker shrugged and Sarah gave him a thumbs up. A warm flutter of happiness bubbled up in her stomach. She wanted to stay here all day with this remarkable to-die-for guy.

As the school day neared to an end, the kids threaded ribbon through their ornaments. Every ornament became a tiny, messy masterpiece, bursting with love, lots of personality, and enough glitter they could rename Snowberry Hill to Glitterberry Hill. The children's eyes twinkled, and their giggles were contagious enough that Sarah couldn't stop her smiles if she wanted to.

"Oh, Nicole, this was so fun." She hugged Nicole. "Thank you."

"Seriously, I should be thanking you." Nicole said to Sarah and Ryker. She sweetly prompted the children to thank their handy-helper elves for stopping by. The munchkins erupted into a unanimous cheer, jumping and clapping their thanks.

Sarah's heart fluttered, and her eyes brimmed with happy tears. The children's appreciation overwhelmed her like a long-lost memory suddenly remembered.

As they reached Ryker's truck, he opened the door for her. "What is this?" He pulled a couple of strands of silver from her hair.

She blinked up at him. "Is that—?"

"Tinsel? Sure is." He chuckled and held it up with a playful smirk. "Looks like you've been: tinsel-touched."

"Nicoooole," Sarah muttered under her breath and looked at the school.

Nicole stood in full view, waving and smiling. Then she tilted her head and shrugged.

Forever Tangled in Tinsel

After delivering the much-needed gingerbread mix to Snowberry's Fellowship Hall, and having a bite to eat at Dayna's Diner, Sarah found herself seated on a wooded bench at Snowberry Hill's ice-skating rink. The scent of a fresh bonfire and hot cocoa drifted through the crisp evening air. Laughter and conversation from the concession stand and the ice rink rippled through the air like the warm glow of twinkling Christmas lights overhead.

"I can't believe I let you talk me into this, Ryker," Sarah grumbled, glancing up at the bustling rink. Her hands trembled as she laced up her skates, the familiar knot in her stomach tightening with each pull.

"Come on, Sar. I promise I won't let you fall." His blue eyes sparkled in amusement. With his gloved hands, he took hold of Sarah's leather-gloved hands, all the while a playful grin tugged at his lips.

Sarah hesitated, memories of wobbling ankles and bruised pride resurfaced. But the warmth in Ryker's amused gaze made her reach out and take his hand. "You better not, Mr. Hockey Star." A smile betrayed her feigned annoyance. "Good grief, it's been … over ten years since I've skated."

As they stepped onto the ice, Sarah's ankles trembled, and her free hand gripped the railing. Ryker's muscular arm wrapped around her waist and steadied her. "Just relax." He whispered in her ear. "I've got you."

They glided forward, his movements fluid and confident, her legs stiff and unsteady, and her heart pounded as she held onto his hand.

"Remember when we used to sneak out here after school?" Ryker pumped his eyebrows. "Shoulda been doing homework, but we were the invincible rebels, remember?"

"You mean when you used to drag me out here and I'd spend more time on my butt than skating?" Sarah's laugh mingled with the scrape of skates and the distant strains of chatter on the ice.

Ryker's eyes crinkled at the corners. "But you always got back up."

"Yeah, with the grace of a newborn giraffe."

"That's what I always admired about you, Sar."

"What? My doppie giraffe side?"

"No, your determination. You tried so hard to learn hockey. It just wasn't your thing. Although, our stolen kisses were another thing." He looked into her eyes.

Heat spread across Sarah's cheeks. Blushing? For goodness' sake, she was twenty-eight.

As they rounded the corner, Sarah's skate caught on a divot, and she pitched forward. Ryker's arms tightened around her, pulling her close. Their faces were inches apart, their breath mingling in the frosty air. Her heart thundered. Their connection so real the warmth spread through her like sunlight melting away the last traces of winter.

"Careful there, twinkle toes. I don't want to lose you again."

The words hung between them, heavy with unspoken emotions, along with an unspoken insinuation she wasn't sure how to handle. "You never lost me, Ryker. We kinda went our separate ways." Sarah swallowed hard. That wasn't totally true. She went her way and left him standing. "Ryker, I ... I'm—"

Before she could finish, a group of laughing teenagers cut her off—right at the beginning of a ten-year-old confession he desperately needed to hear.

Sarah's mind raced like a Christmas light show— flashing emotions, tangled thoughts, and the occasional short circuit. His hand stayed wrapped around hers, steady, warm, like he had no intention of ever letting go.

Maybe, they could figure things out. Was he ready to forgive her? He seemed like it. And maybe, just maybe, she could finally stop running and take a chance on love again.

But then what? Could she really trade her high-stakes event planning career for small-town familiarity and move back to Snowberry Hill? The thought nearly made her stumble. She couldn't do her job remotely, unless she magically sprouted her own business overnight.

Good grief. She'd come here to run a festival, not rewrite her entire life.

"You're doing great." Ryker slipped in front of her and skated backwards.

My word, he could glide across the ice with the same effortless grace as the hockey pucks he used to fire into the net.

As Ryker turned into her, he wrapped an arm around her waist, and Sarah melted into him. Even through their coats, she felt his warmth, the steady beat of his heart against her cheek. For a moment, the years of hurt and distance faded away. Right now, she was just a girl skating with the boy she loved. Through each frost-kissed moment, the walls crumbled around her heart, her icy defenses melting in the glow of his companionship. Their laughter wove into the festive jingles of Christmas music, and for the first time in a long time, she was where she truly belonged. Right here, with him.

"Sarah, I need to say something."

Sarah's heart skipped a beat at the gravity of his voice. "Oh boy, not sure where this is going, but it sounds serious."

Ryker guided her toward the railing and faced her fully. "It is. I know we've had our differences in the past, and I know there's still a lot we need to work through, but I can't ignore what I'm feeling anymore."

Ryker's gloved hand reached out and brushed a stray lock of hair from her face.

"Sammie's death hit me like a wrecking ball—life isn't just fragile, it's cruel, slipping through your fingers before you even realize you're holding it."

"Ryker, I..." Sarah's pulse quickened at the raw, honest vulnerability in his face.

Before she could continue, Ryker gently pressed a finger against her lips. He'd taken his gloves off and the warmth went straight to her soul.

"Wait, let me finish." His eyes locked on hers. "I know we hurt each other in the past. When you left for college, I said some horrible things, downright mean. Things I should have never said. I should have just walked away, but I didn't. Even as you drove off, not looking back, I never stopped caring about you, Sarah, never ... even after all these years."

Sarah's heart melted at his words, and she instinctively reached for his hand, intertwining her gloved fingers with his. It felt so good, so familiar.

"I never stopped thinking about you either," she said softly. "But college ... building a career ... those things mattered to me. I had scholarships and two extremely demanding, overbearing parents who wanted the best for me. I didn't grow up in a family that owned and built a tri-state business conglomerate—like yours." She looked down. Should she even be saying this?

"I was scared, Ryker. Scared of not being happy here, scared of disappointing my parents, scared of losing scholarships, scared of hurting you." The words came faster like a flood she couldn't stop. "And scared of coming back for visits. So, I didn't. I stayed away. I didn't want to come back and find out we'd lost *this*." She motioned her hand between their chests, her heart racing. "Whatever ... *this* is." She motioned again.

Ryker grinned, his thumb gently caressed the back of her free hand, his touch sending shivers down her spine.

"I know, Sarah. I was scared too and bitter as hell. But since Sammie's death and now that you're here for the festival, I don't want to let fear hold us back anymore. I'm tired of being angry. Most of all, I don't want to lose '*this*,' either." He motioned his hand between their chests, and they both laughed at his mockery. "I don't know about you, but the Snowberry Hill folklore has had me tangled in tinsel since you got here. And whether you admit it or not, you're shining in it too. I think the Big Guy from above is offering us a second chance."

Sarah's eyes shimmered with unshed tears, her heart swelling within the fragile space between hope and fear. Ryker's steady presence grounded her in a way she hadn't realized she needed—or missed. Being near him this past week felt like stepping into that old photograph she'd found on the mantle—comforting, yet edged with uncertainty.

Ryker's free hand cupped her cheek, his thumb gently brushing away a stray tear. "I can't promise that it will be easy, Sarah. But I can promise that I'll never stop fighting for you, for us. I'd like to think we've both matured since our high school days."

Sarah's nagging voice of practicality continued its chatter. "What if we're just setting ourselves up for heartbreak?"

Ryker's eyes softened, his gaze filled with a tenderness that made Sarah's breath catch. "Like I said, it's a risk. Give us until after Christmas. Spend Christmas with me, my family, and yours in this small town that loves you. If it's not what you want, then we'll try an alternative ... a long-distance relationship. Sarah, I love you—always have."

His words stole her breath away. *He loved her.* After everything—time, distance, and uncertainty—he loved her. How could she leave without giving them a real chance? She couldn't. She scanned his face, all she saw was steadfast determination and a willingness to fight for the chance at something real and lasting.

She exhaled, a soft smile of relief playing on her lips. "Ryker, I've never stopped loving you—ever. This is the happiest I've been in a long time. And yes, I'll stay until after Christmas. But I'll have to leave on the twenty-sixth or -seventh."

A radiant smile spread across Ryker's face, his eyes shimmering with a blend of relief and pure joy. Sarah drew closer, their bodies swaying gently to the distant sound of Elvis Presley's *Blue Christmas*. "Please tell me that song isn't a sign of things to come." Sarah plugged her ears.

Ryker laughed and took hold of both her hands and brought them to his chest. "Don't start overthinking this, Sar. This is happening. No running."

Before she could fire back a retort, his breath brushed her cheek—then his lips met hers, soft but sure, sending fireworks straight to her toes. Sarah melted into his embrace, her doubts drifting away like tinsel caught in a warm breeze. She kissed him back with a hunger that proved whatever they had was real.

When the kiss ended, their undeniable chemistry snapped, crackled, and popped. "Wow ... " Sarah breathed as she opened her eyes and watched a twirling strand of tinsel fall onto her shoulder. The other end of the tinsel fluttered and landed onto Ryker's—forming a delicate silver bridge, connecting them as one.

Sarah glanced at Ryker the same moment he looked from the tinsel to her. As their eyes connected, Ryker gave her another quick kiss, put one arm around her and held her hand. He then guided her toward the exit. The tinsel fluttered and swayed behind them, like a shimmering ribbon of Christmas blessings drifting down from above.

As they neared the exit, Sarah's breath hitched. She squeezed Ryker's hand, eyes widening. "Oh my goodness, this cannot be happening."

"Oh, it's happening. And I have a feeling we walked right into it." Ryker let out a soft chuckle.

Standing just beyond the rink, a small crowd of smiling, familiar faces stood waiting: Nicole, Margie, and both sets of parents—all waving with unmistakable glee.

Sarah laughed as she leaned into Ryker. "So, what do we have here? Our own tinsel-touched conspirators?"

Ryker squeezed her hand, his breath warm against her temple. "Pretty sure we've been set up. What do you think?"

Before Sarah could answer, Nicole burst out in triumphant delight, "Sometimes the best tinsel-touched surprises are the ones you never see coming!"

Sarah eyed Ryker and said, "Maybe, just maybe, some surprises were meant to be."

THE END

Author's Note

Sarah and Ryker's journey is far from over. With the Christmas Festival fast approaching, secrets will surface, hearts will be tested, and love will hang in the balance. How far can their tinsel stretch before it breaks? Will this holiday season bring heartbreak—or a love strong enough to last a lifetime? Find out as their full story unfolds during Christmas 2025!

About Linda Morgan...

Linda Morgan lives in Northeast Ohio with her husband. Her debut novel, Prayers Under Fire, releases in September. (Spoiler alert: it's a trilogy, so get ready to meet the Jameson brothers, whose entertaining adventures and swoon-worthy romances bring faith, hope, and love to life on every page.)

Linda's had a poem, Little Boy Lost, published, and she's won first place on two devotionals at FaithWriters.com. She also manages an active blog, Spiritual Sparks, where she shares weekly devotions to uplift, inspire, and add a bit of humor to this journey we call life. Stop by and allow her words to touch your heart. You see, writing isn't just what she does—it's how she lives out the purpose God has placed on her heart.

Fun Facts: Linda's a total word geek with a quirky habit of spelling words backwards—silently, of course. Not loud—that would just be weird. After 15 years as a medical transcriptionist, her fingers race across the keyboard—though some might credit her coffee-fueled Snoopy mug for that. She belongs to the WCNG and GLFW writing groups and loves Beta reading when she has time.

Happy Reading!

https://www.inkerspen.com/linda-morgan
https://www.inkerspen.com/linda-morgan#SpiritualSparks
https://www.facebook.com/lindamorganwriter
https://www.instagram.com/spiritualsparks.llm/
lindamorganwrites@gmail.com

Christmas Village

by

Ruth Reifsnyder

Scott Looney and his wife Terry do all the right things to please God and their rich friends. How did they find out what it means to bond with those who need help?

The small group clustered around the fire as the sun sank behind a row of pine trees. Paul tried to dodge the smoke as he spoke to Fred. "So, what did the mayor have to say?"

"Oh, the usual bit of drivel he uses every year at this time. How it's September and we should be thinking about the cold nights."

"As if we haven't had to think about that before. What's it been three straight years now?"

Everyone nodded. Each deep in their own thoughts.

Fred, the head of the tent city, faced the town fathers anytime there was a dispute between the two groups. At seventy, he was the self-appointed patriarch of the fifty or so homeless that managed to find their way to the wooded camp. Like many of the others, Fred was no stranger to hard work and hard times. He was a veteran of the Vietnam

War and afterward provided for his family as a mechanic in a small neighborhood garage. The kind that doesn't exist any longer. Several years ago, he lost his wife and two children in an auto accident. After that, he had his own bout with cancer. That's when he lost everything.

Sitting next to him was Paul. Usually, he wasn't around in the early evening because he worked full time as a security guard for a local plant. His wife, Gladys, worked in a hospital kitchen. Their combined wages weren't enough to let them live anywhere else. They had a seventeen-year-old daughter, Sierra. She not only went to school but also had a job working at a fast-food chain in the nearby mall.

Mario, a young Mexican in his late twenties, sat on a log across from them and extended his hands to warm them from the chilly fall air. Several other residents appeared intermittently, not only to share the warmth but to hear the latest gossip. Nearby, the women laughed and compared stories as they shared their fire.

As usual, any attempt to have a rational conversation was interrupted by the sound of domestic violence triggered by Oscar's alcoholism from his tent tucked away in the back corner. "You know, sometimes I actually feel sorry for that poor fool," said Paul.

"He's a nice guy when he's not drinking," Mario chimed in.

"I don't know why Charlotte puts up with it," said Fred as he mindlessly poked the flames.

"Where could she go?"

***

Meanwhile, not far away, in a Georgian brick mansion situated in the upscale part of town, lived a wealthy ne'er-do-well, Scott Looney, his wife Terry and their three kids. The two older ones, Jordan, eighteen, and Rachel, sixteen, attended prestigious boarding schools. The youngest, Robin, was eight years old, so she still lived at home and attended the local private school. It was not a good day for Terry.

"What do you mean you bought a mall today?" she demanded of her husband as they sat on their fancy brick patio overlooking their sunken garden. "Haven't you bought enough failing businesses? Can't you ever invest in something that can really make some money?"

"It's good for a tax write off."

"Just like that ski resort you bought. And what about that cattle ranch?"

Her fury didn't faze Scott in the least. "I think I can turn this one around. Especially with the holidays coming up."

She rolled her brown eyes and threw up her hands in defeat.

Scott was a kind, well-meaning man, but sometimes, he just didn't make the best decisions. It was only because of his family's money that he even made it through college. "You know, sometimes I think you're dumb as dirt."

"How about I take you down and show it to you? We can grab something to eat at the food court there."

"Why didn't we do that before? Let me tell the cook there will only be Robin tonight."

The enclosed one-story mall was laid out in a predictable manner with a major chain at each end and several small shops along the sides. The food court was tucked behind a line of popular stores. Terry wasn't impressed one way or the other. Just mad that Scott was dumb enough to buy it. It was hard to tell how much serious shopping was being done or if this was the norm. There were only a scant number of shoppers around. It didn't help when a shabbily dressed young woman stumbled up to her and asked for money to buy a meal for her children.

Terry backed away in disgust. "Certainly not!"

Needless to say, this didn't help Scott's business venture.

"Is it always this dead?" she asked after they purchased food and sat down to eat. Before he could answer or take a bite, Scott's phone rang. It was the principal from Jordan's school. Both parents wondered what he did now. The last time they called, he had thrown a firecracker in the class fish tank, which exploded everywhere. Water and flapping fish were all over the classroom floor among the bits of broken glass.

"I see," said Scott with a frown. "Oh no. No. Of course, I'll be right there as soon as I can. It will take several hours, but I will be there."

"Now what did he do?"

"He didn't do anything. That's the trouble. He's flunking out."

"Well, they did give him fair warning. I guess the only thing left is public school."

"We'll discuss that later," he answered before she could have a meltdown right there. He knew what should be done, but this wasn't the time to spring it on her. "Can you call someone to come get you, or should I take you home?"

"I can call Frannie," she said, meaning the cook. Exasperated, she waved him off.

As she waited, the shabby young woman came around the corner, clutching money in her fist. She strode right up to the pizza place and ordered a meal. Terry was close enough to hear the conversation.

"How are those little ones today?" said the dark haired, young beauty that waited on her. "Is Bella over her cold yet?"

"Just about."

"Good. I'm so proud of how well you're doing."

Terry couldn't believe what she was hearing. How could a shabby looking slob be doing so well? With what? Also, how could a girl with so much going for her even associate with such a low life? The next thing she said shocked Terry even more.

"I pray for you and the girls every night." She smiled as the young woman went over to wait for her order at a nearby table.

Frannie and Robin arrived before Terry finished, so she treated them to an ice cream. "This is a nice mall," said Frannie as they sat down.

"You've been here before?"

"Sure. My sister and I come here a lot."

Terry relayed the story about how a "pathetic, shabby looking woman" tried to beg money off her and then she had the nerve to come in here and buy food.

"They live in the tent city. The girl behind the counter is Sierra. The other girl is trying to get off drugs."

Terry almost choked on her pizza. "That's disgusting. Why would they hire such people?"

"Sierra goes to the beauty school at the vo-tech with my niece. They have regular classes half day and learn hairdressing the other half. My niece says they're both going to use their hairdressing to pay for college. They don't want to finish with a whole lot of debt."

Terry shrugged. "I guess that's admirable. I didn't know homeless kids even went to school."

"I think it's the law they have to let them."

"Where is this tent city?"

"It's in the woods right behind the mall."

Terry was stunned. She sat up in her seat with astonishment.

"As a matter of fact, whoever owns this mall owns the woods."

***

"Where's Jordan?" Terry asked at breakfast the following day.

"Still at the school. I talked them into letting him stay until Christmas break."

"That's a good idea."

Scott breathed a sigh of relief until she went on, "that will give us time to sign him up at wherever he's going to go next."

He took a bite of toast to give himself time to approach the next topic. "Well, I talked to him about that, and he won't be going to school anywhere." He took a deep breath as he waited for the bomb to drop.

"Where does he want to go?"

Scott chose his words and answered very carefully. "It's not where *he wants* to go. It's where *I* think he should go."

"All right, Bright Brain, where do *you* think he should go?"

Scott took a deep breath. "He should get a job. Find out what it's like to put in a hard days' work."

Terry thought for a moment. "Not a bad idea. But where would he find a job like that around here?"

"My brothers' quarry."

"Are you crazy? He can't be trusted with a firecracker, and you want him around dynamite?".

"I already talked to Joe, the supervisor. He won't be using dynamite."

"Well, now I've got news for you. It seems there are some occupants in the woods behind your mall."

He thought she meant the kind with four legs. "There's always animals in any woods. We'll deal with them if anything comes up."

Terry let out a disgusted huff. "No, Stupid, there's a tent city set up right behind the mall."

Then she explained what Frannie told her.

"Maybe I should pay a visit to get acquainted." He wasn't sure how he would handle things, but of course, Terry knew exactly what to do; evict them.

"I'm only looking out for their welfare."

"Of course you are, Dear."

"Nobody should be stuck living in a tent during the winter."

"That's very benevolent of you," he teased.

***

Scott only meant to be at the mall for a brief time but something he saw forced him to hang around. It was raining that day and he heard water dripping as soon as he arrived. He couldn't tell if it was from Shoe Palace or Best

Books. He decided to try the bookstore first. One can always use a new book. While browsing through the mystery section in the back, he noticed a bucket strategically placed to catch the steady drops of water. He located the proprietor to ask him about it. He paid for the book and posed his question. "How long has that been leaking like that?"

"You're the one who bought this mall, aren't you?" His tone was friendly enough, but Scott could tell he was going to give him bad news.

"I can see I'm already well known."

"Well, I hope you're going to do better than that last pair that owned this place. They didn't do any maintenance and we've all been losing a lot of customers because of it."

"I'll see to it that it's taken care of."

"I hope so. I would hate to have to close my store."

Scott turned the conversation to small talk and left to look around some more before going to Tent City. As he walked around, he saw a bucket in the Shoe Palace as well as a few other places. One of the stores even had yellow safety strips in front of it. What did he get himself into this time? Nobody told him about any structural damage. True, the inspector said there were a few repairs but nothing major. When was he going to learn to be more proactive in these deals?

***

He had no idea what to expect as he drove his Lincoln SUV back to Tent City. The areas around the tents in the front seemed clean enough, but as he looked towards the back, he noticed debris spread across the region. A small, rickety shed made of red plywood was located directly in the middle.

Out stepped a tall, stalwart, grizzly-looking man with a graying beard and his hair held in place with a folded sweatband. He noticed the luxurious car with a man dressed in khakis and pricey golf shirt getting out. His immediate reaction was a fear that the police were after someone. Despite his attempt to keep unscrupulous characters out, people on drugs and with arrest warrants manage to find their way in. What stumped him was his inability to recognize who it might be. They didn't look like any of the people he had to contend with in the past. Even when Scott extended his hand, Fred was wary. "Good afternoon," said Scott. He had some of his own reservations as well. "Just thought I'd drop in and introduce myself. Scott Looney."

Fred accepted his handshake. "Fred." He liked that this new trespasser had a firm handshake, but it didn't ease his suspicions. "What can I do for you?"

"I just purchased the mall and learned that these woods are part of that real estate, so I thought I'd come out and see how things are going."

"Things are going fine and we don't need anyone checking up on us."

"Of course. That wasn't my intention."

"And we don't need any charity." Fred narrowed his eyes as he sized up this monied stranger. *What is he after?* "What are you going to do with the mall?"

"I hope to keep it as it is."

That would be your first mistake, thought Fred.

***

Not long after their encounter, it was Thanksgiving. Paul's employer gave everyone a turkey, which he cooked over an open fire and shared with everyone. Gladys did a little shopping on her own. Other people chipped in some food. There was enough for everyone, even if some of it was stolen. As they all fell asleep under piles of blankets that chilly night, no one complained of the cold. At least their stomachs were full.

***

In the brick mansion, it was a different kind of Thanksgiving. The two older Looneys were home from school with their tales to tell. Grandma came in from New York, and Uncle Tim and his wife joined them. Frannie prepared a feast while the men watched football, and the women got caught up on the family news. To Terry's credit, she and her girls helped Frannie with her prep work the night before so she could finish early and have her own holiday.

Of course, Scott was waiting for the next day, which was a major shopping day. He made sure the esplanade was gaily decorated for Christmas. Crews were hired to fix the areas of the roof that leaked, but he was hoping Black Friday would help offset that cost. When the big day arrived, Rachel wanted to go to the mall to start Christmas shopping. Plus, she was hoping that she could find some sweaters at a reasonable price. That gave Scott the perfect excuse to see how things were going down there. Terry decided to go along, so it turned into a family event. Frannie was given an extra day off to spend with her sister.

By the time they got there, everything was in full swing. Christmas was in the air. Shoppers were darting around, obviously pleased with whatever bargains they purchased. The increase in sales restored hope to all the merchants.

Scott decided to sit on a bench while the rest of the family went on their spree. It felt good to relax and take it all in. Terry came and joined him after a bit. When she saw him sitting there, she laughed. He never was much of a shopper. "I thought I'd find you on a bench."

He moved over to make room for her. "I love people watching." They were enjoying some casual conversation when the sound of sirens caught their attention. "That sounds awfully close." He waited awhile then told Terry, "It sounds like they're going to Tent City. You round up the kids. I'm going to see what I can find out."

It didn't take long to see what had happened. Flames were engulfing the area's trees and smoke was filling the sky. Fire trucks from all over whizzed past. As he stood there, Terry and the kids joined him. They watched as inhabitants of the woods were guided out by police and firemen. Scott was watching for a big grizzly of a man named Fred, and Terry was watching for a teenage beauty and a shabby mother with two scruffy girls.

He found Fred helping the firemen and police bring people out of the fire. They took them to a spot near where the Looney family stood. Terry hastily moved away. "Do you think it's a good idea to have these people so close to the stores?"

Scott told her, "I'm not about to interfere with the fire company while they're doing their job." Then he added, "Besides, what can it hurt?"

"It might chase the customers away."

Scott rolled his eyes and walked towards some firemen-but not to tell them where to take any victims of the burgeoning flames.

Jordan decided to chime in, "Mom, have a little compassion."

***

As things slowed down, Steve Carr, the fire chief, approached Fred. "I don't think you and your friends should stay here tonight because there might be some hot spots that could flare up overnight."

It took several hours, and it was almost dark by the time the fire was out. Scott looked around for Fred. He wasn't even sure what he would say when he found him.

Steve noticed Scott and instantly went over to him. "There were four who didn't make it."

"Any idea how it got started?"

Steve shrugged. "Probably somebody was careless with an open campfire."

Fred joined them. Unfortunately, he had the grim task of identifying the deceased so they could be taken away. Most of the damage in the woods was outside of the Tent City area. Luckily, the mall and all other small businesses and homes in the area were spared.

Paul appeared and laid his hands on Fred's shoulders. He looked at Steve, "thank you for everything you and your men did tonight, Chief."

"You should find another place for the night at least." Then he repeated his warning about the hot coals. "If you were sleeping, you'd never know it."

Fred looked him in the eye and said with all the strength he could gather, "where can we go? If we had someplace to go, we wouldn't be here."

Before Scott could stop himself, he stepped forward. "There's an empty spot in the mall that's under repair. Maybe they could use that tonight."

Fred was about to protest but Paul spoke up. "I think that would work. Just for tonight."

"Good enough." Steve stepped back to let people pass. "Show us where it is so everyone can bring whatever sleeping bags they have. If anyone lost theirs in the fire, we'll round some up for them. From somewhere."

About half the tent dwellers accepted Scott's offer. The more Nomadic ones took off to parts unknown. Which probably worked out better for all concerned.

Of course, Terry thought Scott was crazy for what he did so he took her home before she could stir up too much of a fuss.

***

After he helped Fred get everyone settled, Paul wandered over to the storefront security gate and looked out at the walkway. There was just enough light to emit a peaceful glow. He noticed the iron benches among the plants and decorations. Bows, bells, Christmas trees decorated with colorful balls and garlands graced the capacity. Artificial pine wreaths were everywhere. In the center was the infamous seat for Santa to greet the kids. Not far away there was a train that ran on an oval track all day for them to ride. No matter where you looked there was every kind of Christmas symbol on display that you could imagine. Except for one. There was no creche. Every year he would build a small one in the Tent City area, and that was one of the spots that burned.

***

Scott felt pretty good about himself when the Looney family went to church the following Sunday. He got the roof fixed on the mall instead of ignoring it like the past owners. So that should make the store merchants think he's all right. Then to top it off he saved the day by giving those homeless people shelter. God is probably pretty pleased with him by now.

Even if Terry won't stop telling him how dumb he is for letting those rogues use him like that.

"After all, they could have robbed everyone blind.".

He stopped gloating long enough to hear the pastor remind the congregation to get an ornament off the tree in front of the foyer.

"They all have an item for someone in need written on them. Choose one and get something for a family in our town who is less fortunate than you. Bring the wrapped gift in by the Sunday before Christmas."

After the service Terry was among the first to head straight back to that tree and take an ornament. The one she chose said, "Sweater for an eight-year-old girl." As she turned around, she was greeted by Mrs. Oswald, the head of the hospitality committee. "Good morning, Terry. I wanted to remind you of the meeting tomorrow to make plans for the Christmas Eve party."

"Of course I'll be there."

"Oh, and bring your daughter. We're trying to get the young girls involved this year." Translated that meant, *we can't get anyone to help so we have to try every avenue we can.*

As soon as they got home, she looked for Frannie to tell her she would be needed again to make the refreshments for Christmas Eve. Frannie was waiting for Terry so she could ask for some time off. "My mother fell and broke her hip. She needs me to take care of her."

Terry was disappointed but Frannie was always good to the family, so she gave her permission to be with her mother. "Take as much time as you need."

***

At the meeting the next day, she had to explain that Frannie wouldn't be available to help.

"That's such a shame about her mother," said Mrs. Oswald. "Would you be able to fill in?" she added hopefully.

Terry swallowed hard. "Of course I can."

Rachel's jaw dropped as she stared at her mother in surprise and disbelief. As soon as they were in the car she said, "What did you do? You can't cook!"

"I know I can't. Shut up." She started the engine and drove. "I'll figure something out."

When she got home and told the others her predicament Jordan and Robin burst out laughing. Scott said, "you're kidding. I think the people who will have to eat your food are the ones we should pray for."

Terry threw a pillow in his direction as she plopped down on the couch causing him to duck.

"I have some good news."

"What? I could use some."

"There's a guy named Paul who lives in the Tent City, and he wants to put a creche in the mall."

"What's a creche?"

"It's a nativity scene."

"That's a nice idea. I didn't even notice there wasn't one."

Jordan and Rachel went back to school the next day. Terry began her search for someone to take Frannie's place. Several weeks passed, the kids were home again, and she still hadn't found anyone to do the meal.

Robin asked her to take her shopping. "I have to get a gift for the class party."

"Might as well. I need to get a sweater for an eight-year-old girl. Maybe you could help me find one."

Robin got something nice for her classmate and they took their time picking out a sweater for the girl from the poor family. When they finished, Terry suggested they go to the food court for a pizza. That way, she wouldn't have to cook. As they got in line, she recognized the girl serving as the friend of Frannie's niece. When it was their turn in line she was as pleasant as could be. She had a way of making everyone she waited on feel like they were the only ones in the room. "How is Frannie's Mom?" she asked Terry as she handed her change and two slices of pizza.

"I think she's doing fine."

"I hear she's going to PT now."

Terry wasn't only surprised that Sierra knew that but she was suddenly ashamed that she hadn't taken the time to call and find out. As they looked for a table Terry felt a little funny.

"What's the matter, Mom?"

"Nothing. I think."

"I'm glad we got that sweater for that girl. I hope she likes it."

"Yeah, me too." She couldn't stop watching the girl behind the counter. There was a long line of patrons to be waited on. Still, she treated each one with easiness and a big smile.

Robin interrupted her thoughts, "didn't Dad say someone was going to build a nativity scene here?"

"Yes, he did."

"Well, I didn't see one."

"We were probably so busy we missed it. Let's look for it on the way out." There was no creche.

They mentioned it to Scott when they got home.

"You didn't see it because there's not going to be one. Paul had it built and ready to put the figures in and some woman called the mayor to complain that it was a religious symbol, and it might offend somebody."

"Who would do that?"

"Try Mrs. Oswald."

"Why, she's nothing but a hypocrite." The words burned inside of her as soon as she said them. *Sure, it's easy to buy for someone you don't have to see. But it's another to judge someone just because they don't live like you. Or maybe they do. Maybe they have the same dreams as you.*

Those same pangs of guilt stayed with her throughout the next day. Was she really that shallow? No matter what she did the image of that girl stayed with her. As she was putting the final touches of decorating on her front door, Galatians 6:10 crossed her mind. "Therefore, as we have opportunity, let us do good to all people, especially to those who belong to the family of believers." She stopped suddenly with the garland still in her hands. *Wow. Where did that come from?*

Without another thought she called Frannie. *I need to see how her mother is anyway.* She was relieved when Frannie answered. After she found out that her mother was doing well, Terry got to the reason for the call. After she explained her reaction to seeing Sierra yesterday, she said,

"I want to give her some money to help her out. How should I do it?"

There was a pause on the other end of the line. "That might not be such a good idea."

"Why not?"

"You might end up insulting her. Maybe if you did it in such a way that she could keep her pride."

"How do I do that?" Then together they discussed a plan.

Later that day there was another meeting to plan the church Christmas party. Mrs. Oswald asked Terry what she planned for the menu.

Terry read the list off to the group.

"Will you be able to do that all by yourself?"

"I won't be doing any of it. I hired a girl and her mother to do it. Frannie assured me

Gladys is a fantastic cook."

"Terrific. Where are these people from?"

Terry's palms started to sweat as she carefully chose her next words. "Well, actually, they are from the Tent City. I'll pay them what I would have paid Frannie."

Mrs. Oswald was aghast. "I can't believe what you're saying. You want some Gypsies to serve our Christmas dinner? I'm afraid that won't do."

Terry stood up. "Fine." She walked out with her head held high. "And there will be a creche in our mall."

Christmas Eve arrived. The Looney family went to their Christmas Eve service as was their tradition. They sang Carols and prayed. Everyone lit their candles and sang Silent Night as the worship team led. After the service they engaged in small talk and smiled at their fellow Christians as always. Then they left and headed for the food court at the mall. Some of their close friends followed.

When they arrived, they were greeted by a few shop owners and some people from Tent City. Sierra and her mother were clad in black pants and crisp white blouses which were donned with Christmas corsages. They served delicious food from eye appealing trays. Paul was at a table nearby ladling out a frothy pink non-alcoholic fruit punch. When everyone finished eating, they gathered in front of the creche and sang carols, *a cappella,* in four-part harmony.

About Ruth Reifsnyder...

Ruth is an award-winning writer. That is if you want to count the Creative Writing Award that she received at 8th grade graduation.

She was impressed by books before she could even read. One day she discovered the library in the home of her father's boss. There were shelves of books from floor to ceiling on all four walls. To a young three-year-old, it was mesmerizing. She didn't want to touch anything. All she wanted to do was gaze at the sight of so many books. Even though she was scolded for going into there, it impressed her so much that she decided right then that when she grew up, she would have a room just like that in her house.

Later on, she discovered books and with the encouragement of her teachers she made up her mind to be a writer. She knew she wanted to get married, send her husband off to work, her kids off to school and stay home and write.

She took the long route to writing by becoming a nurse first. Then she told her husband she wanted to write. He thought it was such a good idea that he bought her an old manual typewriter at a yard sale for $13.00. Thus began her freelance writing on her kitchen table. The first article she ever submitted was published in a nursing journal. When her daughter started school, she covered township meetings for a weekly newspaper.

Now, when she's not going to the grandchildren's sports or piano recitals she's working on her first novel.

To find out more about Ruth and her writing check her out at

https://www.inkerspen.com/ruth-reifsnyder/

The Light of Cleveland

by

John Newton

A grieving father, a bitter winter, and a people divided over a foreign tradition—Samuel Müeller wants nothing more than to escape his pain. But as Christmas approaches and the first tree in Cleveland is lit, he begins to see light where he once saw only darkness.

A howling wind rattled the windows of Samuel and Clara's small home as the snow piled high against the glass, muffling the sounds of the outside world with a thick, white blanket. Samuel sat beside his daughter's bed, watching the shallow rise and fall of Elsa's chest. Her skin, once rosy with life, had turned pale and cold, despite the warmth of the fire crackling in the hearth.

Clara hovered by the bedside, a damp cloth in her hand. She wiped Elsa's brow. The child's face tightened with worry, far more worry than any four-year-old should have. The sickness had come on so quickly, like a wave that drowned them before they had time to prepare. Elsa's breath rasped, her small body shivering beneath the blankets.

"Samuel," Clara whispered, her voice trembling. "She's getting worse."

Samuel nodded, his throat tight. He had been trying to be strong, trying to keep hope alive, but as the hours passed, that hope dwindled like the fading flames in the hearth.

Elsa stirred, her eyes fluttering open with a glassy, distant stare. Samuel leaned forward, taking her tiny hand in his.

"Papa?" she whispered, her voice barely audible.

"I'm here, Elsa," Samuel said, his voice breaking. "I'm right here."

She tried to smile, but it faltered as another wave of pain washed over her. She gasped, her small frame shaking with the effort of each breath.

Her lips moved, but her words were silent.

A sob rose in Samuel's chest, but he forced it back. "I know, sweetheart. I know."

He glanced at Clara, who had turned away with tears streaming down her face. There was nothing more they could do. The doctor had already told them it was only a matter of time.

As time crawled by, a hush fell over the room. The fire in the hearth dimmed, the wind outside a distant roar. Samuel kept his eyes on Elsa, watching as her breaths became shallower, more labored.

Then, with one final, shuddering breath, Elsa's chest stilled.

The silence that followed was deafening. Samuel froze, his hand still gripping Elsa's. Clara let out a quiet sob, falling to her knees beside the bed. The wind howled with sudden fury. A gust from the window slipped through the cracks, snuffing out all three candles in one breath.

Samuel couldn't breathe. He studied Elsa's peaceful face in the dim light, urging movement, hoping for signs of life. Her eyes remained closed, her lips slightly parted as if she had simply fallen asleep.

But she wasn't sleeping. Their only child was gone.

The weight of it crashed over him like a wave, and Samuel finally let the sobs come, his shoulders shaking with the force of his grief. Elsa, their bright daughter once so full of life, was gone.

***

During the funeral, winter showed no sign of easing out of respect for the dead. At the gravesite where a hole had been chiseled into the frozen ground like a cavity made of shadow, their fingers turned numb, and Samuel barely remembered a word spoken by the pastor. Surrounded by friends, he and Clara remained locked in their shared grief.

Once everyone had spoken their final soft words of condolence, Samuel and Clara walked back to the church. The thought of the return home haunted Samuel—the black funeral wreath hung on their front door, their only mirror covered in black cloth as a sign of respect, and every inch reminding him of Elsa. All that remained was silence. They had no other children, no matter how hard they had tried since Elsa's birth. Clara was a healthy twenty-three-year-old woman with no sign of infertility, and Samuel was only two years older in equal, if not better, health.

"If it's all right with you, I would rather not return home," he said.

Clara answered with a quick nod.

The heavy oak door of Zion Lutheran Church creaked as Samuel and Clara entered, their footsteps echoing off the hardwood floor. A warm, comforting sensation greeted them—the subtle scent of burning tallow candles and the aroma of aged wood—a stark contrast to the biting chill of the December afternoon outside.

Clara gently placed a hand on his arm. "Samuel, perhaps we should go home. The house is empty without her, but it's our home."

Samuel shook his head, his eyes welling with tears. "Not yet. I need to pray ... here."

They took a seat in a pew near the back, where the silence enveloped them. The place where Elsa's casket lay barely an hour before was empty. Samuel slipped off the pew to his knees and bowed his head against his clasped hands as he struggled to find the words for his prayer. But no words came, and all he could do was weep in silence. His body wracked with sobs. He felt Clara's comforting hand stroke his back, her own grief mirrored in silent anguish.

Samuel had given up asking the *why* questions. "Why Elsa? Why wasn't she healed? Why, God, why?" His theological training gave satisfactory answers in universal terms, but at this moment, his heart found little comfort in them.

Clara's voice broke through his thoughts. "Samuel, do you think Elsa would have been better off if we had stayed in Prussia?"

The question hung in the air, heavy with unspoken regrets. He didn't have an answer and didn't want to burden her with more questions that led to nowhere.

In Prussia, he had been a scholar, immersed in the world of history, theology, and literature. His father had urged him to join his older brother in the textile business, but Samuel had chosen the path of academia.

Did he make the right choice? Has his education been wasted in this foreign land? If he had come here as an industrialist, he could have given Elsa a better home, better food, a better doctor. What did academics give him? Nothing but a meager wage collating papers in the dank basement of the Cleveland Herald. A clerk's wage—a mere paper miser, days chained to monotonous tasks, leaving no time to exercise his talents. He sighed. *Forgive me, Lord, for my lack of gratitude. Others have it far worse.*

The church's heavy door creaked.

Samuel peered through heavy eyes. An elderly woman entered, her footsteps slow and deliberate. He couldn't remember her name but thought she was a member of the church's benevolent committee. A faint smile tugged at his lips, remembering her kindness and compassion. She approached Clara, her voice soft but firm.

"Mrs. Müeller," the woman began, "we've organized a meal schedule to support you during this difficult time. We want to ensure you have one less thing to worry about."

Clara stood and took her hands. "Thank you," she whispered, her voice barely audible.

Samuel's initial instinct was to refuse the offer, to insist that they didn't need charity. But considering the exhaustion etched on Clara's face, her hollow eyes, he relented. She needed this support. "Thank you," he said, his voice thick with emotion. "We... we appreciate your kindness."

The woman smiled gently and placed a hand on Clara's shoulder before leaving.

As the door closed behind her, Samuel sat back in the pew. He and Clara sat in the stillness, two souls adrift in a sea of grief, clinging to each other for support, yet starting to see a glimmer of hope.

***

A year later, the Cleveland Herald moved Samuel from the basement to the first floor, from a clerk to a historical correspondent, which sounded better than it paid. Still, the moderate pay increase put them in a better position and might move them into a larger house someday soon. But for what purpose? They couldn't fill it with children, but they would submit to God's will.

After dinner, Samuel sat by the window, intending to finish an article he had been writing, but felt no desire. He stared out at the snow-covered street while Clara washed dishes, singing to herself. She stopped mid-verse and walked over to him, mindlessly drying a ladle until it gleamed like a mirror.

He glanced up.

She was staring at him.

"What?" he asked.

"We should go to the church tonight. They're holding a meeting about the Christmas service, and Pastor Schwan has asked for everyone to attend."

Samuel frowned. "A meeting? In this weather?"

"Yes. It's important. He wants to do something special this year. He's been talking about being the light of the world, or did you not pay attention to Sunday's sermon?"

"Light?" Samuel sighed. "I don't know. I'd rather stay here." The truth was, he found the darkness comforting, but he wasn't going to tell her that.

Clara narrowed her eyes and pursed her lips. "It's not just about us, Samuel. It's about hope."

He returned his gaze to the icy streets.

She waved the ladle at Samuel to emphasize her point. "You're not the only one who knows what day this is. I do, and so does the pastor. Remember Elsa? Yes. Mourn her? Definitely, but then do something in her memory. Something good for someone else. The church has been helping people during the cold—providing warmth, food, and a place to come together. I think we have something to contribute, especially now."

Samuel sighed and rubbed his temples. Clara was right, of course. The church had always been a source of support for the people of Cleveland, especially during the harshest winters. And yet, on the anniversary of Elsa's death, the thought of attending a meeting, of putting up with other people—annoyingly happy people, arrogant people, people bickering about trivial matters—seemed almost unbearable to him.

Still, he couldn't bring himself to refuse Clara. She had been his anchor through all of this. Her quiet strength kept him from sinking entirely into despair during the darkest times. If she said they needed this, if she believed that going to this meeting might provide them with some semblance of comfort, of duty, then he would go.

***

The biting November wind lashed across Samuel Müeller's face as he and Clara walked down Lakeside Avenue. Even bundled in woolen coats, the chill penetrated their bones, a grim reminder of last winter's bitter cold. December 4th, 1850—Samuel would never forget. The loss weighed on them in silence, words unnecessary as their hands remained clasped, fingers numb but hearts forever aching.

Ahead, the soft glow of lantern light spilled out from Zion Lutheran Church, beckoning them into the warmth. Tonight's congregational meeting held the promise of something different—something that might bring a flicker of hope into this bleak season. Pastor Henry Schwan had called the meeting to propose a new tradition. Samuel's curiosity outweighed his sorrow, though barely.

Inside the church, voices buzzed with anticipation. Pastor Schwan, standing at the front, greeted his parishioners with a calm smile, though a tension lingered beneath his eyes. Lavinia Hartwell, the ever-watchful critic, swept her sharp gaze across the room, clearly ready to challenge whatever change was coming.

As Samuel and Clara found their seats, Pastor Schwan stepped to the pulpit. "I thank you all for coming," he began, his voice steady. "Tonight, I bring before you a proposal—a new tradition that I hope will bring light to our dark winter. Recently, I visited a family in Wooster. They had in their home a Christmas tree, lit with candles, a symbol of Christ's light. It reminded me of the trees we had in Bavaria."

Murmurs spread through the congregation, but Samuel felt a glimmer of interest. Was it not a time for something that brought hope? Clara leaned toward him, squeezing his arm, her face softened by the suggestion of warmth.

Pastor Schwan continued. "I believe that bringing a Christmas tree into our church could offer a visual reminder of Christ's birth, the light of the world. In this cold and darkness, we need that light."

"Pastor," a gruff voice broke the silence. It was Mr. Wittenberg, a stout city councilman, leaning heavily on his cane. His gray whiskers framed a face wrinkled from years of labor. "Is it not dangerous to bring a tree into the church? We've all heard tales of candles setting homes aflame. What you propose could be a risk to our sanctuary."

Pastor Schwan swallowed hard, his shoulders stiffening. "I understand your concern, Mr. Wittenberg. But the tree would be small—six feet at most. And we would take every precaution with the candles. It is meant to be a symbol of Christ's light in the world, not a danger."

The room murmured again, this time louder. The tension thickened in the air. Clara shifted beside Samuel, her eyes flicking toward the pastor.

Another voice rose from the back, harsh and skeptical. "Why do we need a tree at all?" Mr. Smithson, a man of few words but strong opinions, glared from beneath his thick brows. "This is not a tradition of this new land. It's German, is it not?"

Pastor Schwan hesitated, his hands gripping the pulpit now. His eyes flickered nervously to the crowd. "Yes, it is

German. But the meaning is universal. It is about bringing the light of Christ into our lives, just as He came into the world to save us. The tree is but a symbol, not a replacement for the Word." The pastor's voice wavered slightly, revealing his growing unease. The room, once filled with murmurs, now seemed ready to boil over with dissent.

Lavinia Hartwell rose to her feet, her tall frame casting a long shadow in the candlelight. She smoothed her dark dress with a gloved hand, her voice sharp and filled with authority. "Pastor, I appreciate your sentiment but let us not forget that such symbols—these trees—are rooted in paganism." Her voice dripped with disdain. "According to pagan tradition, when Nimrod was killed, it is said that his blood fell upon a stump, and that stump grew into an evergreen tree overnight. The tree became a symbol of his resurrection—a pagan idol, glorifying a false god. Are we to allow such idolatry in the house of the Lord?"

The air in the room froze. Caught off guard, Pastor Schwan stumbled over his words. "I ... I am not familiar with that story, Mrs. Hartwell ..."

His faltering words hung in the air, and for a moment, Samuel could see the uncertainty flickering across the pastor's face. He shot a glance in Samuel's direction—pleading. The room was silent, waiting for someone to speak, to refute the accusation.

Clara's hand on Samuel's arm tightened. "You must say something," she whispered.

The weight of the moment pressed down on Samuel. He loved books, not public speaking. He stood slowly, his boots creaking against the wooden floor, the fallen leaves still clinging to his soles. The room turned toward him, the anticipation palpable. Lavinia's eyes narrowed, her lips curling in condescension.

He spoke softly at first, but his words carried the weight of his knowledge and grief. "Ah, Mrs. Hartwell, you've read Alexander Hislop's *The Two Babylons*. But I must tell you, scholars agree his claims are without basis. There's no evidence of this connection between Nimrod and the Christmas tree. In fact, the tradition has a Christian origin, one that we can use to share the Gospel."

"Oh, Samuel, please," she said, her voice cold as the windowpanes. "You are a simple clerk and not well read."

He pressed on. "In the Middle Ages, people performed plays during the feast of Adam and Eve on December 24 as they needed a prop, a tree—what they called a Paradise Tree—to represent Eden. Over time, this tree became associated with the celebration of Christ's birth."

Her eyes narrowed. "And what makes you think you know more than those of us who have studied the origins of these symbols?"

"Well, I'm no longer a clerk with the Herald. I'm a historical correspondent." He caught the slightest lift of her eyebrow—a sign of respect? Then she flicked it away with a click of her tongue and a toss of her hand.

A few chuckles and rumbling murmurs echoed through the room. Samuel's jaw tightened, but before he could speak, Pastor Schwan cleared his throat and stepped around the pulpit to address. "Because of his humility, most people here do not know Mr. Müeller is a scholar of antiquities and has studied at the Humboldt University of Berlin. His knowledge of history is well-regarded, and I, for one, value his insight."

The room fell silent, all eyes on Samuel as he continued, his voice gaining strength. "The tree itself is not pagan. It is both a reminder of the Fall and a symbol of the redemption that came through Christ. We were expelled from paradise because of a rebellion that started with a tree, but the story doesn't end there. Christ came to restore what was lost by being hung on a tree. The tree stands not as an idol, but as a symbol, a presentation of the Gospel." He took his seat and let out a deep breath.

Clara hugged his arm, a small tear in her eye.

Lavinia, still standing, her lips trembled as if struggling for words. The murmurs around the room shifted from doubt to consideration, as Samuel's reply seemed to offer a substance of hope.

When Lavinia finally sat down, she muttered, "This is what we get for having such a young pastor."

Heads turned, but no one spoke, except for Clara who whispered in Samuel's ear, "I think the pastor's thirty-two or three."

Pastor Schwan nodded gratefully at Samuel and turned to address the room once more. "This tree, should we decide to bring it into our church, will not be about any pagan symbol. It will point to Christ's light and the hope He brings." He scanned the room. "Any other comments before we take a vote?"

Silence.

Papers were passed down the aisle with instructions to write a simple "yes" or "no." When the final vote was tallied, the decision was clear—by a narrow margin, the congregation had agreed to go forward with the tree.

When the meeting ended, Samuel and Clara stood to leave. The wind outside was still bitter, the loss of their daughter still present, but there was something new now. As they stepped out into the cold, Samuel found himself holding his head a little higher, the idea of a light in the darkness staying with him.

***

On Christmas Eve, as the congregation gathered in the church for the unveiling, the mood was a mixture of anticipation and uncertainty. The tree stood in the center of the church, its branches adorned with simple decorations and tiny candles. Pastor Schwan stood beside it, a quiet smile on his face as he looked out at the gathered crowd.

Samuel and Clara stood near the back of the church, watching as the candles were lit one by one. Mr. Wittenberg, like a one-man fire brigade, held a pail of water at the ready, in case the tree became a symbol of hades instead of hope. But the flickering candles seemed content to cast a warm, golden glow.

In that quiet moment, Samuel leaned toward Clara and said above a whisper, "I think there's something more to light than a physical phenomenon. The psalmist wrote, 'God is clothed in light.' The Apostle John describes the throne of God as being bathed in light, and that's just the tip of the iceberg."

She studied his face. "Sounds like a good word study." She smiled. "It's good to see you come out of the darkness."

"I wonder if there's far more to light than physical brightness that dispels darkness."

She tilted her head. "Doesn't light represent purity, truth, and transformation?"

"Yes, but…" His words trailed off as he studied the gentle dance of the candle flames.

Clara nodded. "It's a metaphor for the divine presence that reveals what is hidden in the dark corners of our lives."

Samuel raised an eyebrow. "Oh? I stand in the presence of a scholar."

"Don't make me laugh. This is a solemn event."

"With Wittenberg and his bucket?"

She snickered until she snorted, turning heads and raising a few eyebrows.

"But it must be something more. What is the relationship between glory and light?"

"You're the scholar. You tell me. I'm more concerned about Wittenberg's aim. With his tremors, he's more likely to douse Lavinia than the flames."

"I'm serious."

"Very well." She cleared her throat. "The word glory means ... recognition of great deeds done."

"Exactly, but before God's throne, glory goes beyond mere applause, or a ribbon pinned to your jacket. Glory is the very radiance of God's presence—a transformative brilliance beyond comprehension. Light, with its ability to reveal and purify, goes hand in hand with glory. It reminds us that we were created with an inherent, God-given worth, a splendor and dignity—"

A stern voice, sharp as a hawk's cry, echoed behind them, "Sounds like vanity." The voice sent shivers down their spines.

Lavinia Hartwell stepped out of the shadows, apparently having escaped Mr. Wittenberg's splash zone.

"Oh, Mrs. Hartwell, I didn't hear you," Clara said.

Lavinia answered in a whisper, "And yet everyone has heard you making a racket back here. And another thing.

This so-called glory you speak of is nothing more than vanity or pride."

"No, it's our intrinsic worth. We long for glory because we want to be with God, a position we were made for."

She straightened her dress. "Nevertheless, I have not come to argue, Mr. Meuller, but to apologize. It seems I was premature in my assessment of you. This tree thing", she waved toward the middle of the sanctuary, "appears to have some merit."

Clara and Samuel exchanged glances.

"Uh," Samuel stuttered. "If ... well, if you're interested in ancient history and cultures, I brought some books from Prussia you might be interested in. Scholarly books."

The hint of a smile crossed her lips and eyes. "That would be fascinating." She pivoted, and with a clack of her shoes, headed for the aisle to the front.

Clara shook her head and caught Samuel's eye. "Well, that was—"

"Unexpected," he finished for her.

As the final candle was lit, a gentle murmur of awe passed through the congregation—each face lit by the soft glow of candlelight. Samuel closed his eyes and whispered a prayer—not only for his and Clara's healing, but for every other soul locked in darkness.

***

In the years that followed, the Christmas tree became an annual tradition for Cleveland's Lutheran congregation. Each winter, as the cold descended on the city, the church would light the candles, reminding the community of the hope that had carried them through that dark winter of 1851.

Samuel and Clara continued their quiet life, and three years later, shared Christmas with their newborn son in the flickering light of another Christmas tree.

Author's Note

This may not have been the first publicly displayed Christmas tree in America, but you can find a plaque at 1254 West Mall Drive in Cleveland, Ohio posted by The Cleveland Landmarks Commission as an historic marker. It reads:

The First Christmas Tree in America
Publicly lighted and displayed in a church Christmas service,
stood where the Cleveland Public Auditorium now stands, a designated Cleveland landmark.

On that site once stood the original Zion Lutheran Church where on Christmas Eve, 1851, its pastor, Henry Schwan (1819-1905) introduced that first historic Christmas tree, a tradition he brought from Germany, which spread from that site throughout America.

The present location of Zion Lutheran Church is 2062 East 30th Street

---

About John Newton...

John Newton is a science fiction and historical fiction author who asks the big question—what if? John attended twelve different schools, finally graduating from a high school in Cyprus where the Cypriots soon realized it was in their national interest to ship him back to the United States as fast as possible. He is currently working as an electrical engineer, robotics programmer, landlord, part-time farmer, father of seven, and married the wife of his dreams. Sometimes he even writes a thing or two.

Website: https://newtonscifi.com/
YouTube: https://www.youtube.com/@NewtonSciFi

Christmas Giving

by
Max Willi Fischer

Private Will Saunders just caught the Golden Triangle flyer out of Pittsburgh on a cold, December's night in 1946. He can't wait to ride the rails in order to make it home to his western Ohio farm in time for the Christmas holiday.

He encounters two worldly strangers—an army corporal and an elderly Belgian woman—who teach him a valuable lesson, which he doesn't immediately comprehend.

Through a tragic accident and inexplicable occurrences, Will learns that the simplest of gifts are often the best.

Late in the evening of December 12, 1946, the 'Golden Triangle' passenger train sped through north central Ohio towards Chicago.

His khaki side cap askew atop his blond buzz cut, the private surveyed the crowded railcar, hoping to find a vacant seat. Half-way down the aisle, his spirits rose as he saw an empty bench seat near the front of the car.

"Excuse me, but is this seat available?" the young soldier asked the two occupants of the other seat.

"Reserved for you, private, if you care to make use of it." A uniformed corporal offered a wry smile.

A wide grin commanded the peach fuzz passing as stubble on the private's face to attention. "Thank you, corporal, I will. I've spent almost half of Ohio stuck sitting on a box in the baggage car. I got to the station in Pittsburgh late and felt lucky just to make the train."

"Well, we've been waiting for you." The corporal chuckled as he reached out and shook the young soldier's hand with his right hand while his left arm lay limp at his waist. "I'm Matt Bentley, and this lovely lady is Madame Simone Cherneau, who comes to us all the way from Belgium."

"Hello, ma'am. It's a pleasure to meet you both. I'm Will... Will Saunders."

"I met Simone in Belgium during the war, and wouldn't you know it," Matt's brown eyes lit up, "she and I run into each other at the terminal right next to the *Golden Triangle* flyer."

"Whoa... What are the odds of that?" Will's eyes popped, and he extended two opened hands.

"Good evening, *Monsieur* Saunders." The elderly woman's wrinkled hand swept some strands of silvery hair out of her bluish-gray eyes from beneath a dark gray bucket hat. Rumpled facial lines straightened as she began to speak. "Please call me Simone. Where might you be headed in ze dark of night on zis speeding train?" an obvious French accent coated her words.

"Convoy, Ohio... near the Indiana state line. Back to see my folks and family before we ship out to Japan. I get off at Fort Wayne, this train's only stop till Chicago."

"You guys in the Eighth Army headed to Hiroshima or Nagasaki?" Corporal Bentley, elbow on an armrest, supported his head with a thumb and forefinger under his chin.

Will heaved his shoulders. "Don't know. Nobody knows until we report to our units in Illinois in a little over twelve days, right after Christmas."

"The bomb was brutal on those two cities." Bentley's eyes wandered toward the window where some city lights illuminated the night. "Welcome to Canton, Ohio folks."

"Well, I'll worry about wherever I'm headed on December 26. Until then, it's Mom's cooking, meeting old friends at Shaney's Tavern, and perhaps a bit of pheasant hunting for Christmas dinner."

"For those caught in it, ze war waz brutal to all, no matter where it zunk its teeth in you." Madame Cherneau looked down the aisle for a moment before turning toward her travel companion. "Surely, Matthew, you know what we experienced in and around Bastogne."

The name *Bastogne* raised Saunders' senses. For the first time in the ten minutes since he found a cherished seat, he noticed Bentley's shoulder patch above his hobbled arm. Unlike most everyone of the hundred and fifty soldiers straight out of basic training on the *Golden Triangle*, the corporal's patch didn't have the octagonal red sections of the Eighth Army. His was a red "A" inside a white, six-pointed star, highlighted with a red perimeter. A bald eagle's head rested above it. Will leaned in towards Bentley. "You're Seventh Army, not Eighth." His spine reverting to attention, the private laid back against his seat, and whispered, "You guys were in the Bulge."

"Yah. 101 Airborne"

"General McAuliffe's outfit?"

Bentley nodded and then looked at Simone Cherneau.

"Yes, Monsieur Saunders—"

"Please call me Will."

"*Oui*, Will." Simone pursed her natural pinkish lips. "I have known Matthew for ze past two years, ever since he parachuted into a field on ze outskirts of Bastogne."

Cherneau looked at Bentley with the softness of a mother's admiration upon her son as she placed her aged hand on his.

The corporal smiled at her and then addressed the young soldier. "My chute got hung up in a tree a couple days before Christmas, and there were Kraut patrols all over the place. Just as I cut the last cord and dropped ten feet to the ground, what looks like a man and woman show up." Bentley nods toward Simone. "One is young and beautiful, the other is Simone, dressed in men's clothing! The young one insists she's going to get the chute, and the two of them are arguing in French."

Will cocked his head and shot a confused look at Simone.

"Renee waz a nurse at ze military aid station in Bastogne." Simone's hands wagged back and forth. "She coveted ze silk from white parachutes as ze perfect dressing for ze wounded."

Bentley continued. "Renee was able to grab the lowest corner of the chute and cut a section off. Then the Germans spotted us and start firing, hitting me in the back of my shoulder. Felt like I got knocked down with a sledgehammer. I don't know how the two of them got me back into town and to that aid station."

"That must have been some Christmas to remember." Will bent forward again.

"Christmas iz a time to celebrate ... even in ze darkest of days. In toze circumstances, just being alive iz worthy of some celebration." Simone's eyes darted around without looking at anyone.

"I sup-pose so," Will said in a halted tone, his hands gripping his slacks at the thighs as he looked out the window into the anonymous darkness. "When I think of Christmas, I think of a big, freshly cut spruce, taking up half of our living room in our farmhouse... my mom ruling the kitchen, roasting a turkey with all the fixin's, including apple pie . . . sitting with my dog, Blue, in front of the wood burning stove, best hunting dog in Van Wert County... a big pile of presents, neatly arranged under the tree." By now, Will's hands had escaped the security of his clothing and danced on their own. "Most importantly, our whole

213

family—my parents, my two younger brothers, and me—all there yakking up a storm around the table or tree, doesn't matter. We always have something to say to each other." Saunders reached inside his khaki jacket and pulled out a well-worn photo. "Blue's my good luck charm. Can't wait to take him out on a hunt." He reached the creased image of him kneeling next to a lop-eared, mottled-colored hound over to the corporal.

A crossing bell dinged briefly, interrupting the incessant clatter of the rails.

"Sometimes," Bentley became misty-eyed looking at Will's photo before passing it back, "sometimes real family is far away, and you celebrate with those around you. Lord knows we had all the cognac and champagne we could want."

Once again, Will turned to Simone with his eyebrows raised.

"*Oui*, it iz so. Most every Belgian household stores cognac and champagne in their cellars, and it waz used in many ways in ze makeshift hospital for ze injured. Ze doctors used it to sterilize instruments, nurses cleaned wounds with ze cognac, and—"

"And injured men drown their pain with it... Right, Simone?" Bentley let out a half-hearted laugh and gently patted her hand.

"So, what happened after you got to the hospital?" Oblivious to the constant rattling of the tracks and buzz of conversation throughout the railcar, Will had been drawn into another world, two years in the past.

"First, do not think of it as you would a normal hospital." Simone shook her index finger while she crossed her legs, exposing the hemline of a lavender dress with a floral pattern. "It waz a large house in Bastogne with three floors... three stories... that ze doctor in charge, Doctor Prior, believed best suited to house ze many injured. It had already been divided into apartments, so we had ward rooms of a sort."

"Well, I slipped into a coma right after Doc Prior took that bullet out of my shoulder blade. Before I passed out, I remember a Black nurse helping him, looking down on me. She had the scent of lilacs and the touch of an angel."

"A darkie?"

"Watch your mouth, boy!" The close-cropped dark hair at the side of the corporal's head sprung to attention as the shadow of his stubble became more visible.

"*Fermez la!*"

In unison, albeit two languages, Bentley and Cherneau pinned Will's tongue to the red plaid fabric of the back rest of his seat.

"Do not let your ignorance of ze canvass of life allow you to paint each person with ze same brush based upon ze color of their skin or their belief about God." For the first time, the elderly woman's voice hardened before calming down to a grandmother's whisper. "If you judge each person you come across without making ze effort to know them, your life will become a hollow shell, void of the richness of ze experiences of others. You will become as shallow as a dried-up pond."

Will felt as if his mother had just washed out his mouth with soap for swearing.

"Listen, Saunders, your attitude toward Miss Augusta, the Black nurse, showed up among a couple of the guys sharing my second-floor room." Bentley took out a smoke from a pack, offering it around without any takers, before lighting it. "There were quite a few of us in there. It must have been a living room at one time. Anyway, I thought I was dreaming when this tender face the color of a Parisienne cappuccino watched over me as she gave me one of the few remaining doses of ether right before the doc was going to operate. She came around after I woke up and wiped my forehead with a damp cloth. For whatever reason, I held up my hand... at least I tried to lift it. She cupped her gentle fingers around it and whispered words in French. I didn't know the language, but I'm certain she was telling me I was going to make it." The corporal took a long drag on his Lucky Strike and vented a stream of bluish smoke from his nose. "A day or two after I came to, I saw two different GIs making a fuss about having Miss Augusta tend to them, calling her all sorts of names, before Prior operated. Doc flat out told them both, *She treats you, or you die*. That shut both of them up."

"She wazn't ze only angel in zhat building. Remember Renee?" Again, Simone's eyes seemingly stared into nothingness.

Matt smiled, creating waves in his face's late day shadow. "Oh yeah. How could I forget her?" He took a final puff from his cigarette before smashing the butt into the attached ashtray under the window. "Striking brunette... too bad she was married."

Simone shot him a nun's side-eye, and he jokingly nudged her with his elbow. "Just kidding, Simone. She, too, had that gentle touch. When she changed my shoulder's bandages, her fingers were like feathers... I felt no pain. Guys could be screaming out in agony, and it seemed like the touch of her hand made everything better. Survival became bearable."

"Both of those young women were only there because of Christmas was ze time to see family." Weary of the long train ride, Simone's head tipped to one side. "On second thought, I will take that cigarette, Matt."

"They didn't live in Bastogne?" Will edged closer.

"They had grown up there but had moved to larger cities to practice nursing." Simone leaned closer to Bentley, allowing him to light her tobacco. "At least one gave everything for total strangers that Christmas." Her words came out between clenched lips and venting smoke.

Will's mouth had just opened when Matt cut off his intended question. "On the night of Christmas Eve,

German bombers hit that aid house and blew it to smithereens. It was a lottery on who got out alive. Some did, some didn't. Miss Renee didn't make it. Doc Prior wrapped her body in one of her precious parachutes and personally carried her to her parents."

"Matt," Simone looked at the corporal and shook her head, "do you know anything about Miss Augusta?"

"I think she made it, but I'm not sure."

"In any case, at Christmas, just as life in general, ze giving iz much more important than ze getting." Simone, cigarette in one hand, raised the other to her neck and clutched a necklace. "I sense all three of us have something of deep personal value we will offer to one of our loved ones zis Christmas." She looked down at a locket pinched between her thumb and forefinger. "Zis," she said, opening it, "is my husband, Pierre, and I on our wedding day... 1906."

Will sensed tears forming at the corner of Simone's eyes and maintained a respectful silence.

"Pierre died early in ze war helping ze resistance against ze *Bosch*. Our son, Albert, was rounded up by ze *Bosch* a year or two later, and I haven't seen him since. Perhaps we should have followed Claire's advice a decade ago. Our daughter warned us of Hitler's intentions and urged us to follow her and her American lover to Chicago."

After a final drag on the cigarette, she surrendered it to Bentley. "Please, Matt, I'm done with zis." While Matt placed it in the ashtray, she reached behind her neck, in front of her coat's collar and unfastened the chain's clasp. "I'm releasing this to Claire when I arrive at her home."

"I wasn't around as long as you, Simone, but I, too, have something of personal value my folks in Omaha will treasure." He reached into his uniform jacket's pocket and pulled out his dog tags. "With these I'll never be missing in their lives."

"*Oui*, my friend, every loved one needs closure."

"What might you have, Will?" Bentley asked.

The private felt his jaw twitch to one side. Searching for words he knew weren't there, he lets his hands slide down his jacket, fingers poking in pockets.

"Oh, come now, Will," Bentley whined in a sarcastic way. "You just showed it to us a couple miles back."

Saunders reached inside his jacket and drew out the crinkled photo. "This?"

Simone and Matt nodded.

"But this is just something important to me. I'd be insulting my folks if I wrapped this up as a present and placed it under the tree."

"They would cherish it forever, Will," Simone said.

"I just don't understand what the two of you have been talking about." Will felt pressure in his facial muscles and blood pumping in his temples. "Christmas giving... yeah, I get your locket for your daughter, Simone, but your dog tags, Matt? What kind of gift is that? This old, dog-eared photo? Geez. I don't get—"

In the chaos of smashing metal, squealing wheels, and cries of distress, the rail car crashed and began a twisting roll. The impact launched Will forward, plastering his face into the seat Matt and Simone had been occupying. He remained conscious just long enough to sense the pull of gravity as the car tumbled, dropping him on its ceiling which exchanged places with the floor.

Monday, December 23 Convoy, Ohio

Like some Currier and Ives' print, snow began to fall on the eve of Christmas Eve, covering the dormant fields of the Saunder's farm with a thin white blanket. Will stood at the kitchen window, propped up with crutches, looking out at the peaceful countryside. After a little more than a week in a Mansfield hospital, he'd returned home to a greatly relieved family.

His hand fidgeted with a small box inside the enlarged pocket of his bathrobe as he inhaled the intoxicating aroma of the sugar cookies his mother was baking. Nothing said *home* like that scent and the sight of her scurrying about the kitchen rolling dough one minute, cutting out Christmas tree and Santa-shaped cookies the next, only to dart to the oven just in time to remove a batch of the perfectly baked treats. He called it her *kitchen dance,* and he hated to interrupt it, but there was something he had to do, preferably when the two of them were alone. His father and two brothers had done some last-minute shopping in Van Wert earlier in the day, so they were occupied with chores in the barn with the livestock.

With the last of the dough having been rolled out and the final tray removed from the oven, his mother offered Will an uniced sample, which he gladly accepted. He bit into the crunchy, yet soft, goodness of the cookie to take the edge off what he was about to say. "Mom, can I tell you something... something strange."

She answered as she looked into one cupboard or drawer after another, gathering ingredients for the icing. "After the past ten days of worrying about you... first whether you were dead or alive, then not knowing exactly how badly you were hurt... I think I'd love to hear about something strange, just as long as it came from *your* voice."

He tired from standing with his broken leg in a cumbersome cast. "Could you pull me a chair to support my leg?" He hobbled to the far corner of the kitchen out of his mother's traffic lanes.

"Surely, son." Even though she hadn't looked at him in the past few minutes, she stopped her search and immediately brought him another wooden, kitchen chair.

After having stood for twenty minutes, relief on both legs became instantaneous. "Remember, yesterday when I told you guys about how someone pulled the wreckage off my pinned leg and got an ambulance crew over to me?"

Mabel Saunders nodded after sitting down at the table to mix milk, sugar, vanilla extract, and green food coloring. "Yes, I remember. You said you'd been talking to him and some elderly woman on the train."

"Yeah, he saved my life, Mom. What I didn't tell you was that they had both been in the Battle of the Bulge. They talked about the horrific Christmas of '44 in some military aid station in Bastogne."

Mabel stopped her stirring and stared at Will seated across from her. "I'd say that man... and woman were heroes. Did you catch their names?"

"Corporal Matt Bentley and Simone Cherneau." Will looked down at his hands, which he kept rubbing together, while his mother refocused on what was happening in her mixing bowl. "Right before the crash, we were talking about Christmas and how giving... that is, giving something of great personal value, is the important part of the season." He started to pull out the small, wrapped box from his bathrobe. It wasn't heavy, but its weight was well-balanced, so nothing shifted from side to side within it.

Without looking up, his mother chewed on her lips for a moment. "I think they were probably right."

Will put the present on the table as his mother's head turned ever so slightly, catching a glimpse of it. "I hope you don't think this is stupid, but I've always cherished it, and ... and I'd love for you to have it." After rushing through his last eight words, he pushed the gift across the table toward her and exhaled.

Mabel's eyes glistened at her son as she touched the decorative wrap with an image of a lit Christmas candle inside a pine wreathe. Her nails were just long enough to separate the tape from the paper. When the rustling of its seasonal packaging stopped, there was a brown box with the word *Stedman's* embossed in gold lettering.

"Stedman's." Her face offered approval. "This must be special."

"I had Ben and Stephen, with some help from Dad, pick it out for me this morning when they went into town."

She opened it and removed the thin, cotton blanket atop its contents. Carefully, she took out the crinkled photograph of Will and Blue enclosed under glass in a dark walnut frame. She stared at it, and a single tear formed in the corner of one eye.

Unsure of her approval, Will cut through the silence as if he were a salesman trying to cash in on new customer. "It's got—"

His mother burst into tears. "My son, my lovely son!" She maneuvered around the outstretched leg and almost strangled her boy as she hugged him around his neck. "Thank you, thank you so much. I will always treasure this more than you can ever know."

Caught off guard, he continued his pitch as if he needed to. "It's got a fold-out support on back, so you can put it on a stand or table, *and* it's got small ring, so you can hang it on the wall if you like."

By now, Mabel had composed herself as a baying Blue and the voices of Mattias, Ben, and Stephen signaled they were about to enter the mudroom attached to the kitchen. She dabbed her eyes with her apron. "I know just the place... on my nightstand. It'll be the first thing I'll lay my eyes on each morning, and last thing before I close them every night." She squeezed Will around his shoulders.

"Something sure smells good," stocky Ben said as he led the procession into the kitchen.

Stephen snatched an uniced Santa cookie off a cooling rack before his mother could intervene.

"You heathens keep your hands to yourselves or their won't be enough cookies for tomorrow night, let alone for after the church service." Mabel still smiled as she ranted from behind her eldest boy.

Blue stormed in wagging his tail before dutifully taking a seat next to Will, who patted his head and side.

"Western Union came by and dropped this off for you, son." Mattias, halfway through removing his overalls, stuck out an arm toward Will with a telegram on his fingertips.

Before Will had the chance to open the message's envelope, his mother shared her joy with the family. "Look what Will gave me." She held up the framed photo, cupping it in the palm of her hand.

"Really?" Seventeen-year-old Ben smirked at his older brother. "I thought you'd never leave home without that picture of you and Blue. I thought—"

"He had that talk on the train with that airborne corporal and Belgian woman." Stephen interrupted. "Didn't you listen to anything Will said yesterday?" he laughed.

Will looked at the telegram, his fingers itching to open it, but his mother had more pressing business for the family. "Listen, there's something I need to tell all of you, especially Will. I was going to share this with your father the morning after he came back from Fort Wayne without Will, but I forgot in the hubbub of the telegram telling us about the accident."

"What, dear?" Mattias narrowed his eyes, intrigued by her secrecy.

"The night Will was to have arrived, and you went to Fort Wayne to pick him up, I fell asleep and had a dream. In it, I *felt* Will had come home, at least for a short while, so I went up into his room to check on him. He wasn't there, but this framed photo—with all its imperfections *and* in a dark wood frame—was lying on top of the bed. To me it was like a sign that, no matter what, things would be alright. Thank you, Will, for the best present ever."

"Mom, you know how whacky that sounds?" Sixteen-year-old Stephen's face twisted in multiple angles as his blond locks greased back toward the nape of his neck.

"Take it easy on your mother, son," Mattias intervened. "I do believe we all have a right to our own dreams, especially the ones that express gratitude and love."

Secretly, Will agreed with Stephen as he watched his brother hug his mother. Deep inside, he thought the dream extremely odd, bordering on frightening. Yet, there were things back on the train which plagued him, although he couldn't put his finger on any of it. This just added one more piece to weigh on his overburdened mind.

As the rest of the family dispersed throughout the house, Will finally got the chance to open the telegram. It was from the army chaplain who'd been sent to the hospital to comfort the troops injured in the wreck. Will had asked him to check on Corporal Bentley's condition.

Did some checking on Cpl. Matthew Bentley as you asked. STOP Never on train. STOP K.I.A. on Dec. 24, 1944 in Bastogne. STOP Simone Cherneau killed same day. STOP Sorry for this news. STOP

Will felt the color drain from his face as he crumpled the telegram into a tight ball. His face and limbs chilled. "I think I need to go into the living room and sit by the fire," he announced to his mother, who began icing the cookies.

"Sure, son, just be careful." She focused on a Christmas tree cookie as if she were da Vinci and the bowl of green icing her palette.

Crutches under his arms, Will hobbled through the kitchen and foyer into the living room, the balled-up notice still in his hand. The aroma of the Christmas tree, a spruce cut just yesterday and decorated last evening, slapped him to attention enough for him to carefully navigate his way to the sofa. He stood in front of the burning fire and tossed the telegram into it.

"What's wrong, son?" His father walked out of the doorway of his makeshift office. "You really look pale. Bad news in that telegram?"

"Remember how I told you Corporal Bentley pulled me out of the rubble at the wreck?" Will grimaced, holding back tears.

"Yeah." His father compressed his lips and sat on the couch. "Sit down, son, sit down "

Will sat, which took a strain off his broken leg. "He died." Will wasn't lying as he looked his father squarely in the eyes, but he'd never go farther down that inexplicable rabbit hole. "Madame Cherneau died as well."

Mattias placed his hands on his eldest son's shoulders and offered an empathetic squeeze. "That has to hurt. I'm sorry, son."

Will gazed into the renewed flames in front of him and reflected on a ten-day-old conversation. "I'm glad I knew them, Dad." He reached hold of one of his father's hands. "It's not just that Bentley saved me, but after talking to him and Simone, I'll always take a bit of both of them into Christmas and beyond."

"I believe you will, son, I believe you will."

Unknowingly, Mattias left a damaged psyche behind on the sofa as he went back into the kitchen.

Questions began to crystallize as they swirled in Will's head.

Why all the talk of odd Christmas gifts from Bentley and Cherneau?

How did they know about Mom's reaction to getting the old photo?

Why didn't I slam into them when the wreck occurred?

If it wasn't Bentley pulling him out of the wreckage, who was it?

Was there another Matt Bentley in the service who'd stowed away on the train?

If Mom was off her nut with her dream, am I ready to be committed?

These thoughts tired him a great deal, and he wanted to lie down on his bed. "Ben! Stephen!"

Ben clumped down the stairs first. "Yeah, whatcha need?"

"I need to lay down. Could you go with me up the stairs?"

"Sure." Ben stepped back, allowing his brother access to the staircase.

At that moment, a pounding drew the attention of both brothers to the front door, where Ben greeted a flustered Western Union messenger.

"I don't know how I forgot to drop this off earlier," the messenger said with a heaving breath, "but this wooden box for Will got buried under a canvass in the back seat." He handed it to Ben before dashing back to his vehicle. "Merry Christmas!"

By now, Will and Ben had been joined by their parents and Stephen. Somewhat larger than a shoe box, the mysterious gift stood vertical. It smelled of pine and had been stamped with a Chicago address. The family retreated to the living room while Stephen raced to the basement, returning with a broad-bladed putty knife.

"A secret admirer, Will?" Stephen snickered, handing him the putty knife.

"Here, son, let me steady it." Mattias grasped the bottom of the box with both hands as Will began to loosen the nails on the top.

As Will pried the top open, curls of wood shavings sprouted over the splintered edges. He reached in and felt glass. "What?"

"Is that a bottle of wine?" Ben's curiosity tried to sprint past Will's revelation.

Slowly, Will eased a dark green bottle from its nest of shavings. He cradled it in both hands and studied the label, written in French with an image of a large manor house. One word stood out since it was the only one he could understand—*Champagne.*

A folded note rose to the surface with the bottom of the bottle, teetering on strands of shavings at the top of the box. Will passed the bottle to his father and reached for the note.

"What's it say?" Only a serious effort at self-control kept Stephen from exploding.

"Who sent it?" Not even could his mother contain her excitement.

Will's mouth opened, but not a word escaped.

Joyeux noël, Will. Simone

He would never question his mother's dreams again.

Author's Note

Christmas Giving, while fictitious, is based upon an actual event. Shortly after midnight on Friday, December 13, 1946, the westbound flyer "The Golden Triangle" turned along a bend in the tracks and crashed into the recent wreckage of two freight trains on the eastbound track about ten miles southeast of Mansfield, Ohio. There were 270 passengers aboard—150 soldiers headed for a ten day leave before shipping out to occupied Japan and 120 civilians. Nineteen people, including fifteen young soldiers, died that night, and twenty-six people were injured.

About Max Willi Fischer...

Born in Akron, Ohio into an immigrant family seeking new opportunity in America after World War II, Max Willi Fischer was raised in a village named after an exotic North African seaport— Mogadore, Ohio. With such a background, little wonder Max grew up with an inborn curiosity about history. After gaining bachelor's and master's degrees from the University of Akron, he spent four decades as a classroom teacher where he realized that history should be a vibrant, well-told story. His goal in writing historical fiction is to engage readers with an exciting, yet accurate, view of our nation's past. He enjoys the discovery of research to ensure that, while his characters are for the most part fictitious, his settings are based on the reality of the era in which he writes, immersing readers in a yesterday of long ago. Retired, Max lives with his wife and trusted four-legged friends Kole, Della, Leo, Bunnie, Lucy, and Izzy.

You can find more on Max at

https://inkerspen.com/Max-fischer

A Timeless Christmas

by

Patricia Miller

What mystery lies within the walls of Hower House? Spooky noises. Furniture moved without reason. Secrets run amuck in this resplendent mansion, and student worker Clarisse is convinced it's a spiritual haunt.

When she teams up with mystery writer Pamela, their investigation goes back in time to A Timeless Christmas.

The lock clicked. My heart sank. Turning back at the Hower House sign displayed in the front yard, my stomach expanded with a deep breath as I pushed a lump down my throat and opened the heavy door ornate with beveled glass inserts with care. *Was I really coming back to this house?* My stinging feet inside snow-covered boots and shivering body answered yes. Even the smoke like cloud that escaped my mouth this snowy December Saturday afternoon agreed. A trap door from within my stomach gave way as I approached. A warm reprieve welcomed me, and yet, I hesitated. I was returning for Clarisse, not for me.

"Mrs. Stillgenbaur, that writer, Pamela, is here," bellowed a familiar voice as I slipped inside the foyer and shut the door.

The student worker, Clarisse, sat at the reception desk dressed in a long red skirt and white blouse, smiling in front of the backdrop of a carved black walnut curved staircase, the handrail draped in deep red velvet with an attached valence of twinkling garland. The rotunda-styled central hall beckoned my obeying eyes, devouring the many shining white lights while the aroma of freshly cut evergreen overtook my sense of smell.

I marveled at the strange coincidence of this house stealing my attention numerous times over thirty years ago, walking along these streets as a college student. And weirder than that, my oldest lived across the street in Fir Hill Apartments as a student thirty years later. The desire to see inside this mansion filled me every time I visited him all those years ago. Little did I know where it would lead me.

***

Standing atop one of Akron's steep inclines, the three-story gem boasted a soaring tower, tall windows, and distinctive moldings. The Christmas spirit lived in each eerie candle glowing in every window. The official pamphlet described the exterior as Italianate. I learned a lot about the history of the house and its generations of owners before it became the property of The University of Akron on my initial visit, but that had nothing to do with why I was returning today.

I shot Clarisse a wink, hoping she remembered our agreement. No one on staff must discover the secrets she shared with me when we met at a local coffee shop a week ago. I can still remember her words today.

"Mrs. Stillgenbaur has heard these same strange noises I've heard. I know it. She just won't admit it, so I don't bring them up anymore. And I was in the basement on many occasions when she and Mrs. Rose asked each other about items being moved or knocked over, I'm telling you. There's something very strange going on inside Hower House."

My next mystery novel needed an imposing setting such as Hower House, which was one reason for my visits. However, Clarisse's fears seemed genuine. How could I not return to investigate further? Who knows? I might just get a kick out of sleuthing again.

"So nice to see you again, Pamela," Mrs. Stillgenbaur declared as she floated into the entry hall in a soft red flowy pantsuit. "I'm so glad you returned for a second visit. It's so exciting to think of a mystery set in Hower House."

Mrs. Stillgenbaur was the head curator, whereas Mrs. Rose worked in the small gift shop called the Cellar Door Boutique. Several other museum workers were working various shifts. But not today—a strategic move on my part.

I shed my outer gear, put my phone on camera, and stood, pen-poised to take notes. Pleasantries aside, I got right to the point.

"So, I would like to get a second look at several areas, if I may, starting with the ballroom on the third floor."

"Mrs. Stillgenbaur," Clarisse chimed in as planned. "I would be happy to take her up."

As we began to climb the grand staircase, I smiled and nodded to applaud her fine efforts. Once upstairs, we could talk in private.

"It happened again," Clarisse whispered as we reached the top landing. "I heard strange noises up here again just yesterday."

I caught sight of Clarisse's' stiffened gaze. My resolve heightened as I surveyed the expanse of the large ballroom. I snapped a few pictures and then turned to her.

"Same or different place?" I asked.

"Same," she answered, leading me into the Ladies' Withdrawing Room right off the ballroom. Mrs. Stillgenbaur already explained that this space was often used for ladies to rest and refresh themselves after climbing three flights of stairs and wearing heavy gowns with multiple layers of undergarments beneath them.

Stepping across the threshold, I took stock of the room and its contents again. A delicately patterned Victorian loveseat sat on the left, and a small armoire with inlaid tiles and a high-back Victorian chair to match the sofa sat off to the right. A marble fireplace graced the east wall, and a small vanity with intricately carved legs and molding sat by the door. As I pondered, I stood in silence before being interrupted by the young student.

"The noises come from just outside this door." Clarisse raised her hand to lead the way out of the door opposite our entry point. I continued to study the room.

I stepped into the center of the room and stopped. "Something has been moved in this room."

"What?" asked Clarisse, also gazing around, her brow furrowed.

I walked back and forth between the furniture and each door. My assessment concluded. I took my place beside my young guide and nodded my head.

"Several things have been moved. There's a different amount of space between the door and the furniture. I suppose cleaners could account for it."

"Wait a minute," Clarisse exclaimed. "How could you know that? I mean, I work here, and I don't see anything different in this room."

"You're going to have to just trust me on this. I notice things like that," I answered.

"Well, in any case, cleaners are not the reason, as we don't allow outside businesses of any kind in here. There's too many priceless items to take a chance."

"That makes sense," I agreed. "Anyone else been up here moving things that you know of?"

"Nope," she returned, eyes wide and still surveying the room. "Did you want to look at the area with the noises?"

"Yeah," I replied, retaking pictures of the room to compare them to the ones taken during my first visit.

I followed Clarisse into the small hallway outside the second door. There wasn't much to investigate. It was just that, a hallway. But my eyes lingered, studying the walls, floorboards, and a small cupboard on the right.

"I'm sure I saw the inside of that cupboard the last time I came, but could you open it again, please?"

My young friend did as I asked without hesitation. I grinned, noticing Clarisse examining the inside. No doubt, hoping to see something out of the ordinary before I did. Both of us came up empty. I shook my head from side to side, signaling Clarisse to shut the cupboard door.

I turned my focus to the hardwood flooring. And in doing so, my attention was piqued by a small knob attached to the baseboard on the left. Stuffing my cell phone in the back pocket of my black leggings, I bent down and touched it with the tip of my index finger.

"You might not remember, but that section of the wood slides open," explained Clarisse.

"For the maids to sweep the dust into," I added.

"Oh, you do remember, then," her cheeks raised in a grin, exposing dimples on either side of her mouth.

"So, there's a duct that goes all the way down to the basement so that the noises could be traveling through that?" I asked, thinking out loud.

"I did think of that, Pamela, but the duct goes to an area of the basement that is sealed off. The dust drops into a pit in the ground." She shot me an ornery grin. "That's one way to avoid looking at your dirt," her grin now accompanied by a quiet laugh.

Smiling back at her, I shut the tiny baseboard opening and swung around while standing up straight. I backed up and glanced over the hallway from a different angle.

"Are you absolutely positive that area is still sealed off?" I asked, hoping this could be the lead we needed. "They might have opened it when they remodeled all those years before you came to work here."

"That's what I was told," she pondered aloud, appearing uncertain now.

Looking from a different vantage point paid off as it had on several other occasions. Something caught my eye, and as I approached, I found it to be an offset in the baseboard wood on the right side below the cupboard we inspected earlier. I squatted down again.

"Well, aren't you interesting, you little devil?" I asked while sliding my finger along the seam in the wood.

Clarisse met me at the same level. "Oh yeah," she interjected. "Mrs. Stillgenbaur told me that was where they were going to put the dust duct, but they realized it would go to an area of the basement they wanted to use for something else."

"I see. Okay," I announced, raising to my feet again, with Clarisse following in kind. "Well, that's something for us to check out further in the basement."

"Maybe I could get away somehow to get a look down there," offered Clarisse. "It's about time for Mrs. Rose to close the gift shop."

At that moment, I heard footsteps approaching. No one could sneak around in this old house with its creaky floorboards unless you were a being without weight. Clarisse might be inclined to entertain such thoughts, but I am not. I tend to look for solutions within the spiritual plain I inhabit.

Winking Clarisse's way once again, we moved to meet whoever it was. Mrs. Stillgenbaur's shiny and voluminous hair bobbing up and down couldn't be mistaken.

"I got everything I needed in the ballroom and just couldn't resist looking at the attention to detail in the woodwork."

As expected, this resulted in a lengthy lecture recounting the woodworking company owned and operated by the original occupants. Successful business owners John Henry Hower and his wife, Susan, created an abode using the best materials available.

I did find this history fascinating, with plans to intertwine it throughout my story; however, since Clarisse was standing behind me, I took this opportunity to hide my hand behind my back, pointing downward, hoping Clarisse would understand.

"Mrs. Stillgenbaur," interrupted Clarisse. "I'm sorry, but would it be alright if I took my break now?"

"Of course, dear."

Clarisse stepped forward and looked at me. "I'll be in the employee lunchroom in the basement. I'll be glad to help you after my break if you need me." I smiled and nodded to her, and she walked through the main threshold, and drifted down the stairs in a carefree, I'm not up to anything manner.

I did my part by keeping the head curator busy. Clarisse relayed her experience to me at a later time.

***

Meanwhile, on the lower level, Clarisse grabbed a drink from the employee refrigerator and sat at an old square lunch table. An older gentleman in jean overalls and a plaid work shirt joined her. He opened a water bottle and smiled, sitting on the other side.

"Well, hello there, young lady," he muttered, nodding, a gesture he learned decades ago.

"Hi, Simon. How are you?" Clarisse answered.

"Not too bad. Been working in the kitchen," he explained. "There's a lot of work needing doing in there."

"Yeah, they left it pretty rough since that fire all those years ago, huh?"

"Yep," he returned. "Mrs. Stillgenbaur is determined to get it restored this next year, so I'm getting a head start." Simon, the maintenance worker turned remodeler, brushed his hand through his greying head of hair and stood. "Well," he relayed. "Just came down for a quick drink, so I better be getting back to work."

Most days, Simon would ask her about her day and chat a bit more; however, Clarisse felt lucky he was too busy today. Knowing Simon was working in the kitchen on the first floor meant more freedom to snoop in the basement.

Looking at the time on her phone, Clarisse moved to the small gift shop to talk with Mrs. Rose, who would be tidying up the Cellar Door Boutique. The shopkeeper had taken the money out of the cash register and was shutting off the lights.

"All done for the day, Mrs. Rose?" asked Clarisse, walking up to a shelf and admiring the crystal.

"Sure am," the shopkeeper answered. Mrs. Rose was a few years younger than Mrs. Stillgenbaur. She wore her short sandy-colored hair parted in the middle and feathered back from her face, a style made popular in the eighties yet still worn to this day by some.

"What have you been up to?" Mrs. Rose asked as she moved towards the door with the keys. Clarisse followed her cue and did the same. Once outside in the middle rotunda-shaped area in the basement, the student continued.

"That writer's up there. I was showing her around some places again, but now I'm on my break."

"I see," responded Mrs. Rose. "I need to get this money to Mrs. Stillgenbaur and get myself home. I'm making lasagna tonight."

"Mmm," Clarisse mumbled. "That sounds yummy. I think she's still on the third floor with the writer."

"I'll just leave it on her desk, then. If I have any leftovers, I'll bring some in for you tomorrow." The gift shop locked; Mrs. Rose relayed her goodbyes and climbed the stairs to the first floor.

Clarisse went to the foot of the steps, listened for the gift shop manager to enter Mrs. Stillgenbaur's office, and then heard the back door shut. Making sure, Clarisse peaked out from a tiny basement window that overlooked the employee parking area.

Convinced she was safe to investigate, Clarisse moved to the basement area below the dust duct. After moving a few autumn floral decorations away from the paneled wall, she then grazed the paneling with both hands. *Too new. They must have installed it during the remodel. I'm not finding any way in.*"

Emulating Pamela, Clarisse backed away from the paneling and paced back and forth to look at it from different angles. After all, Pamela just did that on the third floor.

She stopped when she spied a raised panel nearest the stone outer wall. She doubted anyone had ever noticed it, given that few staff had reason to be in that area. Discarding a few empty boxes, she climbed back to the dimly lit corner. A shiver overcame her body as goosebumps rose upon her exposed arms, and a tingle dripped down her back. She peered behind her, half afraid she would be ambushed from behind by some unknown assailant and drew her phone from her pocket to enable the flashlight.

Alone in the basement, she sniffed an aged smell she assumed emanated from the stone walls. Looking back to the paneling, she examined the abnormal break. It didn't appear properly attached to the next panel, but nevertheless, she couldn't get it to pry apart. She bent down and found the same result from the bottom.

Balancing with her hand on the wall to return to her feet, she almost fell when the wall gave way, acting as a hinged door. Her chest stiffened as she gasped, a breath snagged in her throat. There were just a few minutes left of her break. Fearing Mrs. Stillgenbaur should come looking for her, she replaced the panel and moved all the décor as she first found it. Clarisse climbed the stairs, excited to share her findings with Pamela.

***

Clarisse and Mrs. Stillgenbaur almost collided at the top of the stairs. The student chuckled while the latter nearly swallowed her tongue in surprise.

"Oh, Clarisse," Mrs. Stillgenbaur blurted after catching her breath, her hand to her chest. "I was just coming down to see if you've finished your break."

"I'm done," announced the younger worker. "What can I do for you?"

"I must gather the budget records for tonight's university board meeting. Pamela would like to see the bedrooms again, and I'm sure you can answer any of her questions about that part of the house. Would you accompany her?"

"Of course, Mrs. Stillgenbaur," affirmed Clarisse. "I'd be happy to."

The head curator lowered her voice. "Thank you. I hate to ask you this, but I need to leave in about fifteen minutes. Simon is just about done for the day, too. Can you lock up and set the alarm if she needs to stay later? You know how to, right?"

"I sure can. I locked up a few times over the summer," insisted Clarisse.

Mrs. Stillgenbaur smiled and lowered her hand onto Clarisse's shoulder. "Oh, that's right. Okay. Thanks so much."

I stood, looking down over the balcony railing from the second floor. Clarisse raced up the carpeted stairs and stood beside me in silence. We both observed Mrs. Stillgenbaur scurrying out of her office and heard the closing of the same back door through which Mrs. Rose had exited a few minutes before.

"Well?" I asked.

"You were right. The remodelers paneled the wall in front of the dust pit, but I was clever like you, and I found that one piece of paneling opened like a hinged door." I couldn't help but smile back at my beaming protégé.

"Well, you are clever," I boasted with approval. "I think I hear Simon leaving."

We walked over to a hall window and witnessed him driving his old baby blue pickup truck out of the lot.

"Shall we examine the basement then?" I asked. Without a word, Clarisse nodded, her excited eyes bulging, and she spun on her feet. I followed close behind.

We locked all the doors and shut off all lights before heading for the basement. As the afternoon sun disappeared, the beautiful and charming Hower House of before now took on a darker and more sinister feel. Shadows appeared, it seemed, out of nowhere, and house-settling cracks and creaks began to emerge.

The basement remained lit as per usual. Clarisse led me to the paneled wall she had examined a short time ago. Pulling away the few items stored against the wall, she guided me to the corner where the paneling and stone outer wall met.

I shuddered. "Oh," I blurted. "This part of the basement gives me the creeps for some reason."

Clarisse stared at me as if some force had frozen her. I stared back to see what she would do next for a few seconds before breaking the suffocating silence.

"What?"

"I felt the exact same way when I stood here before," she recounted. I nodded, wondering if this was a coincidental naivete or something else. I refused to entertain the idea of something else.

"So, how does this panel open then?" I asked.

"Like this," boasted Clarisse, pushing on the one panel that bounced back like an opened door.

I pulled a small but powerful flashlight stick from my pocket. The light sifted through the opening as dust particles fluttered in the once-stifled air. As I pushed the paneling door open further, it creaked, bellowing in the basement.

"Could that be the noises you heard on the third floor by the dust opening?" I asked.

"I guess it could be," Clarisse hesitated. "But, how come Mrs. Rose never mentioned hearing it when her gift shop is in the room right next door?"

"Maybe her gift shop wasn't open at the time. The hours are varied. Or, maybe she has but isn't telling anyone," I suggested. "Or, maybe she's the one making them."

"Why?"

"That we don't know yet," I answered. After we stepped inside, Clarisse shut the paneled door behind her with force, which made a resounding thud. "One thing for sure," I added. "No one shut that door like that during the day. That sound would reach all ears within the walls of Hower House and on the grounds as well."

"Well, there's the dust pit," I revealed, beaming my flashlight down the deeper-than-expected opening. Clarisse stepped forward to peer into its depths. "Hey, stand back unless you want to see the bottom from the inside."

Clarisse moved back, swallowing hard at the prospect I had just outlined. I passed the light over the walls and marveled at the discovery made to our right.

"Well, well, well," I interjected. "Will you look at this?"

"Is that a tunnel?" she asked, leaning forward past me. She stepped nearer to its opening. "Pamela, it **is** a tunnel."

"Turn on your cell's flashlight," I instructed. "We're going in, that is, if you don't want to stay back here?"

"No way I'm missing out on this."

The dark cavern was straight for about five to six yards but then made a sharp turn to the left, and after about ten minutes of walking, the winding back and forth had rendered me void of directional sense. Our shoes began to skid over what felt like gravel and dirt but soon returned to solid concrete like we first encountered at the beginning of the tunnel at Hower House.

"Looks like a dead end," Clarisse surmised as we stopped.

In front of us were two concrete steps with what looked like a wooden door, faded and worn by time. Clarisse studied a metal attachment but was no wiser for it.

"There's no door handle. We're stuck. We'll have to go back."

"Now, now," I broke in. "Slow down and let me show you something." I moved in front of her and asked her to hold the flashlight. Pointing to the metal device, I explained. "See this? This is an old-fashioned latch. You raise this part and..." With a snap, the latch and the old wooden door opened.

Bitter and cold temperatures from outside flurried into our once-warm tunnel. My absolute disdain for winter weather returned as I peered outside before heading out of the tunnel. We stepped carefully into a building with glass walls on three sides, colliding with greenery in every direction.

"What is this place?" the young worker asked at full volume.

"Shhh," I answered with authority. "Keep your voice down." We turned off our flashlights immediately, and I stepped forward to peer through one of the glass windows. "Do you recognize this property?"

"Well," Clarisse observed, moving closer to see as well. "I think that's the privacy fence behind Hower House, so I would say this is an adjoining property."

"Interesting," I added. "Let's make our way back the way we came."

As we walked along the somewhat familiar tunnel, Clarisse was deep in thought but not silent. I answered with as many "uh ha's" as possible, allowing me to continue working out things in my mind. I would have much preferred silence. I returned to the present with my cohort in midstream.

"I just can't figure out why there would be a tunnel hooking together these two properties," she yelled, oblivious to the reverberations off the tunnel walls. "Someone back at Hower House has to know about this."

"Oh, someone back at the house does know about it, that's for sure." I paused for thought and continued. "Who all was on staff during the remodel?"

"Mrs. Stillgenbaur told me everyone was hired after that," Clarisse answered. "I've often wondered if Simon had worked there long ago, left, and was re-hired. He seems right at home in the mansion."

"I guess that's possible. Whoever knows about the hinged paneling also knows about this tunnel."

"Pamela," Clarisse addressed me with more seriousness before we reached the basement threshold.

"Do you understand any of this?" I stopped, making eye contact with her furtive eyes.

"Not completely, Clarisse. But I'll figure it out. No, **we'll** figure it out. Not a word to anyone about what we found tonight."

"I won't tell a soul," she promised, eyebrows raised. "Not a soul."

Relieved to be out of the tunnels and back into the Hower House basement, we turned off our flashlights and wiped the soot and dirt we brought back on our clothes, skin, and hair. At that moment, a dark red piece of cloth jammed into the rafters above us caught my eye.

"What's that?" I asked, looking up.

Clarisse climbed onto a wooden frame, as limber young people do. She pulled it down and jumped back to the concrete floor. She flipped it around in her hand before offering a helpful suggestion.

"Hey, that's a bit of luck. We can wipe the dirt off us with this rag." Clarisse wiped her arms and then handed it to me.

"Judging by the little bit of dirt on it when you took it down, I would say it was put there with that same intention by someone else, wouldn't you say?" I grinned and raised my eyebrows at her this time.

"That's brilliant," she gushed. "I wouldn't have thought of that."

"You will next time," I concluded with encouragement.

"What do you mean by next time?"

"Somehow, I doubt this will be your first and last investigation," I asserted. As her face beamed at the prospect, I led the way before we set the alarm and left for the night.

***

The dampness of the next day's rain seeped deep inside me as I shivered, cupped my hands around my coffee, and eyed the flames of the coffee shop fireplace. Fragments of information about Hower House swirled through my mind like flames, none smoldering yet each remaining ablaze.

I shook my head and scrunched my face to shake the cobweb tangles free. Resorting to my notes, I reviewed what I knew, hoping to make sense of our discovery in the basement. *Someone there has to know about the tunnel. Who? It must be connected with the strange noises. What's going on here?*

A set of tennis shoes appeared, perched by my table, and a courteous "Hello" brought my nose from my notes and back to reality. Clarisse stood smiling while holding a hot chocolate. Her ripped jeans and blouse contrasted with my baggy pants and oversized sweatshirt.

"Oh, hello, love," I greeted. "Want to sit down?"

Without answering, she slid into the seat across from me, sipped her warm drink, and, to my surprise, remained silent. I went on with studying my notes. When finished, I raised my eyes and smiled at my young friend.

"So?" she asked.

"I'm trying to make sense of all of this," I returned.

"Anything in your notes helping?"

"I'm not sure," I answered, paging back and forth in my notebook. Stopping at one page, I referenced a point. "So, Mrs. Stillgenbaur told me that when Gracie Hower lived in the house alone, one of their businesses crumbled amidst a larger-scale economic decline."

"Okay?"

"Well, she also said that up to that point, all the land around Hower House was part of their large estate. Gracie had no choice but to sell the land to pay off the debts left by the failed business."

"Yep, I remember hearing about that," acknowledged Clarisse in a candid manner.

"Then," I continued, turning a page. "I remember her telling me that Gracie was distraught because she preferred the opulent look of an estate. So," I explained, leaning in. "Over a period of a few years, she bought back all the properties one by one. Well, the houses built on them had to go."

"So, she had them all torn down," Clarisse retorted.

"Seems so." I sat deep in thought for a few seconds. "I wonder..."

"What do you wonder?" the student asked.

"I think I'm going to see if I can talk to the neighbor who owns the greenhouse. I could tell them it's research for the book and see if any of them are ancestors of the same people involved in the selling and buying."

"Risky," she warned with a hiss. "Nowadays, I don't think people would let strangers in."

"That's true, but they just might."

***

As luck would have it, I found myself sitting in the living room of Levina Toures. A sweet old lady in her eighties, Levina had an aristocratic way about her. Her updo suggested weekly hairdresser visits, and her dress looked like fine brocade material. The tea on a tray with china cups and saucers confirmed my suspicion.

On the other hand, the vibe emanating from her adult granddaughter was anything but inviting. *Who could blame her? I could be a dangerous stranger for all they knew.* Lucky for me, the granddaughter left the room, taking with her the negative vibes.

"I appreciate you letting me ask you some questions about Hower House," I declared after taking a sip and returning my cup to its saucer.

"I'm happy to tell you what I know," she acquiesced as we sat. "Oh, writing a book is wonderful. Your life as an author must be so exciting."

"I'm sure it's not as exciting as you might think. But, at the door, you mentioned your ancestors sold this property back to the Howers and later repurchased it. I can't imagine anything more exciting than that."

"Well," she offered, looking up at the ceiling. "My great, great, great grandmother...or should that be four greats. Oh well, regardless, my ancestors bought this land from the Howers when they needed the money." The latter part of that sentence was diminished to a whisper. "Then, later on, they managed to get it back. Isn't that interesting?"

"Very much so. So, your ancestors built a house on this property, and when the Howers bought it, I understand they tore it down."

"Yes, that is what happened." She paused. "No one minded, though, because they gave them a handsome price for the properties."

"I see," I confirmed, reaching for my notebook. "Well, you have a lovely home now. I notice you have a greenhouse. Did you build that?"

"Oh, that," she replied while coughing and sputtering tea.

"Are you alright?" I asked.

"Oh, Yes, my dear," she answered while replacing cup to saucer. "I forgot about that old thing. Yes, my husband and I built that when we were left this property in my mother's will."

"Oh, really?"

"Why does that interest you?"

"Oh," I smoothed over. "Sometimes, old properties have outside ice houses or small caves for storing canned goods. I wondered if there was something like that on the Hower's property." I scratched my nose, firmly expecting it to begin to grow.

"No, nothing like that here." *Did I detect a hint of reluctance to share further?* Levina looked away and picked up her cup and saucer in what looked to be somewhat of a hurry.

"What can you tell me about the Howers and your ancestors? Were they friends?"

"Couldn't be," she retorted. "Different class. They weren't unkind or snobby, you see. It's just the way things were back then."

Judging by Levina's nervous change in demeanor, I decided I had hit a nerve. After I asked a few trivial questions, I took my leave. "Well, I can't thank you enough for allowing me into your lovely home and for your information."

With pleasantries exchanged, I exited the door, and before I could descend the snowy and icy front porch steps, I couldn't help but hear a short conversation between Levina and her granddaughter.

"I told you not to let her in," the younger admonished. "You know, we need to do something about that." *Whatever that was.*

"This is my house, and I say how things go. It hasn't changed in decades and won't change while I'm alive. It's a part of history."

***

"I don't like the idea of you hiding out in the basement, Clarisse," I argued on the phone. "You could lose your job. It's not worth it."

"I won't lose my job because I won't get caught," she demanded. "I'm doing it. I've made up my mind."

The fearlessness of youth. *I remember those days. I hope she stays well-hidden.*

The next day, pounding on my front door left me jolted. As I answered the door, Clarisse pushed me aside and barreled in. By the looks of it, she didn't get much rest in Hower House's basement. Coffee soothed her a bit.

"Well?" I asked with impatience as she chugged her drink as if dying of thirst.

"It went great," was all she managed, and began to gulp some more. There was no sense pushing her. She continued after a deep breath.

"I hid out behind storage boxes stacked three high. I took an old blanket and covered my whole body. I must have fallen asleep because a noise woke me up. Guess what the noise was?"

"You tell me," I requested, trying to elicit the facts.

"It must have been the cellar door that goes outside because I also was bombarded with freezing air. I started to shiver. It closed, and after hearing a few items being moved, I heard the paneled door creak open. And then you will never guess who I heard talking to each other?"

There was little doubt that she wanted me to guess. I had an idea but didn't want to take the wind out of her investigative sails. "I'm all ears," I replied.

"It was a female voice, and she said, 'Hello Simon. How are you tonight?'"

"Levina's?" I asked.

"Right!" she exclaimed. "Levina and Simon meeting. I think Simon came in through the cellar door. He must have deactivated the alarm somehow. Anyways, Levina must have come through the tunnel. I wouldn't have known who she was, but he called her by name."

"Now that's very interesting," I added. "Please tell me you stayed hidden."

"Of course I did," she insisted. "What do you take me for?"

"Alright. Alright," I tried soothing her. "So, did you hear what they were up to?"

"Well, Simon scolded her a little by telling her she should have waited for him in the tunnel. He insisted it was too uneven and feared she would lose her footing and fall."

"So, I'm wondering if this was their first meeting or if he told her that before," I thought aloud.

"Oh, they've met before last night, that's for sure," Clarisse boasted with a cocky grin.

"Okay," I coaxed. "Keep telling the story. Sounds like you saw and heard a lot more."

She nodded and continued. "She scolded right back by telling him to quit treating her like a dotty old woman. Isn't that funny?" she laughed. "I heard them leave the basement and take the steps to the first floor. When I was sure the coast was clear, I snuck up the stairs, too. I found them both sitting in the East Parlor."

"The East Parlor?" I asked. "Any idea why?"

"Because the last time they met, she insisted on going all the way to the third floor. He reminded her that she became dizzy and shifted the furniture when she fell." I looked at her in awe of her extensive knowledge. "Well, she wanted to go up again, and he told her no because of it." I nodded.

"While sitting in the East Parlor, she chattered on about how beautiful the Christmas tree was, talked about the JHH carved into the fireplace surround, and then said something that floored me."

I had no choice but to sit while she sipped her drink. My mind swirled with what might come next.

"She opened some book she had with her. I didn't dare get any closer or risk being seen or heard. My guess is it was a journal or a diary. She read passages someone wrote describing the wonderful evenings sitting in this room when the servants had the night off, and everyone else was out."

"She has someone's journal," I exulted. "It could be one of the Hower's, but I would bet it's one of her ancestors instead."

"I think it was someone who was in her family a long time ago. She talked to Simon about how nice it was to sit in there again, look at the Christmas trees, and relive what her deceased relative experienced. And Simon's sweet on her." She bit her lip after that tidbit.

"Really?" I asked.

"Why else would he risk his job meeting her at the tunnel and letting her in the house after hours? And that's not all. He laid his hand on hers as she read the diary and reminisced. I imagine he has heard these same diary entries and stories before."

"Did you hear anything else?"

"They spoke of the times being so different back then and how whoever they were had to keep their meetings a secret. And of the pride she felt in her ancestors for helping Susan Hower safely transport her black female servants to the voting booth after the 19th Amendment was passed."

"She told me her relatives and the Howers couldn't be friends because they came from a different class," I reported. " She made a point of saying it was just the way it was back then."

"That might have been it, then," declared Clarisse. "Hold on, you mean that the tunnel's been there for years, and that's how one of the Howers and one of Levina's relatives met in secret?"

"That's what I think," I answered.

"That's amazing." Clarisse sighed. "So sad they couldn't be proper friends."

"I have no doubt they were proper friends, no matter how they had to meet," I answered.

"Simon went on to tell Levina that she should show the journals to Mrs. Stillgenbaur, but Levina refused because she thought the tunnel would be closed off then."

"She's not wrong about that," I sighed.

"Simon agreed with her on that. And then she pleaded, 'Simon, I'm a very old lady. I won't be around forever; please keep my secret.' He assured her he would and walked her down the tunnel and back to the greenhouse. He must have locked up and reset the alarm after I left. Before he returned to the basement, I had already hightailed it out of there."

"Where did you park your car?" I asked.

"In the Fir Hill Apartments parking lot, of course." She noticed my laptop and notes on my end table. "You writing the book?"

"Sure am," I affirmed. "I'll keep all this tunnel stuff out, though. There's no reason to rat them out."

**

A few months later, Levina Toures' obituary was in the Akron Beacon Journal. My young budding investigator came to see me, tears welling in her eyes as she planted herself on my sofa.

"I saw it in the paper," I disclosed with a gentle voice. "How about we go to the funeral together?"

"Could we?" She sniffled. "That would be nice. A lot is happening at Hower House now."

"Like what?" I asked, handing her a drink. I sat opposite her in my usual high-back chair.

"Simon is retiring for one," she burst out. And before leaving work tonight, I heard banging from the basement."

"Banging?"

"I asked Mrs. Stillgenbaur what all that racket was, and she insisted some paneling was coming off the one wall, so Simon was nailing it back on. I went down and saw him building big shelves on that wall, which he attached with huge braces."

"Of course he is," I returned. "When's his last day?"

"It was today," Clarisse sniffled, swallowing hard, tears dripping.

"It was his last job," I concluded. "He kept her secret and stayed loyal all those years. Now that's true love, if you ask me."

Author's Note

The Hower House was built in 1871 by industrialist John Henry Hower and his wife, Susan Youngker Hower. Three generations of Howers lived in the home from the 1870s until the early 1970s.

The home has 28 rooms and was designed by Akron architect Jacob Snyder, who modeled the unique floorplan on the "Akron Plan for Sunday Schools," a design used nationwide until the early 20th century. When it was built, the home had no electricity, coal-burning fireplaces, and, in the absence of running water, a gravity-fed flush system. Eventually, the Hower House was one of the first private homes to get running water, electricity, and a telephone.

The Howers owned and operated 40 businesses, including Hower Oats Company, which later became Quaker Oats, and a woodworking business in Jamaica which supplied all the Mahogany beds in Hower House.

The Hower House Museum has been owned by the University of Akron since the early 1970s. It was sold to the university with the stipulation that the last surviving Hower, Grace, would live there until her death. Hower House has operated as a historic museum since the mid-1980s.

Many thanks to Ann Cousins and all the Hower House staff for providing me with a tour and a wealth of information, which served as a foundation for this mystery story.

About Patricia Miller...

Award-winning author Patricia Miller grew up and lives in a small town in Ohio where she has worked as a mental health counselor for 30 + years.

She writes Agatha Christie-like, who-dun-it cozy mystery collections ("Mysterious Tales of the Unexplained Vols 1-4), which include illustrations by middle and high school art students. She also has published a YA sci-fi trilogy (The Joshua Trilogy) and is a contributing author in a romance anthology (Love on the Lakefront) with Mystery Weekend Romance. Her first two mystery collections were each named finalists in the American Bookfest Best Book Awards, and volume 3 was awarded a 2nd Place Purple Dragonfly award in the mystery category. Miller has presented Character-Driven Writing workshops, including at the 2024 West Virginia Young Writers Celebration at the University of Charleston.

The Abandoned Cottage

by

Judy Cicero

In the heart of a snowy Ohio winter, a brave band of animal misfits — each with their own quirks and past struggles — come together to build something truly magical: a warm and welcoming sanctuary for creatures who feel alone, lost, or unwanted. Through friendship, kindness, and a little holiday magic, they discover that family isn't just about where you come from — it's about who you choose to share your heart with.

A heartwarming tale of hope, belonging, and the power of working together, this story will charm readers of all ages!

The Fearless Foursome

An abandoned cottage in the Forest Hills area of Cleveland Ohio aroused curiosity, annoyance and concern among its neighboring homeowners. This uninhabited structure stood behind the main house on the property as a stark contrast to the historic and well-kept residences that surrounded it. Most particularly, the noises generated from the cottage during the long winter nights interrupted the sleep of many residents and filled them with anxiety. To the adults the eerie creaks, the sudden thuds—each sound seemed to carry an ominous message.

In the midst of this urban mystery, a small, quiet dog felt the need to explore. He was a peculiar little critter himself, with an extraordinary sense of smell and an insatiable curiosity. His glossy, brown eyes sparkled with intelligence, and his nose, always twitching, was a finely tuned instrument of investigation. His name was Scent.

***

One particularly cold winter night, Scent decided it was time to uncover the secrets of the abandoned cottage. He had spent the day with his furry friends; a cat named Luna, a chipmunk called Chatter, and an old, scrawny squirrel who served as this maverick group's lookout when needed, called Teacher. They called themselves The Fearless Foursome. Earlier in the day, at Scent's request they met to plan their first adventure together.

"I called this meeting and am so glad you all could make it. I was slightly snoozing in the sun this afternoon near the abandoned cottage when I overheard the neighbors discuss plans to tear down this noisy, historical eyesore. The Neighborhood Council decided it had to be destroyed," Scent announced.

For many winter seasons, the Fearless Foursome had spent cozy nights huddled together under the porch of the cottage to keep warm. Yet, they had never ventured inside. Scent was well aware with the winter season upon them, and Teacher's aging body struggling to keep warm, they needed to find a more comfortable place inside to spend their nights.

"Well," purred Luna. "I am always up for a new adventure. And I can jump up on places where you, a measly dog, cannot go." She blinked her pretty yellow eyes.

Luna was a beautiful cat of Siamese descent but more importantly for tonight's adventure, she could also serve as the signal corps of one as she could produce a very soulful, frightening and noisy howl when necessary. Ordinarily she was very stealthy and quiet. She smiled, proud of herself and her special abilities. Scent overlooked her boastfulness and turned to Chatter. He would deal with Luna later, he thought.

"Chatter, how about you? Are you ready to explore this old cottage with us tonight?" he asked. Scent knew Chatter was always ready to scurry around and create a bit of dust and chaos in his wake.

Chatter's tiny body quivered with excitement. As an adolescent teenage chipmunk, he was hyperactive when awake and thoroughly annoying to the people who planted spring flower bulbs in their gardens. Without hesitation, each year he dug up as many as he could to provide a stockpile of delicious food for the cold winter months. Now dreams of spending these months in the abandoned cottage, cheerfully munching on his delicious morsels of plant food increased his typical excitement and he quivered nonstop. "Let's go," he stated. "Let's get this show on the road."

"Thanks, Chatter but slow down. We must check in with Teacher first and then make a united plan of action." Scent turned to Teacher. "Are you ready, old guy?"

Teacher was a misfit squirrel, a cross breed of red, yellow, white and black furry forefathers. As such, he spent most of his life searching for a permanent home and friends with whom he could fit. This strange group of critters and Scent's invitation to join in with this grand adventure tickled him to no end. Despite his old age, his hope to finally find a place in which he might belong could be fulfilled.

"Of course. Let's go. I'm ready right now." Teacher shook himself to fluff his varied colored coat of fur and look better than he felt. As a senior squirrel, he suffered from arthritis and struggled in the winter months of the year. A warm home to occupy, good friends, and a few acorns were all he needed to live out his life in peace and comfort. This invitation was a once in a lifetime offer to him and he intended to honor it with all his skill in serving Scent's plan to its fullest.

"I know I am elderly and not as quick as I used to be, but I am still very great at climbing up to high places and becoming a brilliant and weaponized team member as I can toss down acorns at will. I am also a quiet and stealthy look-out for the rest of you."

Scent nodded to his tiny but fearless team of misfits. He, too, understood the need to belong and hoped this experience could provide this foundation for him.

As a puppy, Scent had been adopted from the City Animal Shelter by a wonderful family who lived in Forest Hills. He had been the beloved plaything for a new baby in his human family. As he grew, however, his cuteness and playfulness were overridden by his girth and strength, and the family decided he was simply too much for their baby child to enjoy.

One evening, Scent overheard the adults speaking about him. "You know, while we love Scent, we must get rid of him soon. I am afraid he will accidentally hurt our child if he rolls on top of him. I think we should return him to the City Animal Shelter. Perhaps a family with older children would want him," the mother said.

"I suppose you are right," agreed the dad. "Maybe a large family that lives outside the city where Scent could freely run and play, would take him."

Wishful thinking thought Scent. Sadly, Scent recalled his return to the Shelter and had thoroughly detested it. As a well-meaning but underfunded facility, it was crowded, dirty, cold, and noisy. During outdoor time one day, when the Shelter was being cleaned in preparation of a visit from the Mayor, Scent, along with a few other pups dug under the fence and sprinted to freedom. He never looked back.

"OK," Scent directed. "Let's meet under the large oak tree about midnight and make our way to the cottage with the moon's guidance. The Old Stone Church bells will ring to tell us the correct time. "

Chatter could hardly contain himself. Never in his short life had he expected such an adventure. Running in circles seemed to drain some of his pent-up energy and he became ready to quietly follow Scent and the others to the Cottage.

***

When the church bells of The Old Stone Church struck twelve, with a determined yet cautious gait, Scent trotted through the neighborhood, his paws silent on the cobblestone paths. His three new friends followed with hearts pounding. The air was thick with anticipation, and even the shadows seemed to hold their breath.

As Scent approached the cottage, the noises grew louder, more distinct. He could hear the swoosh of the pine tree branches brushing against the side of the cottage. He thought he heard the distant echo of many footsteps, and a low, mournful sigh that seemed to come from deep within the cottage walls. Undeterred, Scent pressed on, his nose guiding him through the tangled overgrowth that choked the entrance.

Finding the outer door ajar, Scent peaked inside. With quiet caution, Scent slipped in hoping his keen senses would lead him to the source of the disturbances.

Luna followed on soft paws and slinked along the perimeter of the room. The fur on her back was raised and she was prepared to defend herself and the others if need be. She could hiss loudly, arch her back, and show her claws, howling loud enough to scare most humans as well as other critters. A force to be reckoned with, for sure.

Not to be outdone, Chatter scurried along the right-hand wall while his need for speed was satisfied at the free reign he had been given to explore his designated area. Life could not get better than this.

Teacher brought up the rear and shuffled along the left-hand wall. His slow but steady pace allowed him to scan the room and note its sights and hear its sounds for his report back to Scent. It felt good to be needed and appreciated for his special talents despite his senior status.

Scent, without fear, strode down the middle toward the sounds as they grew louder. His nose guided his eyes to safely avoid any unforeseen dangers in his path.

In the heart of the cottage, Scent stopped dead. The others did so as well.

***

Scent discovered a hidden room, concealed behind a rotting wooden door. His nose went into overdrive, sniffing and sorting the multitude of smells seeping under the door. He pushed the rotting door aside and sneaked a peak into the room. The air inside felt colder, the sounds more pronounced and scents more overwhelming. Bravado rather than good sense fueled his behavior.

"Whoa," Scent turned and whispered to the others. "I am not sure what is in here and I think we should have a quiet look around before we all stumble into this inner room. It is important that we have some idea of what we may be dealing with. I would volunteer to lead us but I am too clumsy and would be spotted immediately by the insiders." While Scent truly wished to be recognized as the brave leader, his talents lie in organizing and planning for the group rather than confronting and combating the unknown. Chatter, energetic and adventuresome seemed a more likely sentinel. "Chatter, are you ready to be our look out?"

Chatter, so thrilled at being chosen by Scent to breach the inner room, calmed himself as best he could, relaxed his quivering body, and positioned himself at the entry door waiting for Scent's signal to enter.

Luna, however, was annoyed. Her name as a shining light forecast her role in life, and she felt overlooked and hurt that Scent selected Chatter. She hunkered down and cast a pouty look on her lovely face.

Noticing Luna's disappointment, ever the diplomat, Scent said to the entire group, "While each of us has special and unique skills, sometimes or size and shape will dictate who does what for the sake of our group. Chatter is tiny, unlikely to be observed, and not noticeably a threat to the occupants. Luna, we will need your talents once we know what we are facing inside this room. Is that alright with you?"

Luna's pride restored with Scent's special mention of her, she lifted her head, and graciously accepted Scent's recognition. "I would be happy to assume whatever duties you may have for me," she replied. A few loud purrs later and she was once again her haughty self, eager to join the group as a valued and special member.

The Fearsome Foursome readied themselves for a new adventure.

The Uneasy Encounter

Sniffing deeply, Scent stopped abruptly and said, his voice barely above a whisper, "Wait, I smell something very unusual in here." Chatter, ever curious, almost skidded to a stop and bumped into Luna. He asked "What is it? Can you tell?"

Scent nodded. "It is a mix of musky and sweet. It must be raccoons."

Unfortunately, Scent was all too familiar with the pesky and sometimes frightening raccoons in the neighborhood. Their constant search for food and need for mischief caused several rolling trash cans to careen down the street as the raccoons foraged for whatever delectables they could find.

Scent suddenly signaled the others to stop. "There, look in the back corner, and stay quiet."

"Whoa," whispered Scent to the others. "There is something in here, but I think it may be more afraid of us than we are of it." To his astonishment, Scent found a family of raccoons had made the abandoned cottage their home. These nocturnal creatures had been the source of the evening noises, their movements amplified by the silence of the night.

The father, a rather large and imposing figure, let out a low growl, his eyes fixing on the intruders. He stood in front of the mother and the baby, clearly indicating his intention to protect his family at all costs. The mother's eyes, sharp and wary, scanned the surroundings, while the baby raccoon playfully tugged at her fur, unaware of the potential danger lurking nearby.

"Get away,' growled Papa Raccoon. "This is our home. We claimed it first. You are not like us so we want you gone. We only welcome our own kind." He growled some more.

Mama Raccoon shed a tear, noticed only by Chatter.

Scent backed away as did the others. All except Chatter.

Chatter, sensing a new playmate made a beeline for the baby raccoon. His natural curiosity and kind, friendly spirit took Papa by surprise. Papa's growl and threatening stance softened as Baby waddled up to greet Chatter, nose to nose.

"Why are you waddling in such a strange way?" asked Chatter? His naive and open concern did not seem rude or aggressive to Mama. History had taught her that not all creatures were kind. In fact, she said "Well, if you must know, Baby is not perfect like the other babies were in our family. His right foot is twisted which causes him to walk funny. In our raccoon extended family, he didn't belong. His disability became a handicap for the entire troop of raccoons so our family was ostracized. Unwanted. Feared, made fun of, and a permanent and total misfit to the nature of raccoons."

Another tear glistened as it slid down her cheek. "We were cast out. Thank goodness we found this safe and warm hideaway for a new home," she said softly.

Papa, with a stern expression, stood his ground. "It is not right for you to barge in and disrupt our sanctuary. We are finally settled in here and although we miss the company of other critters, our need for safety comes first."

Scent, though understanding the raccoon's plight, could not ignore the nagging feeling he had that there were probably many other critters who were ridiculed, humiliated, bullied and made to feel unwanted because they were different.

"Papa, I understand your feelings," Scent replied gently, "but this cottage has enough space for many of us. We can even share it with others and create a community where everyone feels safe and valued."

Papa shook his head, his eyes narrowing. "Sharing is not our way. We have our own rules and our own space. Bringing in others will disrupt our life here."

Papa assumed a forceful stance, ready to fight. Scent stood taller to appear stronger. He let out a low, menacing snarl. A tense silence followed as both sides weighed their options. Baby's whimpering broke the silence, drawing attention to the little one's distress. Mama looked pleadingly at Papa, her eyes asking for understanding and compassion.

Scent took a deep breath, trying to find a way to bridge the gap. "Papa, please consider this: we don't want to fight or take anything away from you. Instead, we want to build something together. A place where no one feels outcast or alone. We can all benefit from each other's strengths and create a supportive community."

Papa seemed to soften a bit at these words. He grumbled under his breath and looked at his family, then back at Scent. "We'll think about it," he said finally, his tone less harsh but still uncertain.

At that, Baby emerged from under his Mama's belly and sidled up to Scent. He wiggled under Scent's belly and settled into a cozy snooze.

Papa and Scent looked at each other, locking eyes. Simultaneously their mutual scowls, growls, and stares disappeared. "I am sorry," Papa muttered. "We have our guard up given our recent banishment from our own kind. And strangers worry us also. We feel so alone, yet afraid of all others. You startled us and I reacted instinctively. Aggressive, angry, and afraid. "

Mama smiled at her partner. She continued, "I, too am ashamed of my reception toward you all. How is that a good example for me to give to our little baby. To fear everyone and hide away from the world. No. It is not right. We must face our fears."

Scent, too, felt uncomfortable. He, of all critters, with his band of misfits should have recognized Papa's position with their intrusion into his home. They were the outsiders, the invaders, the threat. Scent, overwhelmed with shame, bowed his head toward the raccoon family. "With great remorse, I ask your forgiveness. We meant no harm and to break into your home was wrong. And thoughtless."

"May I remind you, Scent, that we are a 'family' of misfits so we know how difficult it is to live among those different from us," quipped Luna. "Yet, we are all different from each other in our little group."

Teacher, wise in his ways, offered. "Different but the same. We all want to be loved, cared for, safe and sound, especially in our old age. I know I do. And I welcome the Raccoon family into our circle as well."

With that, Baby awoke, peaked out and spotted Chatter. He instinctively knew he had found a little friend like himself. Rushing to Chatter's side, the two of them then raced around the two groups, ever closing in to bond The Fearless Foursome with the raccoon family.

***

"Now," said Scent. "I have an idea."

The Cottage of Comfort

The raccoon family and the Fearsome Foursome gathered together near each other. Baby snuggled next to Chatter and fell into a much-needed sleep. Her gentle snoring calmed Chatter and for the first time, Chatter discovered the thrill of feeling content and relaxed.

"You know," started Scent. "We do not need all this space in this wonderful cottage. But we do need a sense of permanency for prospective residents. Granted the cottage could use some fixing up inside first but nonetheless it is warm and safe. Then we can figure out how to fix up the outside. Given a new and restored look, the cottage will no longer be of concern to the neighboring residents. And then we owe it to other critters like us who find themselves lost, lonely, and discouraged simply because they did not fit into the mainstream idea that to be the same is to be appreciated, not outcast. Seems, sadly, people and animals share this point of view. Maybe we can do something about this."

Scent, not used to talking quite so much, took a deep breath and sat down next to Luna. He knew he needed her support and then the other critters would then join in. First, though, he relied on Teacher, the elder to offer his words of wisdom at this point. He looked at Teacher, smiled and nodded.

Teacher, in a shaky voice, said, "I think this is a fine idea. I recall when we four first got together. You, Luna were ready to hiss and claw Scent, you long established natural enemy. He didn't look like you, smell like you, sound like you, or play like you. Luna, you are lovely whereas Scent is quite scruffy looking. Never takes care of his appearance or spends time grooming himself like you do. And he is noisy-barking, growling, grumbling. As the stealthy one, Luna, often we don't even know you are around. But you two found common ground. You both opened your hearts to welcome each other as new friends, despite your differences."

"Right on," Chatter chimed in. "And then Luna, you even let me be your friend, once you decided I was more than a small critter you should chase and possibly have for dinner. I know I annoy you with my wild energy and I appreciate that you tolerate this without complaint."

Luna was taken aback with Chatter's comments. She had not given this little chipmuck much credit for being insightful, open, and thoughtful. His accepting, non-critical personality put her to shame for a few moments. Hearing what he had to say, Luna would spend several hours considering her former behavior and opinion of him. That little guy may be tiny but certainly huge with his big, open heart towards others.

"Finally, Teacher, Tell us your story. What makes an old, weary, and pokey squirrel like you become a valued part of our Fearsome Foursome? Why did we take you in?"

"Good question, Scent. In fact, the reason I was out there alone until I met up with you was because I am old. I am weary and I am pokey. And not likely to change at my age. My kind didn't want me around. Thought I would be a handicap to our active squirrel family. Even my younger friends, with whom I spent a lot of time when I was able, thought I was of no worth. No one believed that this old guy with a broken-down body still had a sharp mind and years of wisdom to share with the younger generations. Scent, as your second in command so to speak, I am truly grateful to serve in any way that you and the others wish". His eyes welled up with tears. As did the others.

"Well then, how about this?" Scent continued. "Not only do we clean up this place but create a home for other homeless critters. Not a shelter but a permanent home where we each could feel wanted, valued, loved, and safe.

Chatter, the community run-about knew that the Forest Hills people were preparing their beautiful homes for the winter holiday season. He had seen many folks outdoors putting up lights on their trees, bushes and homes to honor the holiday spirit. Forest Hills Park with its magnificent display of lights welcomed any visitors who drove down the street to enjoy the sights and grace the holiday spirit. A nativity scene and a menorah were placed in the center gazebo. Children skated in the central pond. A silent audience of ducks enjoyed their antics and laughter.

"I have an idea too," Chatter announced surprising himself with his show of confidence. "Let's clean the cottage up and then divide the spaces to set aside places for various functions in our home for everyone. We could designate a small area for a nursery and day care center as many homeless critters will have their children with them. And an area for a kitchen so that anyone can eat without disturbing those who want to rest. A rest area, of course, is needed with warm but comfy blankets to lie on. The space wouldn't have to be large as some residents are night sleepers and others day sleepers. And finally, a common space for socializing, getting to know one another and developing new ideas for our great endeavor."

Truth be told, Papa liked this idea. He missed his evenings spent with other Papas while Mama remained in their den with Baby. And Mama enjoyed some quiet time alone after Baby went to sleep.

"Humph," said Papa, finding himself getting into the spirit of this plan. "Not only can we provide a warm and welcoming space for newcomers but with the winter holiday upon us, we need to decorate like the humans do who live here. We can call on the fireflies to lie on our windowsills and light up when dusk falls. This will light the way for travelers to find us for refuge. And those busy bees and spiders can create a wreath of holly leaves and red berries for our front door. The spiders could then spin a shimmering web around the wreath to further enhance its loveliness. The snow will provide sparkly glimmer around the outside. Finally, the deer family who bed down in the yard could stand upright as a gentle invitation to anyone who may wish to visit us during this holiday season. They can be our stand in for reindeer." Releasing a sigh of relief, Papa felt proud of his contribution. He was again a leader for his family and now a valued member of a small but mighty critter community.

***

In no time, word spread in the animal kingdom and many strays and lonely critters travelled to the abandoned cottage. First to arrive were the bunnies. Nible and curious, they enjoyed the overgrown garden they sensed was under the snow. There they could burrow as usual. Those older generations of bunnies could look forward to moving indoors when the weather became too hard on their frail bodies to remain outdoors. Those critters who ate anything and everything, the raccoons and fox, were given the assignment to gather whatever food they could each day on a rotating schedule beginning with the raccoons who were familiar with the best spots to forage food. Those who had special protection devices, stinkbugs and skunks were assigned to guard duty. Their job was to provide safety for the sick, weak or disabled at night so the others could rest. The inquisitive animals like the martens led weekly outings for the children and adults who wished to explore the many and varied city parks in the area. A wise old owl, with its vast knowledge and keen eyesight, kept watch over the cottage, ensuring greater safety for all who lived there.

Once the cottage was completed inside and the noises subsided, the homeowner repaired the outside to avoid its demolition. He made sure the windows and doors were secure but never looked inside. The critters were safe.

The abandoned cottage now housed each new arrival with their tales of hardship and survival, and offered them a newfound sense of belonging. This former relic was transformed into a vibrant home through the collective efforts of its inhabitants. Together they maintained harmony and order, fostering a community built on the enduring spirit of acceptance.

No one was turned away. Each found a place in the world that had seemed so unwelcoming. The Fearsome Foursome and the raccoon family basked in their success, enriched by each critter who chose the abandoned cottage as their forever home.

The mystery of the abandoned cottage had been solved, and the eerie sounds that had plagued the community were no longer a source of concern. The cottage became a place of curiosity and fascination, thanks to the bravery and determination of one small, quiet dog named Scent.

And so, the cottage remained a silent sentinel in the midst of the city, its secrets laid bare by a little dog with a big heart. The neighborhood returned to its peaceful slumber, knowing that sometimes, the most extraordinary discoveries come from the most unexpected places.

The End

Author's Note

In 1923 John D. Rockefeller, Jr envisioned an upscale residential and commercial development area featuring the distinctive French Norman style of architecture to be located on the near east side of Cleveland. Initially 81 homes were constructed in the lovely Forest Hills area. Forestry land was preserved for parks and recreation areas.

Today the Forest Hills Preservation Society is dedicated to educating, sharing, and preserving the historic integrity of the Rockefeller legacy. (See City of Cleveland Heights, Rockefeller's Forest Hill district)

The Abandoned Cottage is representative of this unique community.

About Judy Cicero...

Judy Cicero, Ph.D. writes from the point of view of whimsey. Don't be fooled however as her stories contain real relational issues and blessings.

She is a retired clinical social worker and university professor whose love of people and desire to understand them are explored throughout her fiction.

Currently she has four children's books and two adult novels available. More in the works …

www.judycicerobooks.com

Sleigh Watch

by

R.W. Schultz

On Christmas Eve, Sector Antler's elves—gruff Frost, earnest Everett, and flamboyant Jangle—scramble to perfect Santa's route.

Frost clings to eighty-five years of tradition, but Everett's push for a softer touch drags the unruly Millers into the mix. With a mischievous cat, a house of chaos, and time ticking down, one wrong move could unravel the night. A whirlwind of elf grit, holiday hijinks, and cocoa-fueled clashes—will Sector Antler's crew keep Christmas on track?

Wooster - December 24th

They sat at the intersection of Cedar and Lemar, watched the snow softly covering the inflatable snowman in the Gilmore's front yard. The irony made Frost chuckle quietly. His pointed ears peeked out from under a snug green cap that was always too tight because of his wildly curly chestnut hair—an appearance many would say didn't suit his personality.

Despite his rough exterior, he genuinely enjoyed this time of year. He often reminisced about the past when children could simply be children without bearing the weight of the world's issues. He recalled a time when a house was adorned with just a few lights in the windows and a wreath on the door, while the real spirit resided in the hearts of those living within.

Lights were still on in two of the four-bedroom windows. Frost knew the Gilmores were night owls, but at this rate the team may need to intervene.

"What's so funny?" Everett asked, followed by a sip of hot chocolate overflowing with marshmallows. Everett donned a bright red sweater instead of the standard tactical green. His blue eyes and elongated nose projected an air of naivety that irritated Frost the instant they met.

"Oh, it just seems funny to me how these people have been decorating these years."

"You know, I kind of like it, it's like there are more ways for everyone to express their spirit."

"I thought you came from records, not interior decorating." Frost took a sip of his own hot chocolate, sweetened with alternative chestnut sugar. Another bedroom light went out at the Gilmore's.

"So, have you heard Nick is looking to retire?" Everett did his best to seem like one of the boys.

"I have, but you and I both know it's not that simple. Rules are rules after all." Frost continued to scan the Gilmore's house. "Besides, this job is great. You really only have to work one night a year. I know I'll never give it up."

"I suppose." Everett took another long sip of hot coco. "But Frosty, you got to admit, this one night is a lot, it's too much for any conductor, let alone of the famous Sector Antler NO7W72. Besides, admin has been wanting to add a softer touch to the operation."

Frost twitched at the sound of his least favorite nickname. "Yeah, well just don't get too many ideas here. I've been doing this for eighty-five years, forty-one of which as a sweeper. And I tell you what, things look a lot different inside the house as opposed to those snow globes you peepers look through."

"We're 'observing', thank you very much." Everett caught a falling marshmallow and threw it in his mouth. "I will admit though, it has been fascinating seeing the houses in real life. They almost don't seem real when you just watch from afar, like it's a TV show or something. Speaking of which, the Scotts live close by, right? They are one of my favorite families."

"Yeah, the Scotts live two houses down the street. They have a new dog this year. That should be fun. The Patterson's next door here have all aged out. Thank goodness, that house had so many decorations, it was a minefield getting around. The Millers down the ways have gone three years now passed up. They've got three eligibles too. I've hardly seen that many passed up for so long."

"Yeah, that's just really sad. I mean, those kids had gone through so much the past year. This is stuff we've never seen before Frosty." He adjusted the mirror on the van as a lady walked her dog down the snow-covered sidewalk. "The stress they are facing from everyone, it's unreal."

"I wouldn't disagree. Times have changed quite a bit, but it's not for us..." Frost squinted at the elf. "Wait a jingle, the Millers were the only ones that didn't make the nice list that were on your watch, weren't they?"

Some of Everett's marshmallows fell out, which he didn't even notice. "There is nothing wrong with Observers forming an attachment to their assigned children. They are actually encouraging it now."

"Well, they had their chance, they all do. The circumstances are different for each kid, but we can't just give every kid a present. Where's the incentive to be good?

"Plus, I know they aren't showing you everything on those globes. I was on that floor once and..." Everett opened his mouth, but a thought struck Frost. "Say, weren't you on that Tinsel Tribunal that decided that our snow globes would not have access to their internet history?"

"I... look... it's a privacy violation!" Everett flung is mug around, spilling even more marshmallows.

"'We see you when you're sleeping, we know when you're awake'! This whole operation is a privacy violation."

The final light went off in the house.

"Hey boss, the sugar plum fairy's finally hit. We need to move." Their radio crackled.

Frost turned in his seat and paused with his hand on the door. "Please don't let your guilt over the Millers influence the operation. It's complicated enough as it is. Just leave it for our Yuletide Review or tell it to the reindeer or something. We've had this Santa for a long time now, and I don't want to lose him tonight."

Everett, about to say something again, was cut off by Frost opening the door leading into the back of the van.

Red and green lights enveloped the two terminals with elves staring into the monitors. Their hands flew over the keyboard, only to pause to deftly reach for their hot chocolate, which they slurped with no reservation.

A dedicated screen on the wall displayed Santa's current location, showing he was about halfway through Orrville. Above it was an antique phonograph with a golden sound horn. On the other side, a map highlighted the twenty-one houses they were in charge of, each one blinking cheerfully. It seemed like there were more homes on the approved list this year, and after speaking with Everett, he may have a good idea why.

"Report Sector Antler - Aurora, status house alpha." Frost stood behind the two sitting elves.

"The house is quiet. Livingroom cleared. No stockings, which is normal for the Gilmores. Only two cookies set out for Santa this year, and they are gluten free." The screen flashed up a live feed of the living room.

"Looks like we got an eggnog spill in front of the couch they didn't clean up very well. We are looking at a sixty-seven percent chance the big man steps in it."

Numbers populated around the suggested area on the screen.

"Where's Jangle?" Frost took another sip of his healthy hot chocolate which was hardly hot at all at this point.

"Our sweeper is ready to breach, sir." Garland, the other elf at the terminal, chimed in. He brought up a screen of Jangle on the porch disguised as a shepherd in their nativity scene.

"Alright, I want those cookies swapped. Santa can't be taking bathroom breaks the rest of the night." Aurora typed away at the board. "Hit the nog with a Merry Mist and head to the hallway ready with a charmer. I know their youngest, Cory, tends to get up in the middle of the night."

"Um, sir Frost, North Pole Accord article 78-HO3 revised this year prohibits direct intervention with any resident of the household."

Frost and the two elves turned to stare at Everett, who had procured a massive book seemingly out of nowhere.

"That's right, Everett." Frost bobbed his head to hide his annoyance. "That was in the briefing. Tell Jangle to get the SleighBell Thrower instead. You at least get more than one shot with the bells."

Aurora updated Jangle, who had been checking the sugar plum in his Charmer blaster under his shepherd's cloak, only to look up at the camera with an expression of 'come on!'

"Make it ginger snappy Antler. We got a block of twenty-one houses here in Wooster, and we are first hit coming from Orrville."

On the monitor, the shepherd's cloak fell to the ground, and in the adjacent monitor, Jangle's tiny frame pranced into view. He held a spray bottle in one hand, cookies in another, and the launcher strapped to his back. With a perfect pirouette he landed in front of the cookies, swapped them, spun three times around, and sprayed the mister. Frost could have sworn he heard the humming of Tchaikovsky's famous score coming through the monitor too.

"Is this... normal?" Everett found himself at the terminal with them like a dog staring at fresh baked cookies. His eyebrows were raised in surprise.

A muscle twitched beside Frost's eye. "Yes Everett. Jangle was taken from the theatrics department for this job."

"Yeah, after he managed to play both the Nutcracker and the Rat King simultaneously." Garland said, a candy cane bobbing in the corner of his mouth. "Frost, wasn't he technically the stage manager for that performance? I think he still pulled that off too."

Everett pursed his lips. "Impressive, if not a bit excessive—"

"Despite the flourishes, Jangle is the fastest elf on the Northeast quadrant. That's why they put him with Evergreen, our other sweeper." Frost managed to roll his eyes, without actually rolling his eyes.

"I still don't think he was as ever good as you Frost." Garland, who happened to be his old comms partner, gave him a knowing smile.

"I don't know about that." Frost watched Jangle's face in pure bliss as he fluffed the couch cushions just for good measure. "We definitely had different ways of getting the job done."

An alert chimed on the monitor.

"Jangle, you got movement from 2C." Aurora proclaimed.

Jangle jerked his head to the side, perfectly frozen despite just landing an arabesque. His ears twitched and he slowly lifted his SleighBell thrower as if in a James Bond movie.

On another monitor, a bedroom door opened, and a seven-year-old boy came out. Jangle remained perfectly still, but somehow managed to point the thrower towards the hallway.

"Looks like a bathroom break Jangle. You should be all clear. Let's skip the second act and move on to the curtain call." She switched her monitor view. "Agent Garland, how is Evergreen looking for house beta?"

Everett laughed and kept talking to Frost, despite what he felt like a decent attempt to try to give him the cold shoulder.

"Well, I was entertained." Everett shrugged, pulling Frost away from their termial. "Frost, I wanted to mention something while we were talking earlier." He hesitated, and Frost knew what was coming. "Just hear me out. I think we should put the Millers on the list. I know! It's last minute."

Frost shut his eyes, resembling someone who had just been spit up on by a baby during a photo session with Santa at the mall.

"We've done it before. You remember 2020, everything was changing so quickly with what was right and wrong. Since then, Santa always carries extra presents when things change on the fly."

Frost squinted. "Is that what this is all about? You came to sneak some presents under the Miller's tree because you feel guilty."

The accusation shot through the van like the sling shots they make back at the pole.

Everett's pointy ears drooped down. "I don't care about the presents. It's about making kids feel included. And why are you so determined to stop kids from getting presents anyway?"

"That's not for me to determine." Frost barked.

"That's right, it's for me and my department, isn't it?"

"No, you and your department report on what you see, and it's up to Red and the List Authorities to make the decision. And they determined that the Millers did not make the cut. Do you know why they didn't? If anyone should, it's you."

Everett lost any twinkle in his eye, any signature glow that an elf would have the night before Christmas. "They had a rough year, okay."

Frost pulled a tablet off the shelf. "Olivia Miller - started a fire in the chemistry lab, burning Alissa Upton's hair and proceeded to blame it on her ADHD. Braxton Miller - four cases of jump scaring his family members, including their great grandma Miller who just got a pacemaker installed. Harper Miller - spent three hours on Chat GPT coming up with a personalized insult for each one of her classmates. That house has the n-list written all over it."

That drained any further argument from Everett. It was as if someone left the van door open with how cold it felt in there. The elves had stopped typing and the only motion in the van was from the screen where Jangle was spinning in circles in the living room.

"Wait, what about the Jubilee Amendment?" Agent Garland pulled the candy cane out of his mouth, which had been in danger of falling out.

"That's right!" Everett inflated like one of those snowmen out on the yard. He whipped his book back up that he had just barely been holding onto at his side. "Jubilee gives sectors the option of adding one house to the list the night of deliveries. This could be the Millers." He found the amendment in his book and pointed at it so hard that glitter fell on the page.

Frost exhaled and made sure to shoot Garland a dirty look before taking Everett's book. "This says we will need to get approval from the following sector and the regional director. That is, of course, if I even agree to add them to our list. It ultimately comes down to me."

"I... Frost, sir. If we could do this, I will personally help prepare the house. My report will be nothing but glowing. The Pole board is looking to promote -"

"Garland, get Sector Blitzen on the horn. We would need to add at least three minutes to our lotted time. That's not nothing. Is the Big Guy cruising or playing catch-up?"

"Looks like a thirty-six second surplus sir." Aurora clicked away at the terminal.

Great, Frost thought. There's still a chance Blitzen won't bite.

"Let me talk to Blitzen, but I doubt they'll go for it."

"Thank you, Frost. I just feel like everyone-"

Frost spun around from the terminal he had been examining and came within an inch of Everett's long nose. "I know we have ideas in our mind of what Christmas means, but tonight is not a night of fuzzy feeling for us. This is an operation of seconds, not presents. And if any one of these dominos fall out of place, the operation is compromised and the single greatest undertaking on earth unravels like a teddy bear made in China. That's what Christmas means to me. So don't make me regret this decision, Everett."

Shock painted over Everett's face like a toy doll, but then he furred his brow and cocked his head slightly. "Okay, Frost, but do this for me. Try not to forget, were Santa's Elves, not the IRS."

"We got Blitzen on the horn Frost."

Frost stare lingered for one second longer before joining Aurora.

"Is that you, Holly, my favorite sector neighbor?" Frost put on a headset and adopted a much cheerier tone than a second ago.

"Without question Frost." Holly's face appeared on the monitor, framed by her silver hair and sharp features. Frost always admired her professionalism, but her blue eyes always seemed to sparkle a bit when talking to Frost. "I heard you folks at Sector Antler are looking to make things interesting tonight. I haven't seen the Jubilee since 2021, and I wasn't expecting it to come from you."

Frost smirked, though whether in amusement or irritation was anyone's guess. "We got someone on our end that's heart just grew three sizes. Just be glad you didn't get a shadow this year. Anyways, we would need three minutes. I told him it wasn't likely knowing that—"

"Oh no! The houses on our block look nice and jolly. I think we can certainly arrange it."

Her eyes smiled at Frost, and the smallest knot formed somewhere in his gut. "Oh, well that's good. But there's regional yet. This doesn't happen often, and I know they don't like snags in their stockings."

"I bet they'd go for it this year. I haven't heard of many bobbles so far, except for that sweeper that mistook espresso for hot chocolate in Italy."

Holly opened her mouth and then paused. "Like I said, I wasn't expecting this. I... think it's awfully sweet of you."

The knot grew into a chestnut.

"Yeah, well..." Frost noticed Everett flashing him a goofy, supportive grin from the side.

Frost tucked a few stray curls behind his ear. "We'll see how it goes. Thanks, Holly."

He switched off the monitor. "Submit a request to Regional," he instructed Aurora. She watched him with a knowing smile, clearly entertained by the situation. "Yes, sir," she replied enthusiastically as she typed. "You know, they say most relationships begin around the holidays—"

"Enough! We... We need to concentrate here," Frost replied, disliking the slight tremor in his voice. "Garland, status report on Red." Frost stared at the progress board on the wall.

"Red's got four more sectors in Orrville and it looks like thirty-eight houses in the rural. Still ahead, but at thirty-one seconds."

"Sir, Regional approved."

Frost closed his eyes, the light from the screen still bleeding through. "Add the Miller's to the list."

"Yes sir."

Frost opened his eyes to see a light blink on the sector map, now up to twenty-two houses. One more frostbitten house to take care of.

Frost downed his healthy, ice-cold hot chocolate. He had an idea and flicked a switch on the board. "Antler, we're now at 'candy cane go.'"

A record revved to life like Frankenstein's monster rising from the grave. The haunting rhythm of "Carol of the Bells" by the renowned Trans-Siberian Orchestra reverberated through the confined van.

"Let's run Rudolph."

"Sir, initiating 'candy cane go.'" Aurora flipped her own switch, causing the red and green lights to flash throughout the van, almost syncing with the music. "Sweepers, we got to make up three minutes with an advantage of thirty-one seconds. That's two and a half minutes, but I want you to move like it's four."

Frost turned the music down a bit as the electric guitar swelled. "Status report."

"Jangle is at charlie and Evergreen is wrapping up beta." Garland pulled up an updated map of their block. "Judging by the map, we fit the Millers into house kilo."

"Good. I'm going to need you to light the yule log under Evergreen. Jangle can only do so much to cover his slack."

Everett had been looking through some new book on his own and now reached to the mic on the terminal.

"What are you doing?" Frost blocked his hand from the mic.

"I was going to contact the sleigh elves to update them on what was on the Miller's Christmas list."

"Oh no, they're getting whatever extra presents Santa's got in his bag. Besides, it's not the presents, it's the feeling of 'being included' remember?"

Everett's scowl resembled the Grinch. "Fine, I will make sure our sweepers are encouraged and not too stressed out by all this excitement." He reached for a headset, which Frost covered with a tactical jumpsuit.

"You are going to put this over that ridiculous red sweater and gear up. If you like the Millers so much, it's time we pay them a visit."

The music took its dark undertone with the bass as he said this.

Perfect timing. Frost thought.

"Wh-what?" He froze there, his hand like a hanger for the jumpsuit. "I am not trained or know the first thing—"

"You said you would personally help. Well, that's what this is." Frost grabbed gear from the closet. "My policy is whoever has a fruitcake of an idea, gets to see it through."

The music hit its stride as they suited up. Good montage set timing.

Frost placed what looked like a peppermint swirl on his neck. "Put this below your chin. It's a Muffler. I'm going to need to communicate with the team without waking up the whole house."

Everett grabbed the Muffler with one of his legs halfway through the jumpsuit and almost fell on his face.

"Frost, are you sure this is a good idea?" Aurora glanced over while trying to keep an eye on the monitors.

"We'll be in constant communications." Frost slung a thrower over his shoulder. "It will be like old times, right?"

Aurora did not send a look of confidence, but Garland's face was lit up with enthusiasm. "Oh, I can send some comms your way. Just ask anything when over there."

"I knew you'd have my back, Garland. Mostly keep an eye on the other sweepers though. Oh, and tell Jangle that every thirty seconds he makes up, the more of his musicals we'll come to see this year."

Frost gave Everett a vest and slid back a panel on the van floor.

"Are you...? Wait, how are we getting to the house?" Everett fastened the clips onto the wrong inserts of his vest.

Frost twisted the handle of a hatch and pulled open a door on the van floor. The crisp cold air sent a shiver down all the elves' spines. They both leaned down to see a manhole cover below them. The music revved back up with violins, bracing for the adventure.

"Oh no, elves were not meant to... I can just walk." Everett backed away.

Frost held a sleigh bell in his hand. He shook it, and it gave off a golden glow. "It is not too late to call this off Everett. You jump first."

Everett exhaled. "Fine. Just… don't be so pushy. I have a mildew allergy."

Right before Everett jumped, Frost tossed the sleigh bell at the manhole, turning it golden. The electric guitar squealed its climactic finish and Frost jumped. A flash of silver filled the van as each elf fell through, exiting at the perfect climax of the song, like it was straight out of a movie. Frost's heart swelled with excitement as they teleported through the sewer system. Maybe this wasn't such a bad idea after all, but he would never tell Everett that.

***

The two Elves popped up onto the snow-covered street.

"Oh, gosh it's cold out here." Everett sprung up off the ground and wiped the snow off his new jumpsuit.

"Just be glad we're not in the sewer. The Bellhatch Express was only invented in the past thirty years." Frost scanned the streets, which were completely still besides the snow that peacefully fell all around them. "Let's more."

The Miller's house stood before them, a grand structure of brick and stone that seemed to dwarf everything around it. The large arched windows gave off an air of arrogance, like eyes looking down on the other houses on the block. Frost likely imagined this, as he still believed these kids didn't truly deserve what they were doing here.

They snuck up to the house and over the snow shovel someone left in the driveway. Their tiny feet barely leaving a trace in the snow. Carol of the Bells played through his head, Frost matching the tempo of the song with his steps.

"Where are we going?" Everett held his arms close as they moved.

"Just over here."

They rounded to the side of the house where the HVAC system sat before them.

"This is the NorthWind Precision Climate Network," Frost set his hand on the unit like he frequented the place. "Top of the line, and our ticket inside."

He nodded over to the external duct sticking out of the house.

"Oh okay, you got one of those bells to throw at it?" Everett's teeth chattered.

"Ha! Using magic to break into people's houses sounds like an invasion of privacy, don't you think? But no, the tech isn't there yet, so..."

Frost pulled out a red and white striped tool, held it to the corners and the vent popped off.

"Wait, can we even fit in there?" Everett asked.

"If you get stuck, I'll push." Frost nudged him forward. "Besides, this is what makes the house warm."

"Okay," Everett inched forward, "Did I mention that I have a dust allergy too?"

The two elves crawled through the vent, their arms and legs scooting forward at what felt like a snail's pace.

"Sector Antler, progress report." Frost touched the peppermint on his neck.

"Things are looking good here sir," Aurora said. " Jangle is already at India, the house not the country in case you... Anyways, you should have seen the move he pulled on that Doberman. It looked more like a poodle with Jangle's handspring door close combo. I haven't seen that one before."

"Good to hear. Garland, what's the status on Red?"

"Wrapping up Orrville. Only a twelve second lead though."

"Crumbs and frosting! What the halls happened over there?"

"Sir, it sounds like a kid was flying his drone at night and spooked Donner. He is still recovering from the petting zoo incident at the Window WonderLand. I told them he should've had a stand in after what that pre-teen did to him!"

Ahead of him, Everett froze.

"What are you doing?" Frost nudged his pointy green shoe.

"I think... I... it's, the..." Everett said in-between breaths. "Ahhew!"

Everett's sneeze sounded like a mouse in a snowbank. "Dander."

He remained frozen and eventually looked back to Frost with a nervous glance.

"It's fine. Remember that muffler I gave you? It will keep your voice concealed. But it won't conceal your movement, remember that. Now move it, this is not my favorite view back here."

They made it to the vent and Everett peered out. "Okay, I know that Olivia likes to sneak out at night sometimes and play the Switch." He gave a sheepish smile. "Not for too long I'd say, but—"

Frost pointed his peppermint driver and opened the grate.

"She won't be up, kids are hardly ever up on Christmas Eve. They are far too eager for the next day."

Frost caught the grate and brought it into the vent.

"Right, good call. And to think, they would be eager for nothing if we didn't put them on the list."

Frost's eyebrow disappeared into his curly hair. "You sure about that?"

They dropped down from the vent and the first thing they saw was a huge Christmas tree loaded with presents underneath. Presents of all shapes and sizes were crammed under the tree so tight, there was little room for anything Santa would bring.

One bright red box was so large that it would have been likely that one of the kids was getting a new playhouse for Christmas. It faced the fireplace and appeared to be the victim of a peeker with a hole roughly cut in the side.

Frost openly rolled his eyes at this. "You still think these kids need the Pole's presents, let alone all this extra stress for us tonight?"

Everett stared at the haul, apparently enough to make one of Santa's elves blush.

"Don't just stand there. You're on clean up duty." Frost pulled a wand from his belt and extended it into a grabber. He gave it a quick test and tossed it towards Everett.

Upon second glance around the living room, the place resembled the main prep floor in the North Pole the day after Christmas Eve. There were clothes everywhere, socks spilling out from under the couch and shoes lay strewn across the carpet. Stockings, hung with care, dangled half-empty, raided early by careless hands. A pristine gingerbread house—freshly piped by Mom no doubt—sat mangled, chunks bitten out and crumbs dusted the couch. What looked like a white scarf lay on one of the armchairs, but Frost knew it wasn't a scarf.

"What the world? How is this place such a mess?" Everett's tiny head cocked to the side.

"My theory has to do with the fact they are on the naughty list. Classic case of spoiled kids." Frost turned to him with a sudden revelation. "Shouldn't you already know all this as their observer?"

"Maybe, but I also see things like this." Everett handed an opened letter from the end table to Frost and started picking up socks with the grabber.

Frost read the letter.

Dear Santa, all I want this year is for my dad to return from service safely so we can enjoy Christmas together again. - Olivia Miller

He noticed small water marks on the bottom of the page.

Frost groaned to himself.

"Frost, come in. I got you one a private channel." Aurora came in through his earpiece.

"Yeah, I'm here." Frost returned the letter, stuffed down the feels, and flipped a spray bottle out and sprung into sweeper mode.

"Frost, why did you head into a house with the shadow? You know that he's only going to slow us down."

"I know, but he needs a reality check." Frost sprayed the floor with a flick of his wrist and patched up the stocking with a stitching gun he pulled from his belt. "He may be giving me one though."

"What do you mean?" Aurora asked.

"I'll tell you after. I'm guessing Jangle is wrapping up lima at this point."

Everett held a pair of socks out with the grabber as if it were reindeer droppings. Frost snatched a shoe up right before Everett would have tripped over it.

"Yeah, he is. I've never seen him move this fast. It's like he's been holding back this whole time. At this rate we should be fine tonight."

"Yeah, okay, just don't let him get sloppy. We can't miss anything just because we are in a hurry."

Everett had spent this whole time putting six socks and a pair of crumpled shorts into a basket. "Okay, think we're nearly done," he muttered, eyes sweeping the room. They landed on a fluffy scarf draped over the couch. "Might as well grab that."

Frost's grin widened, a Grinch-ish smile. "Garland, stand by for bedroom checks."

"Roger, you sensing some—" Garland crackled back.

Everett snatched the scarf with the grabber, and it erupted. A white cat—buried in its woolly cocoon—exploded upward, hissing like a popped champagne cork. Its fur puffed, eyes wild, tail a bristled whip.

"What—no! I thought—" Everett yelped, stumbling back. The cat swiped, claws flashing, and Everett bolted—classic rookie mistake. The chase was on, a slapstick ballet: Everett skidded around the coffee table, the cat vaulting over gingerbread rubble.

Frost gave a couple of sprays with the merry mist, now with a smirk plastered on his face. "How's it looking, Garland?"

"All... clear. No moment around the bedrooms" Garland voice was a mix of concern and amusement. "Remember your first cat encounter Frost?"

"That I do." Frost tidied up any loose candies and toys under the stockings. Everett squealed past him with his arms flailing, almost kicking the giant red present. Frost froze for a second as he thought he saw the box jump slightly. It may have been his imagination, or maybe it was a puppy for Christmas this year and those were air holes on the side.

"Everett is doing pretty well actually." Garland said. "Pretty nimble for a peeper."

Everett reeled around the corner of the couch, cutting off Frost's train of thought. "I sure hope this muffler works," Frost! "Also, how about some help here!"

He ducked under the coffee table right as the cat pounced from atop of the couch. She caught his pointy hat and proceeded to chomp on it like she just caught a mouse.

Frost slung his Charmer Blaster off his shoulder, aimed, and fired—a sugar plum rocketed out, nailing the cat square between its green eyes. Red and white glitter burst like a peppermint firework, swirling in the air as the cat's pupils spun, cross-eyed and baffled. The sparkles fizzled out, and the beast flopped sideways onto Everett's hat, snoring with a wheezy purr.

"Oh, I'm sorry," Frost stashed the empty blaster. "That was in violation of article 'snow-brained' or something?"

"What the kringle did you wait for?" Everett crawled from under the table.

"I was busy doing my job. No time for playing with cats."

Everett sized up the sleeping cat, wonder how to get his hat back. "Is this cat going to wake if—"

"Should be asleep for twenty-five minutes. Just don't step on her tail or something."

Everett yanked his hat out and put it atop his head all crooked. Frost dragged the cat behind the armchair.

"Alright, we got to go." Frost loaded up his tools, including the grabber Everett abandoned, and took one last glance over to that present. Something gave him a funny feeling about it the more he looked at it.

"Thank baby Jesus." Everett fussed with his hat, trying to make it straight.

The two of them slipped out the side door this time, locking it as they left and pranced their way back to the sewers.

***

"How is it looking Antler?" Frost asked the second he popped up into the van.

"Good so far. Evergreen almost tripped an alarm at tango, but he recovered well. Jangle is wrapping up victor. Just one more after that." Aurora said.

"Excellent, where is Red?"

"Cruising through rural Orville. Still only at a thirteen second lead though. ETA at alpha is ten minutes." Garland flipped a switch, bringing up a large countdown clock above the monitors.

"Alright take us out of Candy Cane Go. Code accomplished, well done everyone." Frost clapped the shoulders of his coms team.

"Thank you, sir." Aurora flipped a switch bringing the lights back to their original state.

"You see, everyone, that was a great lesson in perseverance, adaptation, and a dedication to including everyone on Christmas." Everett struggled with the clips to remove his vest. "And Frost, isn't it good to see a more personal side of the kid's story? I know they propose... challenges, but there is so much more going on in their lives then what you see on Christmas eve."

"Yeah, well..." The thought of that letter flashed in Frost's mind. "I'll be the first to raise a coco once the big guy is through."

"Prepare to enter into Silent Night. Let Evergreen wrap up whisky, I want Jangle in position here at alpha. I want him in rotation at the Miller's too."

ETA clock read eight twenty-one.

"Yes sir." Aurora typed away. "Oh, and nice shooting out there. You still got it, sir."

"What about me?" Everett finally got his vest off and went back to trying to fix his hat. "I took the brunt of the feline assailant. And I'm starting to wonder if you knew that scarf was actually a cat the whole time 'Mr. Veteran Sweeper'".

"I'm sorry, are you complaining about one of the biggest favors I've ever done for someone, and putting this whole operation at risk? And mind you, it's still not over, like I said."

"No, I just." Everett gave a look suggesting he just can't win. "Well, what is there even to do now? Just watch Santa go through all the houses? It should be smooth as fresh ice with all that prep work we did."

ETA clock read six ten.

"This is exactly when things go wrong. We've been trying to convince Red to let the sector sweeper go with him in the houses where he needs it the most, but no luck. He doesn't like the image. We have to stay on him like frost on a windowpane, leap frogging from house to house in case something happens."

"I'm willing to bet it would happen down at the Millers too. I should have shoved that cat in a closet or something just in case she wakes up. Something just doesn't feel right in there."

"Sir, Jangle is ready to take position." Aurora announced.

"Good." Frost eyed the clock. Three forty-five

Frost got his annual jolt of adrenaline. He never cared for sweets, but he imagined this is what a sugar rush felt like. Even after eighty-five years, it never failed.

"Does Jangle still have his charmer loaded?"

"Yes sir, just the one shot."

"Good"

On the monitors, they watched Jangle take position, nestled in the bend of a downspout instead of their nativity scene this time. He climbed with such grace and intentionality, you could almost hear his heart thumping.

One minute.

"Entering into Silent Night protocol." Aurora pulled down a level, which soften the whirs and screens that one wouldn't have been able to tell was there until now. The lights stayed on a dim red, just enough to see the perspiration forming on Garland's brow.

Thirty seconds.

"You better watch out, you better not cry." Garland started singing in a slow, dry voice.

"Nope, not this year." Frost remained laser focused on the monitors.

Then, from outside the van, if you listen just carefully enough, you could hear it. The faintest sound of sleigh bells dancing in the air. The apprehension lifted out of the van to be replaced with pure joy. The elves looked at each other, crying laughter in their eyes. This was what they were looking for each year, what made it so good to be an elf.

Aurora brought up the wide cam to spot a sled and nine reindeer landed on the roof like a snowflake on a mitten.

"Red has landed." Aurora reported, a slight tug in her voice. "Switching to internal camera."

The monitors showed the most peaceful living room, something out of a postcard. The tree had a few modest presents under it, but it was begging to be filled by the man of the hour.

Without a moment's notice, black shiny boots appeared inside the fireplace. Jangle watched in reverent stillness as Santa worked his magic. Presents, wrapped in shimmering red and gold tickled the crisp green lower branches of the tree. Six presents, filled with wonders from the north pole was the final touch to the living room that brought it all together. He paused only for a second to wiggle his fingers over the plate of cookies and sneak one of them for a quick snack.

"Evergreen, are we all set for beta?" Aurora broke the silence, and the trance they all seemed to find themself in.

"Yes ma'am." On a side monitor, Evergreen could be seen hiding with in house beta's vent.

"Good, stay sharp Antler. Red is going to move fast. Don't let the magic distract you."

"Right, thank you Aurora." Frost shook himself out of it. "Keep it tight, be proactive. I want all teams to keep their eyes as sharp as a candy cane after an hour of licking."

"Yes sir!"

Frost turned to Everett who hadn't replayed to his command.

"I've never seen him in action before." Tears welled in Everett's eyes. "Truly a beautiful sight. I love being an elf." He looked at Frost, those dumb blue eyes swimming in a pond. "Can we meet him at one of the houses?"

"If you met him at a house, it would be under very different circumstances, one of which you would not be fond of."

The delivery continued, Santa popping in and out of chimes like a sprig of holly twirling in the winter wind. He was such a natural, and it always surprised Frost. When they do their job as Sleigh Watch, it is a majestic operation partnering with him.

House foxtrot presented their first obstacle.

"Target in sight." Jangle peered through the scope of his Charmer. The little blond girl with pig tales and blanket in tow wondered into the living room. "Give me the word."

"Hold your fire. Hold your fire!" Frost yelled. In the monitor, Santa spotted the little girl and turned to her with a huge smile. "The big man lives for these moments."

Santa handed this girl a teddy bear, which she hugged with delight.

"Awwww." The whole van melted.

"We haven't gotten a see an encounter in ages." Garland was practically hugging the monitor.

"Touching," Frost glanced over at the board. "He did just lose two minutes. We can't have any other delays, or I'll be hearing it from regional for sure."

The deliveries continued and the Miller's was on the dock next. A lump of coal fell into Frost's gut when the sleigh landed on the large roof. Maybe it was all in his head. Maybe he still was salty about caving to Everett's request and this house will be just like all the others.

"Jangle, how's it looking?" Aurora asked.

"All's quiet here." Jangle perched himself in the a-frame of the porch, his night vision goggles scanned the living room. "I have taken an aggressive posture."

"Come on guys, just because they were on the naughty list doesn't mean you need to paint them in the worst light possible." Everett threw his tiny arms in the air. "What could they possibly do at this point?"

And that's when it hit Frost. The box. The giant present was no present at all. And that movement was no puppy.

At that very moment, the boots appeared in the fireplace.

Frost went into full black Friday freak out.

"Jangle, it's the red present!" Frost clasped his headset and the back of the seat.

Santa stepped out of the fireplace and only had a second of taking in the scene before the giant present erupted. The lid flew open, and Braxton Miller leapt out with a loud "Gotcha!"

He swung a large net through the air and caught Santa Claus mid stride.

Santa yelped and flew backwards. He tried to catch himself, but with bag in hand, he ended up hitting the fireplace brick.

Jangle somehow had dove into the living room, and if he had been there a split second sooner, his sugarplum would have hit before Braxton got the net on him.

It still hit Braxton true, right on the back of his head. He crumpled onto the side of the box, fast asleep.

Jangle landed on all fours, his right foot landing on the large white tail of the cat. It sprung to life, and with Jangle's only sugarplum spent, he was forced to engage in hand-to-hand combat.

"Code red. I repeat, Santa is down. Dispatch medical team." Aurora flipped a plastic box and slammed a red button. An alarm sounded, throwing a red light around the van.

Frost turned to Everett and threw him the worst glare ever seen on an elf's face. Everett had nothing, a mixture of shock and horror etched his small features. His mouth open, blue eyes lost in what he just did.

"I'm going in." Frost grabbed a bell and Charmer and yanked the van floor open. He lit the manhole and jumped in. While in mid-air, he saw Everett look up with determination and moved to the manhole himself.

Great. He's coming to make things even worse.

Frost popped up in the street in front of the Miller's and hit the ground running. He heard another pair of feet land behind him. He knew it was Everett, but he didn't have time to address him. In the window, the silhouette of Jangle and the cat bounced around the living room. He ran up the porch and pepper mint sticked the lock.

"Frost, I got regional on the coms. They want to talk with you." Aurora chimed in his ear.

"I'm busy saving Christmas." Frost huffed. "Just send them the feed of the Miller's. They can watch this nightmare before Christmas unfold."

Frost barreled into the Miller's living room, Charmer loaded with the only sugar plum. The cat, a white blur, leaped from the coffee table, claws slashing like a cymbal crash. Jangle met it mid-air with a Nutcracker jeté, empty Charmer Blaster twirling like a soldier's rifle, landing next to the tree. He snatched a ribbon from the branches, cracking it like a whip in a crisp pirouette; the cat recoiled, then lunged resembling the Rat King. Jangle countered with a grand battement, kicking a throw pillow into its path—feathers stayed sealed, floor pristine.

Well jingle my bells. Frost recognized the exact same moves Jangle was pulling off from the Nutcracker.

His astonishment was brought short upon remembering Santa. He glanced over to the hearth. Braxton hung over the present's edge, snoring loudly. The red suit was limp, out cold.

I need to get to him.

Everett stumbled in from behind. "Frost—"

"Check on Red," Frost barked.

Without hesitation, Everett scurried over to Santa, still careful to avoid the cat.

Frost returned his attention to the fight. This needed to stop first.

"Antler, you got movement from bedroom A2." Garland called over the coms.

Yank my tinsel! Frost glanced to the creak of footsteps above him. We have a code red on our hands and now the whole operation is going to get unwrapped.

Upon hearing this, Jangle grabbed a clip off his belt, ducked another leap from the Rat King, and loaded his blaster with bells. He spun around just in time for the first foot to appear in the stairwell. He shot the bell towards the stairs. The most intoxicating jingle and twinkle followed the bell. The cat's eyes grew wide with desire. She took after it like Vixen getting his tail yanked by a three-year-old.

The bell bounced off the wall and up the stairs like a pinball machine. The cat jerked her head with every bounce, determined to catch her new prey.

"Snowball, what are you—" Mrs. Miller stopped before she could see the living room, now distracted by the cat running under her legs after the bell. "Get back here."

She ran off after the cat. Jangle and Frost looked at each other for a second.

"Sir, the med elves have arrived." Aurora said.

Frost ran over to Santa and Everett. Jangle moved to join him.

"I want you on guard." Frost said. "Take this."

He tossed his blaster over to him. Jangle caught it and nodded. Luckily, they could still hear Mrs. Miller chasing after the cat above them.

"I don't think he's... dead." Everett said when Frost joined them.

The net Braxton used lay to the side. Santa slumped against the Miller's hearth, red suit twisted, hat tipped over his brow. His chest lay still, a white-gloved hand still grasping his bag of presents.

Before he could answer, three medical elves popped out of the chimney.

They descended on Santa, their green scrubs crisp under the tree's glow.

"Stand back." The first, a wiry elf with a stethoscope, pressed it to Santa's chest, muttering, "Pulse steady, just rattled." The second, round-faced with a med kit, dabbed a peppermint salve on Santa's soot-streaked forehead, the sharp scent cutting the air. The third with a syringe of glittering fluid, jabbed it into Santa's arm—his fingers twitched, glove flexing.

The wiry one waved a sugar stick under Santa's nose; his eyelids fluttered. The round-faced elf propped his head with a stocking, coaxing, "Easy, big guy." A faint groan escaped as the dust kicked in—Santa blinked, bleary, bag still clutched, coming around slow but sure.

"I... don't know if I'll make it." Santa's voice was grim, almost foreign to his normal jolly demeanor. "This might be my time. I had a good run. Who will be replacing me?"

"Sir... you should be fine," one of the med elves said.

"Who did this?" Santa insisted. "Who is going to be the new Santa?"

"Braxton Miller, sir." Frost gestured over to the kid, still sleeping over the edge of the present.

"Braxton Miller!" Santa sat up with a jolt, not a trace of weakness. "How did we end up at the Miller's? They have been on the naughty list for years."

Frost cocked his head in surprise. "Sir, it was..." He glanced to Everett.

"It was my idea sir. I suggested the Jubilee rule." Everett rubbed the back of his head. "But, sir, are you really wanting someone to take your place? You are the best—"

"Well not like this. Do you know what would happen if this kid took my place? Christmas would be just a giant prank." Santa stood up. The med elves were taken aback, and half tried to stop him from getting up. "I'm fine, this isn't my first time getting knocked down. Although, I was hoping my last."

Frost didn't know what to say to this. He looked at his watch. "Sir, we are eight minutes behind. Also, this is an awake house. May I suggest we get on with the night?"

"Yes, yes. Let's get on with it." Santa grabbed his bag and turned to leave. "I think it's safe to say this house will be put back on the naughty list. What would you say Everett?"

Everett looked as if he just took a large bite of black licorice. "Yes... yeah. I just thought... Well, I suppose I got carried away."

Santa looked at him with sharp beady eyes. "I'd say. How about you join me the rest of the night? I need someone to clean up any messes the reindeer make on the roof."

"Yes, sir."

"Oh, and Frost, regional has my earpiece going off like a broken kazoo. You're going to want to talk with them. Good luck explaining this at the Yule Tide Review."

"Yes, sir."

Jangle came into the living room backwards, blaster aimed and ready. He twirled his finger in the air and pointed at the stairs. Creaks sounded to that direction.

The seven of them stepped into the chimney and disappeared right as Mrs. Miller glanced into the living room.

"Huh, could have sworn..." She said, coming around the landing. "Braxton! Honey what happened?"

She jogged up to him and knelt down.

Braxton groaned. "I..."

"Yes honey, what is it?" She felt his forehead.

"I... I was this close to becoming Santa. That's the rules. That's what an elf told me."

"Braxton, what on earth? You must have been dreaming."

A thumping came from the chimney, and three large pieces of coal came tumbling out, landing right in front of them.

Frosty's Christmas Cocoa

Serving Size: 1 cup
Servings: 1 - 2
Approximate Calories: 120

Ingredients:
- 2 cups milk (whole or 2%)
- 2 tablespoons unsweetened cocoa powder
- 2 tablespoons granulated sugar
- 1/4 cup semi-sweet chocolate chips
- pinch of salt
- 1/2 teaspoon vanilla extract
- 1/2 cup mini marshmallows.
- marshmallow fluff for garnish

Extra Toppings - Optional
- crushed candy canes
- Red and green sugar sprinkles

Instructions:
1. In a medium saucepan, whisk together the cocoa powder, sugar, and salt.

2. Gradually pour in the milk while whisking to ensure a smooth mixture.

3. Gradually Place the saucepan over medium heat. Stir continuously until the mixture is hot but not boiling.

4. Add the semi-sweet chocolate chips to the hot mixture. Continue stirring until the chocolate has completely melted and the mixture is smooth.

5. Remove the saucepan from heat and stir in the vanilla extract.

6. Pour the hot cocoa into mugs. Top each serving with marshmallow fluff and, if desired, sprinkle crushed candy canes or red and green sprinkles on top for a festive touch.

7. Serve with Christmas cookies.

Nutritional Value:

Based on a 2000 calorie diet		
Total Fat:	9	g
Saturated Fat:	5	g
Cholesterol:	29	mg
Carbohydrates:	53	g
Sugar:	44	g
Sodium:	94	mg
Fiber:	4	g
Protein:	10	g

About R.W. Schultz...

R. W. Schultz is a videographer and photographer living in Holmes and Wayne County, Ohio, for the past 12 years.

Married with a two-year-old son and another child on the way, he balances family life with a passion for storytelling.

A sci-fi novel 15 years in the making simmers alongside his love for game design and baking. As a Young Life leader at West Holmes High School, he invests into kids' lives and as well as volunteers at the local teen center. One day, he'll finish that darn book.

For more information find him at

https://www.inkerspen.com/rw-shultz/

Notable Ohio Holiday Celebrations

Although the stories you'll read are filled with a touch of fiction, the places, events, and even some of the characters are as real as a fresh snowfall in Ohio! From charming small towns twinkling with holiday lights to grand winter festivals filled with laughter and cheer, these locations offer a true taste of the Buckeye State's seasonal magic. Whether you're ice skating in a historic village, sipping hot cocoa at a centuries-old holiday market, or watching a dazzling Christmas parade, Ohio's winter traditions are alive and well—just waiting for you to step into the festive spirit!

Ohio is brimming with traditional winter holiday events that attract tourists from near and far. Here are some cherished celebrations you might consider:

Christmas & Hanukkah Events in Ohio

Ohio Christmas Factory – Cincinnati
A massive 50,000-square-foot indoor venue with holiday shopping, activities, and entertainment.
📅 November – December | 🔗 ohiochristmasfactory.com

Eight Nights of Fun: Columbus Chanukah Festival – Columbus

A lively celebration featuring Chanukah music, food, and entertainment.

📅 December | 🔗 columbusjcc.org

Home for the Holidays – Orrville

Kick off the holiday season and spend the evening with family and friends in downtown Orrville enjoying the sights and sounds of the season. Ice sculptures

📅 November-December | 🔗 www.orrvilleareaunitedway.org

Menorah on Mayfield – Lyndhurst

A community menorah lighting event with festive music, traditional refreshments, and giveaways.

📅 December | 🔗 www.chabadofcleveland.com

Maltz Museum Chanukah Candle Lighting – Beachwood

A family-friendly event with traditional songs, storytelling, and a menorah lighting.

📅 December | 🔗 www.maltzmuseum.org

Israeli Hanukkah – Cincinnati

A vibrant celebration with music, games, and traditional Israeli Hanukkah treats.

📅 December | 🔗 jewishcincinnati.org

Places to Meet Santa & Holiday Shopping

Castle Noel – Medina

America's largest year-round Christmas entertainment attraction with holiday movie props, animated window displays, and Santa visits.

📅 Year-round | 🔗 castlenoel.com

Crocker Park – Westlake
A festive shopping destination featuring Santa's House for visits and a 50-foot Christmas tree.
📅 November – December | 🔗 crockerpark.com

Cabela's Santa's Wonderland – Avon
Free photos with Santa, holiday crafts, and festive games. Reservations recommended.
📅 November – December | 🔗 cabelas.com

Lock 3 Winter Fest – Akron
Features breakfast with Santa, ice skating, ice bumper cars, and admission to the Akron Children's Museum.
📅 November – January | 🔗 lock3live.com

Winter Wonderland - Santa Comes to town – Wooster
A charming event of lights, decorations, tree lighting, and voting on the best Christmas window display all while waiting for Santa's arrival downtown on Wooster's historical square. Starts Friday night after Thanksgiving.
📅 November – December | 🔗 www.mainstreetwooster.com

Christmas Towns & Light Displays

Steubenville Nutcracker Village – *Steubenville*
Features over 150 life-sized nutcrackers displayed throughout town.

📅 November – January |

🔗 steubenvillenutcrackervillage.com

Horse-Drawn Carriage Parade & Festival – *Lebanon*
A charming Christmas festival with horse-drawn carriage parades in a historic downtown setting.

📅 December | 🔗 lebanonchamber.org

Legendary Lights at Clifton Mill – *Clifton*
A dazzling display of millions of lights covering the historic mill and surrounding area.

📅 November – December | 🔗 cliftonmill.com

Historic Roscoe Village Candle Lighting Festival – *Coshocton*
A holiday celebration in a restored 19th-century canal town with Santa visits and mulled cider.

📅 December | 🔗 roscoevillage.com

Medina Christmas on the Square – *Medina*
A nationally recognized holiday destination with charming Christmas decorations and festive events.

📅 December | 🔗 mainstreetmedina.com

Dickens-Themed Christmas Events

Dickens Victorian Village — *Cambridge*
The town transforms into a Victorian-era holiday wonderland, featuring nearly 100 life-sized figures in period attire.
📅 November – December | 🔗 visitguernseycounty.com

Belmont County Victorian Mansion Museum — "A Christmas Carol" Theme — *Belmont*
A historic mansion decorated annually in a Victorian Christmas theme, often featuring "A Christmas Carol."
📅 November – December | 🔗 belmontcountymuseum.com

Christmas Concerts, Plays, and Live Nativities in Ohio

Plays & Theatrical Performances
A Christmas Carol — *Ohio Theatre, Columbus*
A beloved annual production of Charles Dickens' A Christmas Carol, bringing the holiday classic to life on stage.
📅 November –December |
🔗 AChristmasCaroAtOhioTheatre.com

Live Nativities

Englewood Christian Assembly of God Live Nativity — *Englewood, Ohio*
An interactive outdoor live nativity featuring live animals, including camels, cows, sheep, and a donkey, set amidst professionally crafted scenery.
📅 December Exact dates to be announced) |

 EnglewoodAGLiveNativity.com

Harmony Springs Christian Church Drive-Thru Live Nativity – Uniontown, Ohio

A drive-thru live nativity experience featuring live actors, animals, carolers, and complimentary hot cocoa and cookies.

 December | HarmonySpringsLiveNativity.com

Zion Lutheran Church Live Nativity – *Youngstown, Ohio*

An annual live nativity with multiple performances, followed by soup and sandwich servings after each show.

 December | ZionLutheranLiveNativity.com

Paul R. Young Funeral Home Wax Nativity – *Cincinnati and Hamilton, Ohio*

A life-sized wax nativity display, a tradition for over 70 years, featuring live donkeys and sheep, with live Christmas music and carriage rides during the unveiling event.

 December | PaulRYoungFuneralHomeNativity.com

Christmas Concerts

Capital University Christmas Festival – *Mees Hall, Capital University, Columbus*

An annual concert featuring various choirs and instrumentalists from Capital University, celebrating the holiday season through music.

 December | CapitalUniversityChristmasFestival.com

The Nutcracker Performances

Cleveland Ballet's "The Nutcracker" – *Connor Palace, Playhouse Square, Cleveland*
An enchanting adaptation of the traditional ballet, promising to inspire audiences of all ages.
📅 December | 🔗 CLEVELANDBALLET.com

BalletMet's "The Nutcracker" – *Ohio Theatre, Columbus*
A beloved holiday favorite, BalletMet brings the magic of The Nutcracker to life with captivating performances.
📅 December | 🔗 BALLETMET.com

Canton Ballet's "The Nutcracker" – *Canton Palace Theatre, Canton*
Canton Ballet presents this classic holiday ballet, enchanting audiences with its timeless story and choreography.
📅 December | 🔗 ARTSINSTARK.COM

Polar Express and Holiday Train Rides

The Polar Express™ Train Ride – Dennison Railroad Depot Museum – *Dennison*
Passengers are immersed in the magic of The Polar Express, enjoying hot chocolate, cookies, and a visit from Santa during the ride.
Ticket Sales: Tickets go on sale to museum members in April and to the public in August.
📅 December |
🔗 DENNISONRAILROADDEPOTMUSEUM.com

North Pole Express – Lebanon Mason and Monroe Railroad – *Lebanon*

A festive 1-hour and 15-minute train ride featuring Santa and his elves, with cars adorned in holiday decorations.
▦ December | ✆
LEBANONMASONMONROERAILROAD.com

Cuyahoga Valley Scenic Railroad Holiday Rides –
Akron Northside Station and Peninsula Depot
Seasonal train rides through the scenic Cuyahoga Valley, offering a unique holiday experience.
▦ December | ✆ HOME |
CUYAHOGAVALLEYSCENICRAILROAD.com

These lists highlights some of Ohio's most magical winter events and destinations, perfect for tourists looking to experience the holiday season! ❄ 🎄

But if you feel we've left something out, don't hesitate to share it with us. We'd love to include it . Send your update to prickleforrestllc@sssnet.com.

About Ohio

A Whirlwind History of Ohio

Ohio's history is a rollercoaster of adventure, starting long before it was even a state! Originally home to many Native American tribes, including the Shawnee and Miami, Ohio saw European settlers arrive in the late 1700s. Fast forward to March 1, 1803, and Ohio became the 17th state in the Union! Ohio wasn't just watching history from the sidelines—it was making it. The state played a huge role in the Underground Railroad, and its factories helped fuel the Industrial Revolution. Plus, Ohio's roads are filled with the stories of early pioneers and innovators.

Famous Faces from Ohio

Oh, you'd be surprised how many Ohioans have made their mark on the world. Oh, and let's not forget one of Ohio's crown jewels. And yes, we're talking football.

When it comes to football — we must mention Canton, home to the **Pro Football Hall of Fame!** It's the ultimate pilgrimage for football fans, where legends are forever enshrined and where you can walk in the footsteps of the greats. Located in the heart of the state, this Hall of Fame is like the ultimate celebration of all things football. From interactive exhibits to memorabilia showcasing the best of the best, it's a must-see destination that'll make any fan's heart skip a beat.

And speaking of legends, let's get back to talking about two Ohio icons who have left an indelible mark on the football world: Paul Brown and Jim Brown.

Paul Brown – The coach who didn't just change the game, he revolutionized it! From pioneering the use of game film to creating the Cleveland Browns and yes, the Cincinnati Bengals too, Paul Brown was a true innovator in the sport. His influence on the game is still felt today, and his legacy lives on through the teams he helped build.

Jim Brown – Known as one of the greatest football players of all time. He was a powerhouse on the field. With his incredible speed and strength, he was a force to be reckoned with, leading the Cleveland Browns to numerous victories. Even after his career, Jim Brown's impact went beyond football—he's a philanthropist and activist whose memory continues to inspire people across the world.

Even though Ohio is football country, we have lots of other notable Buckeyes to boast about.

Ulysses S. Grant – The 18th President and Union general who helped lead the country through the Civil War.

Thomas Edison – The man who brought light to the world—literally! Born in Milan, Ohio, his work with electricity changed the way we live.

Neil Armstrong – You've heard it: "That's one small step for man, one giant leap for mankind." Ohio can proudly say the first person to walk on the moon was one of its own.

Toni Morrison – A literary giant who captured the essence of African-American life in her Nobel Prize-winning works, like Beloved.

Harriet Beecher Stowe – The author of Uncle Tom's Cabin, which sparked change on the national stage.

Ralph Waldo Emerson – Not just a famous philosopher, but also a well-known writer who spent part of his life in Ohio.

Paul Newman – The man who could melt hearts with a smile and a racecar, born in Shaker Heights.

LeBron James – Akron's very own basketball phenom. He might have left for the NBA, but his Ohio roots run deep.

Ohio's Famous Foods

And what goes better with a big game than some mouthwatering food? Ohio's cuisine is all about comfort, flavors, and tradition.

Cincinnati Chili – A dish that's a mix of sweet and savory goodness, served over spaghetti or hot dogs, topped with cheese, onions, and more.

Pierogis – Delicious potato-filled dumplings from Ohio's Polish heritage, perfect for a snack or a hearty meal.

Buckeyes – A sweet treat made of peanut butter and chocolate that'll have you feeling like a kid at Christmas.

Goetta – A hearty sausage dish, especially popular in Cincinnati, made of ground pork, beef, and steel-cut oats.

Lake Erie Perch – Fresh, local fish that's crispy and delicious—ideal for those lakeside picnics!

Coccia House Pizza – Handmade fresh every day, mouthwatering, so good you cry when they take their two-week vacation each year and voted number one pizza in the state.

Fun Facts and Symbols

State Bird – The Northern Cardinal—this bright red bird brings cheer to Ohio's cold winters.

State Tree – The Buckeye Tree—you'll find Ohioans proudly carrying buckeye nuts, especially during football season!

State Flower – The Carnation—it's a symbol of Ohio's rich agricultural roots.

Ohio's Cool Cities

Columbus – The capital city, full of life and home to Ohio State University. It's also got a killer arts scene and some of the best food in the state.

Cleveland – A city with personality! Known for its sports, music scene (hello, Rock and Roll Hall of Fame), and gorgeous lakefront.

Cincinnati – With a mix of German history and modern flair, Cincinnati boasts world-famous chili, stunning riverfront views, and great architecture.

Akron – Known as the "Rubber Capital of the World," Akron is where the rubber industry boomed, and it's still a hub for innovation and fun!

Dayton – The birthplace of aviation, thanks to the Wright brothers. Visit the National Museum of the U.S. Air Force for a look at Ohio's influence in the skies!

Wooster – Home of the Wayne Novelist Guild, Coccia House Pizzeria, the College of Wooster, Ohio Agriculture Research and Development Center of The Ohio State University, and the hometown of August Imgard who started in 1847 the tradition of decorating Christmas trees in America with candy canes .

Ohio's Innovations

You might be surprised at how many things were invented right here in Ohio:

The Airplane – That's right, the Wright brothers from Dayton changed the world forever with their flight in 1903.

The Lightbulb – Thanks to Thomas Edison, we're no longer in the dark! He worked on perfecting the incandescent light bulb in his laboratory.

The Cash Register – Invented by James Ritty in Dayton in 1879, this nifty device changed how businesses counted their money.

The Typewriter – Christopher Latham Sholes invented the first successful typewriter right here in Ohio in 1868.

Population & Economy

Ohio is the 7th most populous state, with around 11.8 million people. It's a mix of urban excitement, like Columbus and Cleveland, and peaceful rural areas where you can kick back and enjoy the countryside. Ohio's economy is strong, powered by a mix of manufacturing, agriculture, and emerging industries in healthcare and technology. Plus, Ohio's agricultural output is top-notch, growing everything from corn to tomatoes, with apples and grapes being especially popular.

Outdoor Excitement

Ohio is a playground for outdoor fun! If you love the great outdoors, you'll find no shortage of adventures here. Spend a sunny day at Lake Erie, where you can boat, fish, or just relax by the shore. Thrill-seekers head straight to Cedar Point, the "Roller Coaster Capital of the World," or King's Island, where the rides are legendary and the fun never ends. Love a good festival? Ohio's Canal Town

Festivals are the place to be, offering everything from craft vendors to live music and plenty of local eats. For nature lovers, Mohican State Park provides serene trails, gorgeous views, and the perfect spot for hiking or camping. And if you're in the mood for some live tunes, Ohio's outdoor music venues — like the Blossom Music Center — bring a great lineup of performances under the stars. And don't forget about our Ohio Amish. They got a way of life that's simple and beautiful. So desired Our Amish heritage with food, farming, life-style, and crafts are highly sought after, in fact, only Cedar Point ranks one step higher on the popularity ladder.

So, whether you're seeking thrills, chills, or just a good time, Ohio has something for everyone to enjoy in the great outdoors!

State Motto

Our state motto is...
"With God, all things are possible"
reflecting Ohio's history and the importance of faith in the lives of many of its residents.

Ohio's Spirit

Ohio is a state that welcomes everyone with open arms and a warm heart. Whether you're cheering on your team, enjoying a summer day by Lake Erie, or savoring a plate of Cincinnati chili, Ohio's got a little something for everyone.

So, come to Ohio , have some fun, and make a memory that'll last a lifetime!

And that, my friend, is Ohio: a state full of adventure, history, and fun as a touchdown in the final seconds of the game.

About The

Wayne Novelist Guild

Welcome to our little corner of Northeast Ohio, where stories come to life and writers become published authors!

Tucked away in the heart of Wayne County where the seasons paint a picture-perfect backdrop for creativity, our eclectic group of award-winning authors has been gathering for over 13 years to support, inspire, and cheer each other on. Through crisp autumn evenings, snowy winter nights, fresh spring breezes, and warm summer gatherings, The Wayne Novelist Guild located in and around Wooster, Ohio has built more than just a writing group—we've built a family.

Meeting twice a month, primarily via Zoom now, but occasionally in person, we share our works-in-progress, critique with care, and lift each other up on the journey to publication. With over half of our members now published, we know firsthand the value of a strong support system. Whether it's exchanging articles on craft, reviewing each other's books, or showing up to celebrate a fellow writer at a presentation, we believe in the power of community.

We love to mix in a little festivity, too! From impromptu holiday-themed writing sprints to gathering at book festivals and conferences, we make time to celebrate our shared passion. Living just a stone's throw from each other makes it easy to connect, collaborate, and toast to new successes.

While we are always open to new members, we do have a vetting process to ensure our group remains dedicated to our shared goal: getting everyone's novels published. No matter our differences, we are united by one thing—helping each other's stories whether it be romance, sci-fi, YA, fantasy, historical fiction, or short stories reach the world.

So, as the holiday season reminds us of the warmth of camaraderie and the joy of giving, we invite you to be part of our writing journey. After all, every great story starts with a strong opening—why not begin yours with us?

For more information, contact the Wayne Novelist Guild through our publisher at prickleforrestllc@sssnet.com.

Thanks for taking time to share in our stories.

About Prickle Forrest Books

Christina H. Benchoff established Prickle Forrest Books through Prickle Forrest LLC now Prickle Forrest Books LLC in 2023. Due to the stigma attached to self-published and Indie authors, Prickle Forrest Books took up the call to help promote these fabulously talented authors to the readers of the world. And by doing this they have provided an affordable service to get the word out. Prickle Forrest Books loves all authors, but indie and self-published take priority in her heart. Prickle Forrest Books hopes one day all authors can publish on a level page. We wish all authors the greatest success in their writing careers. Thank you for letting us help you reach your dreams! https://PrickleForrestBooks.com/

Happy reading!

MERRY CHRISTMAS and Happy Hanukkah!